Boom, Boom, Boom
Ian Kirkpatrick

STEAK HOUSE
BOOKS

First publication in the USA
Steak House edition published in 2022
Copyright © 2022 by Ian Kirkpatrick

Paperback ISBN: 978-17368870-2-8
ebook ISBN: 978-17368870-3-5
LCCN: 2022901885

Our books may be purchased in bulk for promotional, educational, or business use. Please contact your local bookseller to order.

Cover by Samuel Johnson
www.SpoopySamuel.com

Printed in the United States of America.

01   05   22   1

CONTENTS

This One's Pretty Good #137

JananananananaXD   Views: 29
5 Subscribers

Description: I have been experimenting with some easy-to-find ingredients. Petrol, ammonium, nitrate, nitroglycerin, acetone peroxide, nitrocellulose, gunpowder, dish soap… There are so many combustible things around us all the time, you would be surprised by what you can find in your home or grocery store. Although, petrol is easy enough unless it's too cold and you're running low on oil for the heater or the power is out. Then it feels like there is never enough anywhere, lol. I always have extra petrol around though. But, when in doubt, a nice boom and a little excitement will do a lot to keep you warm! Trust me! I'm always surprised by what different compositions can do.

I'm not going to tell you what's in today's video. I want to see you guess! Tell me in the comments if you think you know what I used to get this reaction!

Looking forward to hearing from you!

Boom, boom, boom! Salute!

ONE

I take the cereal box out of the shipping container. Frigid Flakes. It's a dark blue box with a person wearing a light blue parka pulled over their head, covering all of their features. Their skin is pale and their beady, black eyes stare out from the hood opening. The person holds a fishing rod in one hand and a spoon in the other. A box of the cereal hangs from the person's hook. These are supposed to be dusted in white sugar, but every time I've opened a box of them, they are more than *gently* dusted with *something* not right. Coated is more accurate and the coating doesn't smell sweet. It's not sugar, but at least it's not arsenic. Not bitter enough. Maybe it's a little bit of dirt mixed with something else. Coal dust cut with sugar and flour because the factory that makes them ran out of the proper ingredients and couldn't order more?

It doesn't matter. The dust comes off when the flakes are drenched in milk or water, but that's when you notice the little black specks floating in the mix. The flakes retain their crunch regardless of how long they've been sitting in the milk. I still don't know what the black stuff is, but I've found it in every box I've ever had. I turn the box over.

The off-shelf date was four months ago.

This is one of the freshest boxes I've seen in my store.

I pull the other boxes off the shelf and stick this one in the back, then re-stack the boxes on the shelf. When I'm done, it still looks half empty, but that's normal.

"Scarcity creates desire," Boris says. "Desire creates sales."

I'm not sure if that's true, but Boris is my boss and when I'm on the clock, I'm at work. And when I'm at work, I'm doing what he says. That was the agreement I made.

I flip the empty cardboard box over. A quick slit with my pocketknife and the box collapses flat. I tuck it under my arm, exit the aisle, and walk through the store.

My steps are quiet. There's no sound in the shop. No one else is in the store. My right ear rings softly, but after a couple of seconds, it gets louder until I wince, and then it sinks back to a soft buzz. I tuck my thumbnail into my teeth, looking for debris from last night. There's only a little bit of gunpowder, but it's enough to be soothing.

I hum softly to tame the buzzing in my ear. My head bobs off-beat to the sound. I stop next to an end cap, peeking down the aisle to find an empty spot. My voice cracks, interrupting the tune. I clear my throat, then start humming again.

There's never any music playing during the night. Boris turns it off before even the last customer leaves because "They won't notice there's no music when they're talking to the cashier. If they notice there's no music, someone's not doing their job." He says it's better to turn off the music a couple of minutes before closing anyway. You don't want people coming in when you're getting ready to close and music makes people feel welcome. At five til seven, customers aren't welcome anymore. Then he says, "Since I know music makes people comfortable, you can't have it at night. Music doesn't stock shelves; it puts you to sleep in the backroom. Scarcity makes desire, yes, but scant makes desperation, and satisfaction makes you lazy."

Only half of the store lights are on to save on power and even the heater is allowed to go cold. My fingers are ice when they touch my lips. I hold them there for a moment longer just to breathe on them, then I keep walking. While scarcity is normal in the store, it's still hard to tell where the right empty spots are in the dark.

Finally, I spot a hole in the aisle four soup cans. I return to the back room to grab another box from shipping.

The loading room smells of smoke and bits of it catch in the light. I toss the compressed box I have into the stack of broken-down boxes by the back wall. The storage room is even colder than the storefront and has even fewer lights on. Two. One over the trash and one over the small shipping area to read box labels. Outside the windows, the world is nothing more than a void eaten by the night.

There are no lights outside the back of the store.

Well… None that work. There had been one right outside the door, but the light bulb died six months ago, and Boris isn't interested in changing it. "No one uses the back door at night anyway and by the time you leave, you're going out the front when morning shift gets in. We're not wasting the labor costs on something that won't change the work," Boris says. He's very practical like that. If it is not something that will affect the store's income in a positive manner or the productivity of the staff, he doesn't want to spend money on it.

Papa is also very practical and so is Aleks. Calculating possibilities, the future, investments, harm. It's why Aleks is in Sumy right now and I'm still in Nide. There is no extraordinary future for me in Nide; it's nowhere, but I like this sort of quiet. Thinking about tomorrow or next week or next month is pointless when there is so much going on in front of me all the time. It might not seem like a lot when I'm standing in a grocery store at two in the morning stocking shelves, but there is a lot to consider in what you can do with nothing.

I look over the stack of boxes, reading over the marker messages on the side to discover their contents. I turn around to assess the room. I know I will not find any other boxes. Everything we have is stacked in this corner, but I still survey, thinking maybe the box I'm looking for got lost somewhere. Symon squats in the darkest corner of the back room. His cellphone screen lights up his face while the red end of a cigarette ignites when he inhales.

"Symon, have you seen the soup?" I say.

He doesn't answer. He doesn't move. He doesn't even pretend to see me.

"The cans are looking scant, Symon." I look over the boxes again, getting closer this time. I take out my cellphone and flick on the light. It's not until the fourth time that I go over the same box on the right that it registers in my head that's what I'm looking for. "Found it!" I say. "Thanks!"

I slip my phone away and grab the box.

The end of Symon's cigarette lights up again.

"Be careful with that," I say, "could blow up any moment. That's what *hot stuff* tends to do, you know? Like me." I pause in front of the door that leads back to the storefront to see if Symon's going to say anything, but the pause isn't long when I know he won't. I could go on for hours about fire and explosions and which element combinations will lead to the quickest heat build-up leading to the biggest explosion—But he wouldn't say anything. I could tell him about the minute scent of petrol that if you pay close attention to, you'll smell it in the backroom, something like dirt and lots of water and even the mild scent of vegetable like in vegetable oil. If you smell that, there's a little bit of spilled gas, but not enough to be a gas leak yet and you should be careful putting out your cigarette on the floor. I've tried sharing my hobby with him before, but he's never paid me much mind. Even when I was mixing nitromethane with erythritol or a little bit of gunpowder, he wasn't interested in the outcome.

I know the camera never really captures the explosions well, but on that one, you can still see the green ring if you look really close at the smoke before it goes boom.

That's the worst part about what I do: everything is a one-shot. If you want to see what you've made, you have to pay attention, be in the moment and if you're not, you'll miss everything beautiful.

I return to the storefront and walk down the aisles until I've reached the soup. There are only ten cans. The box I'm holding has gotten much heavier by the time I put it down, the cans rattle against each other from how the box slips out of my grip. I look around to see if anyone's there, but it's just me.

Working at night will do that, sometimes. Every small sound in the shop could be a stray cat or a rat or a ghost. I'm sure that there are ghosts in this store for how long it has been standing. In fact, I'm most certain one of the previous employees haunts this place.

Thinking about it, I touch the back of my neck. Chilly air sneaks under the metal loading gate. The cold moves across the cement and comes up through the bottom of my boots and wool socks, chilling my toes next. Cold air can be a vicious beast, you know? Pulling at your ears until they sting, deepening the color of your face without pause, and nipping at every bit of skin, regardless of whether you're wearing a jacket or not. Actually, sometimes the cold is meaner if you're wearing a jacket and it plucks through the cotton like tiny needles, digging for your bones.

I empty the box, crush it, and bring it to the pile by the door. I forgot to look at the shelves before coming back in, so I'm not sure what I need to grab next. I stop at the exit with my foot in the door. Symon's phone still lights his face in the corner. The red dot at the end of his finger seems brighter. "Did you see—" I say, but stop.

Symon flicks his finger over the screen and the colors of the video he's watching reflect in his eyes. I smile toothily. My tongue runs over the bottom of my lip, then I bring my fingers to my mouth, checking under my fingernail with the edge of my tooth again, looking for anything left behind. When I'm done with that finger, I move on to the next one.

I hope he's watching my latest video. It capped at twenty-nine views the last time I checked it. That's the best one of my videos has ever done. Soon enough, everyone in Nide will have seen my work. I'm waiting for the day when Symon admits to watching them and then he will say, "This is impressive. How did you do it?" and I will say, "You think so? This is one of my favorites, honestly." And Symon might be a little starstruck, as people tend to be in front of celebrities, so he will not be sure if he can even say yes, but after a moment, he will say, "Let me buy you a drink, friend, then you can tell me all the details." With a smack to my back, Symon will laugh. I will laugh. Then I'll say, "I will do you better than that: I will show you!"

That day will be the same day everyone in town cannot stop talking about me. I will find a never-ending stream of people proud to say my name.

"That is my neighbor, Jan."

"I went to school with him."

"I thought about dating him once. I think I will think about it a second and third time."

My name will just feel so good in their mouths. The best part of it will be when I come home and Papa finally sees me, he will wrap his arms around me and pull me in tight and say, "I heard that Symon spoke with you about one of your videos. I watched it too. I'm so proud; I cannot believe you are *my* son. Let me take you to work and show you off!"

I stay in the doorway, waiting for Symon to look up from his screen, but he still hasn't. I clear my throat. He still doesn't look up. I say, "what are you watching, Symon?" and lean forward. Symon still says nothing. "Must be something good," I say.

Symon mashes his cigarette's butt into the cement floor, then leaves it there. He slips his phone into his pocket and steps out of the dark corner. His feet drag, making a sound as they move across the floor. He walks past me and into the single toilet bathroom beside Boris's office. He leaves the door open and the light off. Seconds later, he's pissing. He comes back out while the toilet's still flushing, then squats back in the corner. He takes his phone out and picks up his cigarette. The end lights up weakly as he sucks in.

"You know, Symon… I'm going to blow up someday."

"I know," Symon finally says without looking up at me. "Make it sooner rather than later, yeah?"

I laugh and rub the back of my neck as I return to the floor.

I know my shift is ending when the sky gains some color again. The sun isn't up yet, but it's peeking over the horizon. It won't be long before the sky is bright, so I have only a limited amount of time to shoot my next video. As the clock winds down, I'm antsy, pacing aimlessly down the store aisles as I wait for Boris to get here to unlock the door and dismiss us.

The key jingles the lock. The door pushes open. "Good morning, Boris," I say.

"What did Symon do tonight?" Boris says.

"He watched me well," I say.

Boris grumbles, then says, "good night."

Symon says nothing.

I put on my parka and leave the store. Polina, my Vespa, waits for me in the parking lot. I sit on her. Phone in hand, I check the stats on my newest video. It is up to thirty-three views! I trade my phone for my Vespa key. "Did you see that, Polina?" I ask. "We're nearly going viral!" She growls meekly as I press my foot to the gas. We speed off; she knows we have work to do.

It's a thirty-minute drive from the grocery store to my usual spot and I have to walk another ten minutes off a trail to get to the clearing in the trees where I like to shoot. I park Polina off the side of the road, tucked behind a couple of bushes. I pull my bag over my shoulders and pick up the collapsible tripod from under my seat. Most of the snow around my blasting spot is gone and all that's left underneath is the dirty ground, darkened by more than a couple rounds of explosives. There are no trees left very close to the blasting site. I chopped a couple down to avoid lighting them on fire. That happened once.

I set my backpack down in the blasting spot. It acts as a dummy while I walk around with the tripod. I usually place it in the same spot, looking to make the shot symmetrical with trees in the background framing where I'll sit. I know the trees don't move, but still, sometimes they look like they're in a different place. I extend the tripod legs as much as I can, then clip my phone to the mount. I access my phone's camera and use that to find the correct frame.

Orange lights up behind the trees like its own small explosion. Through the camera lens, the warm colored lines streak through the purples, pinks, and blues of twilight. I like the trees on the east side behind the back of the camera better. I don't dislike the summer for the shorter nights because it is much harder to create explosives in complete darkness, but the added daylight makes it harder to make a video that stands out like it should.

My ear's ringing again. I dip my head to the side and shake it a little in an attempt to get rid of the sound. The ringing causes me to wince. I take extra steps to make the snow crunch under my boot, letting the sound be the extra lullaby to put the ringing to sleep again, at least for a little while.

The ringing subsides. I return to my bag and sit on the ground beside it. I shuffle through a couple of bottles marked with numbers, instructions, and shorthand names for what's inside. As much as I would like to just sit and experiment on the spot, I don't have the time. The sun is my clock and when time is this short, I cannot play around and shoot. If it weren't for the thirty-three views on my newest video, maybe I could've played around tonight, but with momentum like that, I know I need new content. If someone left a comment on one of my videos, it would be the greatest thing ever. Even my best friend has never left a comment on my channel. Honestly, I do not think he even watches at all. The last time we spoke of it, he said, "Jan… It's dangerous. What is the purpose, even? Come to Sumy. There are many jobs here you could have," and when I asked him if there was room for this sort of thing in Sumy, he said, "You probably do not want to set off bombs in Sumy."

"Then why would I want to go there?" I said.

"To get out of *Nowhere*."

My chest is tight and my heart pounding as I place each jar of ingredients on the ground. I flop onto my butt. With the first jar in hand, I unscrew the lid. I don't have to bring it to my nose to catch the strong smell. It burns the outside of my nose. The dryness of the air doesn't help. I lid the jar again.

Did you know that the smell of something can tell you how big the explosion will be? Sometimes, it can even tell you what color it will be. Though chemicals don't actually talk to you, if you close your eyes and smell the compound, the colors will light up behind your eyelids and you can almost see a small cloud like you're playing an explosion before it happens. If it's hard to see from the smell, then if you dip your finger in and press that little bit to your tongue, you should definitely see something. You just have to be careful with the compounds. Too much of some of them and you'll burn your tongue. The last time I did that was a couple of years ago. I don't remember the name of the compound, but I could tell you immediately from the smell of it if you put it in front of me. Back then, I got too much on my finger, I wiped it on my tongue, I couldn't taste anything on that side of my mouth for thirteen months.

The contents of my bag are laid out on the blasting spot. Three jars with compounds, a box of matches, and a roll of twine. I pick up my bag and take it over to the tripod. I check the clock on my phone. Then the battery. Only 30% left. That should be enough. From the front pocket of my bag, I withdraw a pair of thick, round goggles. The lenses look copper on the outside and dim the light from the inside. Explosions may not be as true through them, but they also protect me from blindness at least. I put in a couple of earplugs. My goggles slide over my short, wavy hair, flattening it to my crown. I then trade my winter gloves for a protective glove. Before I put it on one hand, I tap the 'record' button on my phone. Once the light confirms I'm rolling, I step back and wave.

"Hello, Boomers!" I keep stepping back, glancing over my shoulder a moment to check for my blasting site. My attention doesn't stray too long from the camera though. "My name is Janananana! How are you feeling this morning? I'm good, thank you. Do you know why? It is because I have been thinking of that last blast we did together. Number thirty-seven, yeah? I did like the green that came in the smoke. Watch the video again in slow motion. There's a green tint to the smoke and along the outer edge of the blast, like it's radioactive. Though, I wish there had been a little more glow. I think if I'd put a little

bit more of ingredient two in, there might've been more."
I stop walking when there's dirt under my feet instead of
snow. "I know you're wondering about the ingredients,
but I can't tell you. Sorry. Even if I say this is for
'educational purposes only,' I do not think that is seen as
a 'good enough reason' to share for *certain people*. Then…"
I lean in, pressing my fingers to the side of my lips.
"People might come looking for me, talking to me, asking
how I got certain things. The less *certain people* know about
me, the better." I wink, turn to my gear on the ground.
Pause. Turn back to the camera. "Not you, though."

I look up at the sky. The orange and yellow are
spreading further into the purple and pink, devouring the
night sky too eagerly. "Sorry. Today's show might be a
little harder to see. I took a little longer getting here this
morning. My legs are stiff." I laugh. "I'm tired, but I have
been waiting all day to do this with you! I just wish it was
a little darker, you know? But… let's get started anyway
before it gets worse."

I pull my goggles over my eyes, sit down on the ground,
and open each jar. The smell of the chemicals is easy to
pick up immediately. It's almost overwhelming, just being
so close. Every bit of mild aroma fills my nose before I
can even pick a jar up. The base jar has clear liquid in it,
maybe one-third of the way full. I pick it up and move it
to the front and center of me.

The next jar I hold is tin and has a dark powder in it.
Without much light, the powder might look black, but it's
really a kind of purple-blue thing when in direct light. I
sniff it first. Then I lick the tip of my finger and stick it in
the dust. Gently, I rub the crystals off on my tongue. I wait
as saliva mixes with the powder. My throat constricts a
little. I swish my tongue around. It glides along my lower
lip, leaving a slight tingle in its wake. My eyes flutter closed
and as the burn soaks in, I gently rock back and forth. I
pinch some of the purple dust with my gloved hand and

sprinkle it into the clear liquid jar.

At first touch, each purple crystal causes the clear liquid to bubble and heat. Fumes rise from the jar as it gets warmer. I slowly sprinkle in another pinch full, then swirl the jar around. The liquid turns darker and opaque, but not totally so. I put the lid on the purple dust, reach for the next jar. Should be a bottle. Pause.

A laugh comes out. "Sorry." I knock myself in the head with my palm. "Forgot the palate cleanser." I go back to my bag with the purple dust jar in hand. I trade it for a bottle of homemade Spotykach: vodka, spice, and rowanberries. I take the cap off and take a swig while walking back to my blast sight. My lips are pressed to the bottle before I'm even sitting again. My mouth comes away with a loud, POP.

"It's a good break." I sigh. "You know, if you don't clean the palate between ingredients, it can be harder to tell what you're looking at exactly." I take a quick shot. The rowanberry silences the soft tingle that had still been on my tongue. I put my finger up, just so the audience will know to give me a moment. I wipe my mouth with the back of my arm. "It's not impossible, but it can be harder. More surprising when you light up, you know? And that's not always a good thing when you're dealing with chemicals. It's like going to make bread, but instead of using flour, you use lots of baking soda. You don't know what's going to come out of your oven. All you know is that you don't want to eat it. Granted, I would be surprised if the oven didn't blow up when you put a loaf of baking soda in it." I laugh again. The bottle comes to my lips to silence me. I'm a little light-headed, a little warm, a little snappy. It's not the alcohol. It's the morning vibrations of the coming boom.

I set the bottle down and exchange it for a new jar. The lid's on the ground. There's a kind of yellow goo inside. I tip the jar to show off its thickness. "You want to know what this is?" I look through the jar at the camera. I lower it. My lips pull into a wider smile. I shake my head. "Can't tell you. Sorry. I could get in… eh, moderate trouble… if a certain person found out I had this and where I got it from. But I will tell you I found it a couple of days ago and the second I had it, I wondered what it would look like if I put it into this solution. It has a very nice burn to it, even just putting my fingers in it." I slide my fingers into the jar. My nails barely touch the top of the liquid, but the heat pulses all the way to my palm. Blood rushes through my left arm, quick to the elbow like tickling under the skin, then to my head. My chest is tight, but my heart races. "You know that feeling you get when something is strong and big and threatening? It's like someone walking into the bar, tapping you hard on the shoulder, and saying, 'let's go outside and fight' right before they punch you. That's what this feels like."

I dip my fingers into the goo. It doesn't stick as easily as the crystal powder, but a little bit slicks the tips of my fingers. I bend my fingers to scoop it. Still, it falls off, leaving a minor amount of residue behind. I stick my fingers in my mouth. My tongue is quickly covered by a fuzzy, soft burn. I close my eyes, reaching for my bottle of vodka as the heat escalates. My lips smack and my throat is drier than before, getting a little tight. "Yeah." The word comes out more like a cough. "The two of them… together…" I bring the bottle to my lips. A fast drink, I swish it around before swallowing. "It's going to be something nice. This blue and yellow… What we want is something unique, yeah?"

I withdraw a small, metal spoon out of my pocket and dip it into the yellow goo. The edge carves out some of the element and holds onto it. I set the yellow goo jar down and bring my attention to the main solution jar. Slowly, I lower the spoon into the liquid mixture, letting it taste the yellow goo bit by bit. "I know, I know I'm going a little slow, but you need to know—If you get too excited, too impatient, and move too fast, things get tricky. You overfeed a combustible solution, its heat gets hot fast and when it gets hot fast, it explodes too fast and no one likes getting hot and exploding too fast in any situation that I know. It's definitely not a good time here. Maybe I'll show you what I mean some time."

I have remnants of that memory as blotchy, red scars down my left arm and thigh. It's a good thing I like to wear sweaters because I never want my Mama to worry and I think if she saw some of those blotches, she would very much worry. She thinks I'm going to get hurt doing this. Everyone does, but I know what I'm doing.

The more I feed the spoon into the purple liquid, the thicker the goo becomes until there's nothing left to give.

I withdraw the spoon from the jar and wipe it on my pants. I slip the spoon back into my pocket, grab my vodka, and take a swig. My eyes land on the camera. My bottle's in the air. I smile into it.

The best companion for an explosion is a kiss.

Our lips part with a loud pop. "Are you ready for this? It's going to come fast. Don't blink."

I take out my pocketknife and use it to cut a hole in the jar lid. I return all the remaining ingredients to my bag so they can't catch on what's coming. My tongue smacks against my lips again. It's still burning from that little bit of yellow goo I tasted. I take another sip of vodka. I turn on my toes. It's definitely the snow under the ice that's making me walk a little less straight than I mean to.

Back at the jar, I sit on my legs and tuck a line of twine through the hole in the lid. "Now, you don't want to close the jar too early. You might not feel it where you are, but the jar is warm in my hands and it's making a lot of fumes already. If you cover the opening for too long, the heat will build faster, the air thicker and fuller, and it will blast, probably while you're still holding it. Then you could lose your hands and it becomes a bloody mess and we don't really want that… But we're ready now."

Once standing, I twist the jar lid on. I grab the box of matches from the ground next and pull one out. "On the count of three. Odyn, va… try!" I drag the match across the emery and toss the lit match down on the twine.

The jar's fuse lights. I'm running fast and take cover behind the nearby rock. My hand grips the vodka bottle's neck, hard. I lean out from behind my tree to watch the flame eat the wick. It climbs into the bottle and warms the darkened liquid. The fuse disappears into the purple mixture and goes darker, deeper.

Instantly, the jar fills with black fumes. A spark of orange cracks through the darkness like a bolt of lightning, and in the next second, boom! The glass jar explodes into a cloud. First, it's black, then purple, then it combusts into a bright orange-red flash that releases more purple clouds into the sky rapidly. The clouds have a glow around them. Maybe it's just the sun. Maybe they're catching and reflecting the sun's beams, but the rising purple clouds glow against the sky and the snow. My ears ring. The right ear is still worse than the left.

A roar from the initial explosion rolls through the trees, echoes through the sky, and comes back at me like a cloud of rolling thunder. The energy of it builds inside of me, much like the fumes in a closed jar, I can't contain myself. The heat is under my skin, it makes me bounce where I stand, it fills me with energy even when I have worked all night. I pump my fist into the air with a high-pitched, woo!

A small patch of weed roots by the blasting spot burn in a fresh fire beside where the bomb had laid, but without anything to feed it, the fire dies quickly.

I'm laughing. I lift my goggles to my head and approach the blast site. A few stray pieces of glass lay at the bottom of the tree I was behind. Some might have flown past me, but they're lost somewhere in the snow and

I'm not sure I care too much about finding them right then. The tripod lays tipped over. "When did that happen? Hopefully, you saw that." I turn it upright again. "It was beautiful, yeah? Purple. You mix it with the yellow goo and you get a purple glow. If you have any guesses for what I put together, tell me in the comments below! You could blindfold me and give me this stuff and I would know what it is. I just wish it wasn't so hard to get, you know?" I pick up the camera tripod and carry it over to the blasting spot. My heart's still racing, throbbing in my ears, adding to the continual, gentle ring. I turn so I'm in front of the camera and the blasting spot is behind me. "I think we could actually get something pretty big… That is… I'm planning to show you guys something pretty huge if I can make it happen, okay? So, get ready for that. Until next time though." I press my forefinger and middle finger to my head and bounce it forward in a straight line. "Boom, boom, boom, salute!"

I switch the camera off and dismount it from the tripod. Still holding it, I take a couple of pictures of the blasting spot, now with a little more spillage from the sun peeking over the trees. I play the video back to myself. I zoom in on the jar just as I drop the match in the video. The fuse lights. I slow the video down and watch the fire devour the fuse, sink into the jar, and change the composition of its contents. Thick, thick, thick. The clouds grow instantly. The slow-motion shows the glass stretching just before it snaps, elongating the moment of purple lightning as the dark clouds are replaced with hot, orange bursts of energy… and then it goes, "boom." I take a screenshot and send it to Aleks in a text message.

Even with the sound muted from slow-motion, I still hear the roar deep in my ears, like the vibrations are stuck inside of me. Like the growl of a mystical creature, it's deep. I lick my lips again. I wipe them with my softly burning fingers. My hands are trembling; everything's trembling and I can't hold it in as I yell into the sky.

My phone nearly flies out of my hand. I grip it hard to compensate for my loose fingers.

Smiling, I turn back to where my bag is. The cold seeps in around. I remove my earplugs and pick up my tripod. The morning becomes quiet, all but for the reminder of the explosion. Still, my heart races with excitement, energy, power. Something I hope will infect everyone in Nide to have a better day. With my things collected again, I make my way back to my Vespa. My skin's warm and sweaty by the time I reach the road. My shirt sticks to my skin. My face is hot, but my smile never fades. I start Polina and we go home.

TWO

My home is still quiet when I open the door; the morning still younger than the time anyone is up. Mama and Papa shouldn't wake for another hour and Mila some time after that. I take off my shoes when I come in the door and carry them through the house so I don't wake anyone with noise. I close my bedroom door before I can breathe again. I drop my backpack into my desk chair. My shoulders sag. They're heavy. My legs are heavy too and my eyes do not want to stay open. Once the adrenaline wears off, everything's just heavy. My phone's almost dead and I'm starting to feel the same. Tears gather in my eyes when I yawn. I rub them away weakly. I take the jars out of my backpack and place them on my bedroom shelf, each marked with tape stating liquid, powder, or base. There are only a couple of jars on both liquid and powder shelves and I don't let any of them touch. I try to keep them away from each other because it would be a pretty bad thing if they spilled.

The base shelf is filled more with long, square boxes marked with a label saying what's inside each of them. The uppermost shelf holds books on chemicals, heating, and

19

geology, mostly for the articles about where you can find combustible materials when mining. Then, just a few books on the shelf are about spacecrafts and rocket fuel.

Beneath the chemical shelves are two more shelves of empty jars and plastic bottles that I save every time I drink a bottle or find one sitting in a trash bin.

I take off my coat. My face is so hot, the room's instantly freezing. My shirt's sticking to my skin and the sweat is chilled by the air. My phone's plugged in and charging. I fall onto my bed and climb under the sheets. On my back, I work my pants off and toss them across the room. I pull my phone under the sheets. My head comes under the covers to keep me warm. I'm navigating through my videos and my YouTube channel until I've selected the video I recorded tonight and have it uploading. The video isn't long, just around eight minutes with all the prep, but still, the uploader says it's going to take a few hours for the video to finish.

I type in all the meta data. The title, a description, a couple of keywords, then put the phone back on my side table. A yawn escapes my lips again. With the blankets pulled up to my neck, I quickly fall to sleep. Even so, the rhythm of the explosion pulses under my skin.

Some might think of explosions as destructive, but I can't see them as anything more than an incredible combination of life elements. Combustion is real-life magic, putting colors in the sky and making things disappear. Yes, you could call it destructive because it can do harm, but it doesn't have to be that way. We're all looking for moments like explosions all the time, aren't we? One-of-a-kind moments that make us feel alive, chasing the things we love to find, a little bit of fireworks and spark in our lives? There's only one thing missing from it.

Somebody to do it with.

To wake me, a fist knocks on my door. It crashes like

a soft boom in my mind and I think I'm dreaming of a small explosion I created before starting a YouTube channel. The knock is so soft, then it comes again, a little harder. "Jani, are you awake?" Mama says.

I sit up slowly. The morning air's colder than it had been a couple of hours ago. I glance at my phone to see what time it is. A little after ten. I pull down my phone information screen to see that my upload has finished.

I go to the video's page. It automatically starts playing and I'm watching myself carry jars out to the blast spot and come back for some twine and vodka. There's a click and my voice tells me, "It can be hard to tell what you're looking at," while my eyes go out of focus on the screen and the words and numbers blur together and I think that I'm just tired because of what I'm seeing. My heart's racing. I'm saying something else, but my voice in the video sounds distant when I'm looking at the numbers on the view counter.

Two hundred and twenty-six.

The video is saying two hundred and twenty-six people have viewed it since I uploaded it and none of those views are mine.

I scroll further down on the page and the comments section shows someone has said something to me. A user named NotTheEggman671 says:

> cool vid.

"'Cool vid,'" I say to myself. I stare across the room. My closet goes out of focus. "'Cool vid.'" A wide smile pulls at my lips. "'*Cool vid!*'" My voice drops deeper that time.

"Jani," Mama says, "are you awake?" She pushes the door open to peek inside at me.

"Mama! You'll never believe this!"

"What?"

"Somebody left a comment on last night's upload!

They said—Mama—They said, 'cool vid'!"

"That's wonderful—"

"I wonder if there are more!"

"Jan."

"Yes, Mama?" My finger flicks across the screen as I click into different videos because even though I don't have any notifications for other comments, that doesn't mean they aren't there. Maybe I just never got any notifications for them.

"There's someone here to see you," Mama says.

"Someone's here to see me?"

"Yes."

"I was not expecting Aleks today." I open the messages on my phone to see if I'd missed a notification. Maybe he'd seen the picture I sent him; maybe he wanted to visit. I open the text messages. He's seen the picture, but he didn't say anything.

Mama pushes the door open a little more and stands more inside my room than out. Her hair is straight but pulled back into a tidy bun. She's wearing a woven sweater, mostly light blue and white with dark blue and white diamond patterns in it. Her voice is lower when she says, "It's not Aleks."

I look up at her. "Symon?"

She shakes her head.

"Boris?"

"I don't know who they are. They're from out of town. I've never seen them before and they have accents." Mama pauses. She crosses the room to come to my bed. Her eyes squint when she's close. She purses her lips, looks over my face, smiles, then licks her thumb. She rubs it against my cheek. Pulling back, her thumb's blackened by a bit by soot. "Get dressed and come out soon, yeah?"

"Yeah."

"I'll put on some tea."

I nod. Mama leaves the room and closes the door. I'm

not wearing pants, but I'm still wearing my shirt from work. I take it off, drop it into my laundry basket at the end of my bed, then put on a sweater with blue and white diamonds, not like my mama's. I run my fingers through my hair a couple of times to make it look less like I just got out of bed. I don't have a mirror in my room, but because it's wavy and short, running my fingers through it usually looks the same as if I used a comb. I rub my eyes to wipe the sleep from them. They're still heavy, a little red, and burn a bit, but I'm not entirely sure if that's because I didn't wash my hands after touching ingredients last night or because I wish I was still sleeping.

I return to my bed and grab my phone off the blanket. I send Aleks a text message.

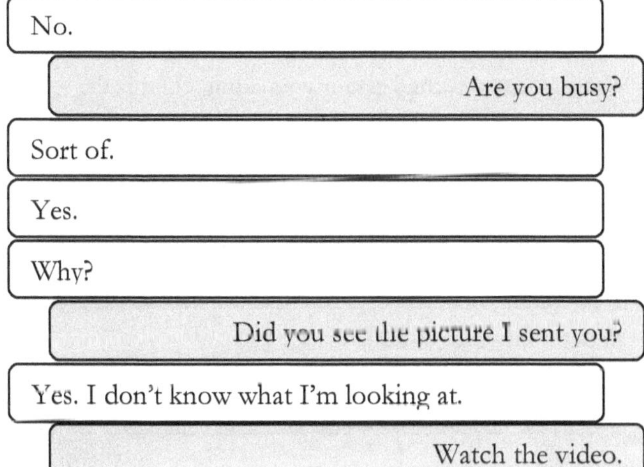

It takes him a minute, but he does respond.

A few more minutes pass.

You need to be careful.

I know what I'm doing.

I don't think you do.

I have a comment, Aleks!

He doesn't know what you're doing either.

And visitors.

Everyone has visitors, Jan.

At my house?

They're not related to your comment.

How do you know?

Because I know.

I'm more concerned about you eating chemicals.

Everyone has visitors, Jan.

Was that NCl3?

I know what I'm doing.

Where did you get that?

Sorry, Aleks.

Visitors.

I slip my phone into my pocket. On the way to my door, my eyes catch on the neck of my vodka bottle sticking out of my otherwise empty backpack. I shake my head and go out the door without taking a drink.

My bedroom is down a long hall that passes Mama and Papa's room. My sister Mila's room is on the other side of the house, while my brother Yavik's old room, now a small library, is across from my parent's room. Every time I walk by, I still expect to see him lying on his bed with a cigarette in his mouth and a magazine in his hand while his computer softly plays something metal. The writing desk, shelf, mirror, and Papa's collection of painted eggs, Petrykivka plates, and small potted plants give me pause. The end of the hall opens into the kitchen which is opposite the dining room and on the other side of those, the living room and front door.

When I enter the living room, Mama has already finished the tea and is pouring it into a couple of cups. Sugar and cream sit in small containers on the coffee table in the living room where a pair of men sit on one of the couches. I've never seen men looking like them before. They both wear khaki slacks, the same color. They're both wearing Hawaiian shirts of flowers and leaves, but different colors. Purple, blue, and white on one, black, green, and red on the other. They both wear thick, square sunglasses and straw hats. They both have watches with shiny faces and black leather straps on their right wrists. The only difference is one man looks bald under his straw hat while the other man has a thick mustache over his lip and dark hair, flattened by his hat. A closed metal box sits on the floor beside the couch.

"Hello?" I say, coming into the room.

They stand at the same time.

"Good morning," the man with the mustache says, his voice a little stiff.

"You know, you can take those off inside?" I point to where the sunglasses would be on my face.

Both men are unmoving.

"No," says the man with the mustache.

"Are you…" The bald man looks down at his phone in his palm. "Jananananana… XD?" He says the name slowly like he's counting each 'nana' until he gets to the end and his pronunciation of XD seems unsure. He speaks Ukrainian, but with an American accent. He has a big nose. I try not to notice, but I can't not.

A hand slides along my back. Mama stands there. I blink a couple of times, then clear my throat. "Yes. That's me. I am Jan." I approach the coffee table.

"Good," the man with the mustache says.

"My name is Bob Dylan." The bald man extends his hand toward me. He looks sidelong at his partner as his hand hangs in the air, waiting for me to take it. His lips curl at the edge, flatten, curl again. He smiles with his teeth. They're straight, white, and clean. I take his hand slowly. His grip is tight, arm flexes, muscular. He shakes my hand hard. I release before he does.

"And I'm Tom Cruise." Tom extends his hand. He tosses a glance toward Bob as he waits for me to take his. My fingers barely touch his before his grip firms around my hand and he's shaking it, fingers tight around my palm. At the very least, it is not a proper handshake and my fingers are crushed in his grip. I pull back. He's still holding on. I pull back harder, and he lets go.

The grip was so hard, my hand continues to hurt even once it's free. I let my hand hang at my side for only a moment. It pulses with pain. I raise it to my chest and stroke it with my free hand. "You're Tom Cruise and Bob Dylan?"

"Yes," Tom says. "We are."

"Is that a problem?" Bob says, his smile looks wider now. More teeth showing, but there shouldn't be more teeth just because someone is smiling wider, yeah? Maybe it's an American thing. I lean in with squinting eyes to try and see if Americans do have more teeth or if this is an optical illusion.

"I don't think so… They sound familiar, though," I say. "Have I heard them somewhere before?"

"Couldn't tell you," Tom says.

"But we wanted to ask you a couple of questions," Bob says.

I look back to Mama standing behind me with the pot of tea. She's watching both men, but she notices when I look at her. She runs her fingers along the area under her eye, subtly pointing before she brings the teapot to the table, pouring the contents into each cup. I thank her for the drink but don't sit down yet. "Are you sure you don't want to take off your sunglasses? It must be dark in here that way."

Tom laughs, then harshly stops. "No."

"Okay… What would you like to know, then?" I say.

"Who do you work for?" Tom says.

"One Stop Shop in the town center."

"What do you do for them?"

"I am a night stocker."

"What about your parents? What do they do?" Tom says.

Bob and Tom drop their head to the side at the same time to look past me. I follow their stares to Mama standing in the kitchen with her eyes on us and her elbows pressed to the counter.

"Papa is a miner. Mama stays home, cooks, makes things in her spare time, and is a good wife," I say.

"And… that's   all that's going on here?" Tom says. He and Bob straighten their necks.

"Yes…?" I say, watching the two for any change in expression, but they hardly have any expression at all anymore. Not even the oddly large smile from before. "Is… there another answer you're looking for..?"

"Not at all," Tom says, finally smiling again. Bob follows his lead, but his smile doesn't manifest, like his lips are weighted down. "I'm—We're fans," he says.

"Fans?" I say slowly. Seconds pass. Probably too many before it makes sense. "You're a couple of Boomers?"

"Boomers?" Tom says, pauses, laughs. "I'm not *that* old. I'm a Gen Exer."

"Gen Exer?" I say. "I've never heard of that creator."

"No," Bob says. "We're fans of *your* channel."

"Oh!" My voice surprises me when it comes out. Out of nowhere, there's pain in my face from my smile. I turn around to face Mama. "Did you hear that, Mama? They like my channel!"

"I heard them, Jani," Mama says. She smiles at me, but remains against the counter, her eyes not leaving their focus on the guests. Her smile fades just as soon as her voice does.

I turn back around. "I'm glad you like my work. You're the first fans I've ever met, if you can believe that."

The two men exchange a glance. "It is amazing that no one else has found you yet," Bob says.

"Right? That is what I've thought for years!" I say. I pull the chair by the coffee table up so it's right in front of me with little foot room. When I sit down, I barely have to lean to pick up the cup of tea Mama poured for me. The cup's already room temperature, but I don't let it stop me. I spoon a little bit of sugar into the tea and stir it in.

"Indeed," says Bob.

"Even my best friend keeps telling me I should stop and focus on *something real*. He doesn't think this is real, but you know what I do on my channel, I can feel it inside of me every time I light something up. Maybe I don't measure like the scientists do, but who is to tell me what I'm doing is not real? You don't even understand how many times I've argued with him. Every time we talk, he tries to convince me to give up what I'm doing and come to Sumy, but I'm like, what is there for me in Sumy? Nothing. That's what. University, politics, and nothing.

You know, people that live in the city are crazy, yeah? I think it's because there's no quiet. It's always go, go, go in the city and people think they have to be doing something and they can't relax or else they are bad but look at Symon. He's perfectly fulfilled by smoking in the back room of the supermarket—"

"Indeed," Bob says. "Symon is fulfilled, isn't he?"

"Oh! You know Symon?" I say.

"Yes," Bob says.

"He never mentioned knowing Americans before." I sip the tea. My tongue laps up some of the liquid left behind. The two men stare ahead with mildly pursed lips. "I guess that's not so surprising. There are a lot of people who don't like Americans, huh? Don't worry. That's not me. I don't hate anybody."

The room falls silent, only interrupted by the kettle's soft whistle on the back stove in the kitchen and the grandfather clock in the corner ticking every time the pendulum swings to the side.

"Why do you say we're American?" Tom says.

"Well… The accent, the way that you dress. I don't think I know anyone who dresses quite as eccentric as Americans. I mean, do you even have a jacket?" I say.

"No. We're on vacation," Bob says.

"Who brings a jacket on vacation?" Tom laughs.

"Vacation?" I say.

They nod.

"In Nide?" I say.

They nod.

"We don't receive many visitors here. No museums or big historical sites to see. We do have one old church though, but so does every town in Ukraine, huh?" I laugh. They don't. "I didn't think foreigners even knew Nide existed. It's not even on internet maps. It doesn't matter. Everyone usually visits Sumy or Kyiv and stays closer to the cities. People like it much more over there. I'm not sure why. Everyone would notice if you made noise in one of the cities. Out here? No one bothers you."

Tom and Bob share another look. Tom's eyebrows raise. Bob's head drops to the side. Tom purses his lips, making his mustache stand out farther than it already seemed to, then Bob's eyes squinted as if in response. Tom claps his hands once. With his palms pressed together, he points his hands forward. Then, Bob taps his knees, left, right-left, faster, left, right, right, left, right, left-right, ending in a clap.

I feel like I should be picking up on some conversation that's not happening and the feeling sinks in that maybe I've made a mistake. They might have been fans, but they've never talked to me in person, and maybe now that they have, they're thinking I'm not the person they thought I was.

"There's nothing wrong with Kyiv or Sumy," I say, mostly testing to see if I can hear my voice and if they respond to it. They do. The clapping stops and so do the strange facial expressions. "But what I mean is, if I lived there, I would have to drive much farther when I got off work to make my videos and I like to waste as little time as possible. Out here, it's not so hard to find a nice clearing that won't bother anyone."

"It's a good decision," Tom says. "To avoid being bothered. We understand a desire for privacy. Only an idiot would do secret business in broad daylight."

"I'm not really *hiding* per se. That makes it sound like I'm doing something wrong," I say.

Bob picks up his tea cup. Without adding anything to it, he sips it, throwing the whole cup back like he's taking a shot, and then he sets it down on the saucer. "Privacy is good," he says. "Especially when you want to talk business." He's staring at Mama.

Mama straightens. "What sort of business?"

"Confidential," Bob says. "Need to know basis.

Assuming your son is an adult, you're unneeded here."

"You don't have to speak to Mama like that," I say.

"We're not trying to be rude, but business is business," Bob says. "If you would like the opportunity of your lifetime, you will need your mother to leave. Confidential is confidential."

Goosebumps form on my skin. It's unnerving to be unable to see the men's eyes. Mama's always warned against trusting people when you can't see their eyes and even without looking back at her, I know that she is probably thinking the same thing. These men could be devils of some kind and even if they aren't, they're untrustworthy by virtue of covering their eyes and wearing hats indoors. I look over the men and I know I should ask them to leave, but instead, I straighten my posture and set my teacup down. "Mama, could you please give us some privacy?" As much as I'd like to check on Mama's face for judgment, I don't turn away from the men.

"Are you sure, Jan?" Mama says.

"I'm sure. I understand why a couple of Americans might be embarrassed to talk about their favorite hobby in front of you. People have never been so good at understanding my interest in this either." I smile at the two men. Tom smiles too big, Bob doesn't smile. Tom nudges Bob with his foot. Bob's lips twitch at the edge, but the smile doesn't stick.

Mama's fingers slide through my hair. I look up and she's standing right behind my chair. She leans down and places a gentle kiss on my head. Her hands slip down my shoulders. She watches the men over me, then lets her glance drop as if evaluating me. "Call if you need me."

"I will, Mama. Thank you."

The grandfather clock's tick accompanies her footsteps until the door to her bedroom clicks and I'm left in silence with the Americans. Something about the room shifts and the smile on my face slowly goes away. They're more different than I had ever imagined Americans to be, these two. My fingers slide along my leg, reaching for my pocket, wishing for Aleks's thoughtful eye and voice to look over this situation, even if he's not here. I'm not sure what bothers me more about this: Americans are in Nide, someone strange has come to see me, or they've watched my channel on the same day I have a comment on my videos.

I'm shifting between the two of them, waiting for one of them to speak, but neither of them do. My lips part, so do Tom's. I say, "What is this business?" at the same time Tom says, "About that business.

"Sorry, go ahead," I say. "I would like to know." A laugh brings the smile back to my lips, though my shoulders are tense and tension aches through my entire body. "Usually, it's not such a good thing when Mama has to leave the room." I smelled the gunpowder the moment I woke up. It's not lit, but it's loaded. It's not what's in my jars, it's something more bitter and compounded. I can't see their guns, but I know they're both wearing one. Something small, something that's not going to stand out. It's not so strange that men might be wearing guns to my house. Everyone I know hunts, but there's something different about these two men—more than their accents. An air of danger, maybe. I think that might be something that comes with speaking to foreigners or maybe it just comes with Americans. Aleks is never too excited to speak with foreigners in general, but he has spoken with exceptional skepticism when speaking of American guests.

He calls it all a farce—The images I have in my head from the programs I've seen on television and online. "Don't trust foreigners," he'd say and, "why are you talking to Americans? Why have you let them into your house? They are not friendly, Jan, even when they're smiling."

I might be more worried if they were wearing Russian

fatigues, but that wouldn't make me distrust them either.

Bob nods. Tom picks up the box from the floor beside the couch. It looks like steel, but it's black and sealed. "We want to sponsor you," Tom says. Tension drops into the air with the celebratory smile on his face, his teeth very white, very long again.

"Sponsor?" I say. "What do you mean?"

Tom presses something invisible attached to his hip and the locks on the box click open. He takes the lid off, then places the box on the floor and pushes it toward me. The smells are immediately intoxicating, I don't know if I can breathe while my heart races and a strike of dizziness comes and goes straight through me. I unfold my legs and lean closer to the edge of the chair. Inside the box are smaller boxes and containers of what smells like different kinds of combustible ingredients. Some of them I recognize as Uranium, Amatol, and Ammonal. A paper sticks to the roof of the box, explaining its contents. I can't read most of it, though I recognize some of the Latin letters of English.

I wave my hand over the box to try and push some of the smells away. It doesn't work. I know it won't, but they're so strong. I plug my nose and lean back. "Put the lid back on, please," I say.

Tom complies.

I lean back breathing deep. My face is burning hot. I think about stepping outside for a bit just to cool off. Instead, I bring my thumb to my mouth and dig at my nail with my tooth while my eyes trail along the edge of the box. My heart is going to throw itself out of my chest if I don't do something, so I end up rocking a little, bouncing my back against the chair, making my eyes focus on different things around the room, counting backward from ten and starting over again.

"Something wrong?" Bob says, his body engaged, sitting upright. His hand moves to his thigh. Tom subtly shakes his head.

"Sorry." I shake my head. "I'm not sure how to respond. I'm trying—I don't know if I can… words."

"You don't want it?" Bob says, stiff.

"Do I want it? Do I want it? Are you joking?" A chuckle bubbles out, half flat, half-hysterical. "I've never seen so many rare chemicals in my life. I can only imagine what I could do with them, but where did you get them? Why did you bring them here?"

"To give them to you," Tom says.

"Me? In exchange for what?"

"Nothing," Tom says with an unbelieving laugh.

"Nothing?" I lick my lip, then press my tooth harder into my nail. I lick the tip of my finger, move onto the next, then pull back. "Does *nothing* mean the same thing in America as it does in Ukraine?

"Yes..?" Tom says, slowly looking over to Bob then back to me. "We're pretty sure it does…"

"You didn't mean to say like *servitude* or *soul?*" I say.

"…Is that what *nothing* means here?"

"Sometimes." I nod with pursed lips. I reach for the box to take off the lid. Part of me—Most of me—Doesn't believe I saw what I think I saw, but I pull my hands back knowing that if what I just saw was there, then I would make myself dizzy with all the smells again.

"Well…" Tom claps his hands against his thighs. "That's not what we mean."

I look between the two of them, examining their faces for change or anger or any sign that they may be lying, but it's hard to tell when half their faces are covered. Still, Tom smiles wide and Bob isn't smiling, but he at least doesn't seem angry. His hand has fallen away from his lap and is instead laced into a fist with his other hand between his legs, elbows propped on his knees.

"Positive," Tom says.

"You really don't want anything from me for this?" I

say.

"Correction," Bob says. "We would like one thing."

Bob and Tom exchange a glance. With how much they keep looking at each other and the exchange of intimacy behind their glances, I'm starting to think they aren't who they say they are and there's something else going on. If they don't want servitude or soul for the box, I'm kind of worried they may want a kind of adult service instead. It's the glances. You don't look at another man like that or that often for it to be meaningless.

"Make it go, boom, boom, boom," Tom says. "Salute?"

"What?" Everything else in my mind disappears as my own familiar words are said to me by someone else.

"Look, we like what you do," Tom says. He leans back, throwing his hands in the air when he speaks. "We want you to keep doing it, but maybe make it bigger. Have some fun with this stuff and don't get yourself killed." He chuckles.

The words are familiar, but not with the chuckle after. Aleks has never laughed when saying those words to me. That's the major difference. For the first time, maybe ever, I think I've found *my* people. Boomers who understand me. I don't dislike Aleks or anything. He's just not a Boomer and so I know he's never understood my need to do what I do, but finally someone does.

"Think you can do that?" Tom says.

I nod.

"Good."

"Very good," Bob echoes, deep and throaty.

"Oh, right—There's something else. Something small—" Tom says.

"An assassination?" I say.

Tom's face turns to stone, his laugh and smile drop for a couple of seconds, then they're back. "Why would you say that? That's ridiculous."

"I don't know," I say. "A feeling I have?"

"No," Tom says. "All I was going to say is that you can't tell anyone about this sponsorship yet."

"What?" I say. "Why?"

Tom pauses a while before saying, "because it's a secret and you can keep a secret, right?"

I nod slowly, still confused, but I don't know business like they do.

"We'll look forward to your next film." Bob waves his hand like he's dismissing me.

"Film?" I say.

Bob purses his dry-looking lips. He licks the top one only, turns away, turns back to me. "Movie?" His voice loses some of its stiffness.

"Video..?" I say.

"Is that all they're called?" Bob rubs the back of his neck. His hat slips down his face, tapping his sunglasses and pushing them down too. Bob turns himself away, covering so that his unshielded face may not be seen. He quickly pulls his hat back and adjusts his glasses so they aren't lopsided, then he straightens again.

Tom's lips pull back into a cringing smile. I'd like to imagine he's rolling his eyes behind his glasses with this look of, "can you believe this guy?" Which, he would then be saying, "I can definitely believe this guy," with the way his teeth grind together.

"I don't know what else you'd call them," I say. "They are just short videos I take with my phone." I pause. "Did you want to see me record one?"

"No!" Tom says fast, loud, his voice echoes down the hall once. "I mean, no, that's fine. While Bob and I would love to see your work in person, we have a flight to catch back in Kyiv. We're supposed to fly out tonight."

"Supposed to?" I say. "How would you miss it?"

"Well, a bomb show for one." Tom stands up. His lift comes with softly cracking knees and hands that reach down his legs, straightening his fingers for a few seconds before slipping them into his pockets.

"Maybe next time," Bob says. His standing is accompanied by even more cracking bones. He groans, cuts off into a grunt, and turns away. "Thanks for the talk." He quickly makes his way for the door. His foot catches on the coffee table. It slides, he mutters, "ow! Damn it!"

Tom puts his hand on Bob's back, he mutters something short. I don't hear it. Then Bob is moving again. "Genuinely, we are starstruck, Mr. XD," Tom says. The two men step out the door without saying another word. They walk down the driveway to their slick, black car, something shinier and newer than anything I've ever seen driving around Nide. The windows are tinted black. The car beeps when Bob holds out a remote. He climbs in the driver's side.

"Mr. XD?" I stand on the stoop; my socks are getting wet from the snow.

Tom stands at the passenger side with one leg in. He slips the straw hat off to run his fingers through his hair then put it back on. "Hm?" he says.

"What do you mean XD?"

"From your name," Tom says. "The XD at the end?"

"Oh." I stare. "You don't say that part."

"How do you say your name then?"

"Janananana, but with a big smile. Doesn't matter." I shake my head. "My surname is Bagan.

"Ah, right," Tom says. "So, Jananana…nana Bagan?"

I laugh, shake my head. "*Nii.* Just Jan Bagan. That other one is my online name only."

"Ok. Good," Tom says. He looks sidelong into the car at Bob but seems to miss whatever he was looking for. "What does 'XD' mean then?"

I'm not sure if he's asking a serious question, so I shrug. "It's just a face, like, the face you make when you're having a good time, you know?"

"Hmm…" Tom says, then, "Maybe." He slaps the top of the car. "But I think my face looks a little different when I'm having a good time, wouldn't you say, Bob?" Tom laughs while he's climbing into the car.

My smile gets smaller with confusion. "Isn't that kind of a strange thing to ask your friend?" I say, but Tom is not listening to me and is closing the car door while Bob turns on the car with a roar loud enough to overpower my voice. The smell of gasoline is thick. They pull out of the driveway in one fast, smooth movement, then they're gone at the end of the street. I lock the door behind me once I enter the house. I pick up the cups from the coffee table and take them to the sink, then I go tell Mama the meeting is over.

Her arms instantly wrap around me when she's near and she pulls me close like she thought she wouldn't see me again. Her lips press to my head. I put my arms around her too, but even when I release, she still holds on. "What did they want, Jan?" She kisses my head again. "Are you in trouble?"

"No, Mama. I just—Something really good happened."

"What was it?" She lets me go.

I can't help the smile. I can't help chewing the edge of my nail then licking my lips as the cold air makes them crack. "It was… Mama… My videos are about to get much, much bigger."

I fish my phone out of my pocket and shoot a quick text to Aleks, saying, "you'll never guess what just happened to me."

THREE

I take the box of supplies to my room without telling Mama what they are. I'm not ashamed of them, but I don't want her to worry. It's the same reason I don't tell her what else I have collected on my shelf. It's the same reason the labels don't directly say what's inside of them. Instead, there are a couple of coded letters and numbers I use for my own understanding. Some might think it's the chemical code, but it's not that either, because I also don't need someone who knows how to read NCl3 and point right at it. The smell, color, and texture are enough to tell me what they are, but in some cases where they look similar, an A, B, or C3 helps me keep things straight. I'll have to create new labels for the new ingredients.

Putting them on the shelf as they are now doesn't seem safe, so I just set the box on the floor and push it under my bed. I grab my phone and call my boss saying, "I can't come in today."

"Bullshit," he says. "You need to come in. Symon doesn't do shit, but make loading smell like cigarette ass."

I grab my vodka from my backpack. It's not smart, but I take a sip and let it choke me up so I'm coughing into the phone. I turn away to cough into my arm while saying, "sorry, Boris—Sorry." I breathe in hard, take another sip, choke up again. My nostrils burn with the vodka coming back out of a place it never should've gone. "If you really want me to come in… I'm more worried about the products. I'm feeling so… unbalanced. I could trip and break something, knock over a shelf, then there's waste everywhere and I don't want to do that to you. But I think it's okay—A twenty-four-hour bug. Everything should be fine if I come in tomorrow like normal."

The line goes quiet for a long time. Somebody drops something and Boris yells, "You're going to buy that, yeah?" The person in the distance says something I can't hear. Boris says, "cashier's that way. No discount for products you damaged." He grunts. I feel him watching the customer through the phone. Then, when he says "fine," he's exhaling. "But you better hope the bug's a single day. Work's not a wolf—It won't run into the woods. If you're not back tomorrow, I will replace you." He hangs up without a pause.

I don't notice I'm sucking my lip in until I say, "Thank you, Boris, goodbye," and lower the phone.

It's fine. I didn't have anything else to say to him anyway and that went a lot better than I thought it would. I send a quick message to Aleks saying, "you'll never believe what I got," followed by a picture of the box and then, "watch my channel later."

He doesn't say anything. I toss my phone onto my bed, lock the door, and pull the box back out. They're stacked on my desk chair. I go through each container, looking at both the jars and the paper that came with them. It's unfortunate that the labeling the sponsors gave me is entirely in English. For each case I take out of the box, I jostle the contents around a little, open the lid, give a sniff, then put the container on my writing desk and go for another.

With all the containers laid out, I have fifteen different ingredients, some similar in color, but very different in makeup. My tongue runs over my bottom lip. I take a drink of the Spotykach and put it in an easy-to-reach location. I pick up the first container and take the lid off. It's metal and has a silvery-gray material. I decide not to stick my finger in it. The next container has a large chunk of stone glittering with silvery-white in it. The next container is lightweight, but when I open it, there's a silvery-gray stone with jagged edges. The smell's immediately familiar.

My tongue eagerly licks my bottom lip, but I don't imbibe—Not yet. I grab a pair of rubber gloves and slip them on. Then, the stone's in my hand and my tongue's against it. Beryllium. I mostly recognize it from juicing batteries.

Cadmium, lithium, manganese oxide, nickel, ammonium chloride… batteries have always been a really good way to find different materials. Most of the time, you don't necessarily know what kind of ingredients they use until you get into them. I take a swig of vodka to wash the taste down. The next container holds a slab of yellow sulfur. The smell is so pungent, I put the lid back on it fast. The smell lingers, so I open the window. I push the sulfur container to the back corner of the desk, but stand waiting to see if Mama smells it and comes looking.

I know I've always been a bit strange. I didn't realize it at first, but my sense of smell and taste are a little stronger than others—Much stronger than others. I first noticed when I couldn't eat the same foods as my family sometimes because of the strong flavor buried into some vegetables or meats we'd have that was just… too much that they made me sick. Papa didn't believe me the first time I said I couldn't eat a piece of lamb because of the sick flavor in the meat. I don't know how else to describe it other than if the colors gray and green had a flavor, that was the taste, more gray than green, darker gray, not lighter. He made me eat it saying there was nothing wrong with it. My siblings all ate it without problem too, but when I put it in my mouth, I nearly vomited. When I swallowed, I finished the job.

My tongue runs along my lip again. I take another drink. My fingers tingle as I reach for the next container. My phone rattles hard against my desk, the ring tone going off at the same time. I look over the name on the screen. Aleks Diduch appears in the title line. I pick it up after three rings saying, "Aleks! You'll never guess who was at my door this morning!"

"Ruskies?"

I laugh. "No! Why would Ruskies visit me?"

"Why are you yelling into the phone?"

"Sorry." I swallow like it'll catch my voice back. "I'm excited." My finger strokes the vodka bottle's neck. I walk over to my bed, sit down, immediately stand up. "What are you doing tonight?"

"Work. Important meetings. Things are tense right now, Jan. Have you been paying attention at all?"

"Paying attention to what?" I pace across my room, turn around, pace back to my bed, and repeat.

"The news. Government notices. Anything."

"Ah." I turn away as if I'm turning away from Aleks's stare. It's like he's standing in front of me. "No." I should be ashamed by what I don't know. Aleks has told me this before, but I don't."

"You're going to get yourself killed if you don't, Jan—"

"And you should come here tonight."

"I don't have time."

"I got a sponsor!" I say.

"A sponsor?"

"Yeah, yeah!"

The line is quiet. I go back to the desk to grab the

vodka. Instead of drinking, I swirl the bottle's contents around, consider taking another drink, but then puts it back down and pace away.

"What exactly do you mean by sponsors?" Aleks says.

"Some Americans—Fans of my channel—Just came to my house and gave me big gifts. Really big. You wouldn't even believe it if you thought last night's video was amazing."

"Last night's video is going to make you a target, Jan," Aleks says.

I laugh again, turning away from the desk. Suddenly it's like he's seeing what I have and I don't want him to see it; he's judging me for the new chemicals, he's judging me for the extra things I'm about to do. I like Aleks, but my chest grows tighter with each passing moment. I pace the room faster. All I wanted was to hear him speak with pride, congratulate me on the sponsors, tell me he knew all along that he believed in me.

I knew better than to think that would happen when I saw his name, but I still wanted to hope for something different. I grab the bottle of vodka and take a long sip. "You'll be sad if you miss it," I say against the bottle's lips. "I promise that. Do you know how amazing the show's gonna be tonight? You don't—"

"How much have you been drinking today, Jan?"

"Not that much." My feet plant firmly. A moment later, they wobble. "I'm not a stereotype, Aleks. I'm not a drunk Ukrainian at all hours of the day because I live in the woods, thank you."

"You're slurring—"

"I am not slurring, Alice—Aleks! Take that back!"

"Why are Americans visiting you?"

"I told you—Because they're fans!"

"They are not fans—"

"They *are* fans! I might even say more like friends than you because they watch my videos without me having to remind them or bug them and they like what I do and they encourage me—Unlike you—"

"What you're doing is dangerous. Because I tell you to slow down doesn't mean I don't care." Aleks sighs into the phone.

My skin's hot with anger and I'm still holding the vodka bottle, but I don't want to take another sip, feeling like it just confirms what Aleks is thinking about me now. I know how they talk about Nide in Sumy. Aleks doesn't spare the details when he tries to convince me to move every time he comes for a visit. Ignorant, simple, alcoholics with nothing better to do and nothing to contribute to society. Dead weight, dead mind, dead meat. My jaw's tight. I'm pacing again, but my room isn't big enough to get the energy out. I don't want to be here. I stop walking and tap my foot rapidly instead. "Fine."

"Fine what, Jan?"

"I understand. I won't bother you again."

"That's not what I'm saying."

"Then what are you saying, Aleks?"

The line's quiet for a while again. In the background, people are talking, I don't know how many, but they're all men. I've never been to Aleks's job. He left Nide to go to school, but I don't hear him talk about it often. I don't even know if he's still going. Sometimes he mentions research, but it's a passing thought, not a subject of conversation. The line is fuzzy for a bit, then he says. "Be safe, alright?"

I exhale. The heat of stress tries to get out, but it's not successful and my body's still stiff. My heart hurts. I look over the contents on my desk and turn away. "Always. I'm just having fun."

"I know," Aleks says. Someone yells something at him. "I have to go, Jan."

"See you in the comments, Aleks… Boom, boom, boom, salute." Even though he can't see me, I tap my fingers to my forehead and give a half salute, the same as I do in my videos.

"Salute," he says.

The line goes dead. I stare at the lit screen until it goes black, partially waiting to see if he'd call me back to say he forgot something or that he was pranking me, even though Aleks has never been the type of guy to commit pranks and definitely judges people for doing them. When he first found out about my hobby, he stopped talking to me for two weeks until he determined it was actually pretty cool, it was just scary and kind of weird, and who wants to make bombs except for terrorists?

The phone doesn't wake, so I hook it back up to the charger and return to my counter of ingredients. I move the box to the floor to take the chair for myself. It was time to pick the stars of tonight's show.

I'm drawn to a jar of reddish, mostly transparent liquid. Thick. Dark. Almost like blood. It's weird. I've never seen anything like it and I can't even pretend to know what to call it from chemistry. Carefully, I turn the lid. It's not even off the whole way when the smell seeps into the room.

Powerful.

My nose burns. I don't take the lid all the way off. I think I probably could die if I did. I close my eyes for a moment and see white stars behind them. Whatever this stuff is, I want to use it. Even without tasting it first, I know I want to use it tonight.

It might not make sense to others, but I can get a sort of vision of what the outcome of some element is going to be by experiencing it through my other senses. My nose is pretty good at assessing the burn and projecting chemical reactions in my head, the taste does the job even better.

It's difficult to describe, but behind the burn that carves pieces of your nose raw, imagine a stench so thick, you feel it crawl down your throat, and at the end of those scent-shaped fingers, there's this momentary flash of bitterness that sometimes goes sweet, sometimes goes hot, and sometimes it alternates. Those are the ones you don't want to put in your mouth, sometimes they burn right through your tongue. It's been a while since I've made that mistake, but I've had a few close calls, getting too excited—I want to try everything.

The flavor profiles of some explosions stick with you, but no one talks about that. I can maybe understand why, especially in American videos about gunpowder and chemistry, but you end up missing out on a big part of education that way. The last time I burned my tongue raw was when I was fourteen. I don't remember what it was called, but I had been mixing nitrocellulose with something else. Nitro has a smell that says *don't eat me*, a bitter, sweet thing that disappears, then goes hot, hot, hot, fast. I wasn't going to try it, but I thought I had a chance because the compound had been weakened by the mix.

Yeah, no. Don't ever think that with the very strong chemicals. It never works out how you think it will. It burned my tongue so bad, I lost the ability to taste anywhere the nitro had touched. Even today, my tongue hasn't fully recovered. Sometimes it's alright since I don't suffer from soup burning my mouth like it used to. Some flavors are lost now and I might over-season things from time to time. Mama used to worry her cooking was not satisfying me, but I told her it wasn't her cooking, it's my tongue. She asked what I meant, but I didn't tell her what I did. I didn't want her to worry. I don't think she ever believed me though.

I tuck the paper label underneath one of the containers and straighten out my backpack for putting things inside. A pair of new bottles from the sponsors, my vodka, an empty container from my shelf, and the matches and twine go to the front pocket. I take one other ingredient off the shelf, though I'm still not sure if I want to use it. I grab one more empty jar, but this one isn't going to stay empty. I wave Mama goodbye as I head out to prepare for the night. I considered bringing my bag with me because it felt wrong to leave all those new chemicals in there without supervision, like they might disappear by the time I come back and the sponsors will have become a dream.

While out, I get petrol for one of the empty jars, a sandwich for lunch, and another bottle of vodka, this time it's plain. The vodka is supposed to act as a palate cleanser to give a more accurate idea of what chemicals taste like. I can use it with chemicals I'm familiar with, but using it on brand new chemicals is asking for trouble.

The evening doesn't come fast enough, taunting me by drawing out the day. Finally, when the sky's melting from blue to orange, I leave the house. The sun isn't anywhere near the horizon, but it will fall fast and be dark just after I finish setting myself up if I take too long. My blast site looks different at dusk than it does at dawn, as if the darkness is sweeping over the trees and sky while making the snow glow with the coming moonlight. With my tripod in place, I set my phone up to record, then empty my bag on the spot.

I pull my goggles over my eyes and run my fingers through my bangs, just to make sure none of it stuck beneath the elastic band. I push the goggles up to wipe at my eyes, then slip them back on. The gloves come next. I make sure the phone's recording before I step back, waving.

"Hello, Boomers!" My voice echoes off the trees. "I have a *special* treat tonight. You don't even know—Some new ingredients from a secret source and I think tonight is going to be really, really fantastic. I brought many ingredients that I've never heard of before. I can't tell you what they are though—You might start asking questions and you know nothing good comes out of asking questions. Everyone always wants to get angry when you ask questions. 'Why are you asking so many questions? Who are you? Are you trying to start trouble?' It's better to know nothing or if you know something, pretend you know nothing. Less people bother you that way…"

I sit down at the blasting spot behind my jars. The first one I pick up is the reddish-black thick slime. I tilt the jar to watch the stuff move, slowly creeping further along the glass then back down as I straighten it out. The top flattens immediately, no splashes, no rush, no waves. "They say this kind of chemical is very rare, created mostly in very secure labs through chemical mixtures developed by foreign governments…" I pause, look up at the camera, look back at the jars, and up again. "Oh—But this one isn't from a government though. I found it in a shop off the side of a road you've never heard of and would never be able to pronounce if you don't speak Ukrainian. Trust me. It's not on the maps for a reason. They have oddities and things, that's how I found it." The warmth from the jarred energy makes the bottle warm and heats my fingers, even through the gloves and cool air.

"Now… Bear with me. I'm not *entirely* sure what the show tonight will look like since I've never put these things together before…" The words are mostly muttered while I scoop a bit of the red mixture into the empty jar. The smell of it makes my skin hot. Not like an excited hot, but like the air around the mixture gets hot and burns your skin by being near it. I scoop a little more out, another spoonful, then jar it. I switch to the off-white, yellow base. It's more watery than the red stuff. Lid off, I pour that on top of the red. After that, a pinch of gunpowder. Always a pinch of gunpowder. Gives everything it's mixed with an extra kick in the end.

I grab the final jar, another new mixture, this one a forest green powder from rocks. I lick the tip of my finger and dip it into the powder. I wipe the substance off on my tongue. "Oh… Oh no…" The stinging hits instantly. I grab the vodka to wash it out. Swishing the drink does not lessen the burn. "Yeah, yeah, yeah, yeah, yeah," I keep saying as I return to my backpack. The plain vodka is doing nothing to help me. There's a little bit of blueberry in my bag and I try drinking that. The flavor helps to cover the burn, but I'm out of blueberry before the tingling stops. I spit into the snow, lick the vodka bottle lip. My tongue's still tingling.

I grab a handful of snow and put that in my mouth then, I return to the blast spot and try the plain vodka again. This time it works. "Yeah, not a good idea," I finally say, my words like an exhale. "Whatever that is—Don't put it in your mouth. A smell should be good enough." I sit back down at my spot and scoop out some of the green powder, a little more than half of what I did for the gunpowder. I gave the full solution jar one long smell. The heat rises to the back of my nose and catches in my throat. I prepare the lid with the twine, but don't put it on yet. Everything else is returned to my bag. "Important to pick up before putting the cap on. Stuff gets hot fast. Sometimes, really, really fast," I say without facing the camera.

Lifting the jar, it's already hot. Small bubbles rise to the surface and pop. There's not going to be much time once the fire ignites. My hands shake. The night sky went dark fast, drenching the forest in shadows. I run my tongue over my bottom lip, looking for a drop of vodka left behind. "Let's kick this pig." I breathe out.

Lid on. Match lit.

On the ground, the twine catches fire. I'm running away instantly. I grab my bag from where it lays beside the tripod and move behind a nearby tree. As the fuse shortens, my heart's slamming into my ears. I'm smelling something—Something hot, tingling, my blood pulses under my skin. I set my bag down and run back out for the tripod. "I don't know why, but I get the feeling we need to step back a little more. Don't mind me." With the camera still trained on the blasting spot, I step back rapidly. "Don't worry—I won't drop the camera." I step behind some trees, but I make sure I can still see the bottle. The fire hits. The contents ignite, glow, and crash all in the same instant.

Time slows.

The *boom* is a roaring dragon, echoing off trees, clouds, and deep space. Seconds are counted by waves of the explosion hitting with smaller pressures, but none of them lacked the urgency of the first boom.

A whispering urge. I stumbled, uneasy. The pressure built in my ear. I worked my jaw to ease the pressure.

Prolonged and getting deeper, it just keeps going while the sky lights up in a whirlwind of white, red, and purple. Fire catches on something in the air, making it look like it's raining black fire, making it look like the end of the world. My skin's hot and I'm sweating through my jacket for uncountable seconds until I pull it off.

The blast should already be over, but it starts again. The roars build with a second wind, like a chorus of thunder, announcing that the lightning is ready to strike. The ground shakes so hard, that if I wasn't holding it, the tripod would have fallen over. Then, the light switches off with a groan. Everything's dark and I can't see. My eyes do not adjust to the change quickly.

A couple of leaves on nearby trees remain lit with hungry, but anemic fires that soon go out. I return to the blasting spot, careful in my steps as if the ground could fall in at any time. From my pocket, I retrieve my keys and the small torch attached to them. There's a deep dip in the ground where the bomb once sat. I tip the tripod around so my camera can catch the fresh ring of color buried in the soot. A purple and white dust mix into the rest.

The energy is too much. I lift my fist into the air with a rushing scream of, "woo!" I turn the camera around so that I'll be in frame. "Did you see that? My God—Did you see that?! Incredible!" With my torch in one hand and the camera in the other, I turn both around the blasting site to catch some of what's left. Cracked wooden bases, broken open, jagged, snapped from pressure. Branches hanging loose, mostly broken, waiting to snap off entirely. "I don't know if you saw it all in there, but that lit up the *entire* sky. It was amazing. It was… Wow." I'm panting. I'm light-headed. I can't think. I kinda wanna go again, but I can't. I didn't bring another empty jar. "I don't think there's any way we can top that tonight, boys. I want to see the damage in daylight though. Don't worry—I'll share that with you too. But until then, boom, boom, boom, salute, my friends."

I salute the camera, then turn it off.

I take the phone off the tripod and carry it around the space to take a couple of pictures. The flash messes up the true color of anything I try to capture, between the trees, burnt leaves, snapped wood, or mixed soot, so I only take a few pictures before leaving.

When I return to the street, Polina's laying on her side. The shake had been hard enough, it reached even half a mile away. "That's so cool." A laugh comes out like a punctuation. Then, I'm heading home to start my video upload.

FOUR

My phone is vibrating against my desk when I wake up. My body aches with a pain under my skin I've never felt before. Everything's heavy. I don't want to move. The phone stops vibrating, but moments later, it starts up again. I reach over. My hand knocks against it before I grab it. The screen reads ALEKS. I've missed a couple of calls and have a few messages. Suddenly, my skin's hot, my heart's racing, and I'm sweating.

"Hello?" I answer the phone.

"Jan?" Aleks says.

"Yeah"

"Thank God."

"Why? What's the matter?" I sit up, rubbing my eyes in an attempt to make them stay open. It doesn't work. When I yawn, my eyes water. "What's the matter? You sound weird." I laugh a little.

"Didn't you see what happened last night?"

"No..? I was..." I trail off, considering if I should tell Aleks what I was doing last night when I should've been at work. If he follows my channel, he'll see the video and he'll know anyway. "What happened?"

"Russia launched an attack by Nide. Whatever they used changed the color of the sky," he says.

My throat goes dry. I can't swallow. "You saw that?"

"How could anyone miss it? It looked like everything was on fire, the moon was gone—"

"I know! Wasn't it cool?"

"No, it wasn't. The *katsap* have been getting pushy lately and doing that on our border—Do you understand what the hell that means?"

"No, no, no, no, Aleks. You're thinking wrong. That wasn't Ruskies. That was me."

The line is quiet for a long while. I can't even hear Aleks breathing. I think he's hung up on me, but then finally he says, "You?"

"Yeah. Me. I was making videos last night—"

"Why would you lie for the Russians, Jan? That was not your homemade explosives. That was a military-grade bomb."

"Military-grade? You really think so?"

"Be serious for a moment, Jan. That was dangerous and it was right in your backyard. The Russians are getting daring, impatient, pushy. Haven't you been watching the news at all?"

"Of course not." I lay back down and turn onto my side. "I don't follow any news."

"Jan—"

"It's always so depressing. You know, sometimes I think it's only designed to make us fight each other—"

"It's not telling us anything that's not already out in the universe. The Russians hate us."

"I don't think *all* Russians hate us—"

"The ones that matter do. It was not that long ago we were subject to the Soviet Union—"

"And that's gone and over with now, Aleks. It has been for decades. You have to let it go."

"No. You let go of the past, you become victim to its

descendants. You're going to get yourself killed if you continue to think in the infantile ways you do, Jan."

I sit up. My legs fall over the side of the bed. My eyes land on the new, unboxed containers still sitting on my writing desk. They're so new, I haven't even put them away yet. My lips part, but I'm not sure what to say. "I just… I don't think it's as bad as you think, Aleks. There weren't any Ruskies attacking us last night."

"You say while you know nothing."

"If there had been anyone in Nide, we'd know. There is no hiding visitors here, not like in Sumy."

"Despite what you think, Jan, there's no hiding visitors in Sumy either."

"It's so much bigger, though—"

"And yet, there's always at least one person who knows when a visitor is here and they tell someone who tells someone else, and eventually, we all know."

I chew my thumbnail, finding just a bit of gunpowder still underneath from last night. My heart still throbs in my ears. I switch the hand that's holding the phone to wipe my sweaty palm on my pants. I swallow hard. "Did a couple of Americans visit Sumy yesterday? Did you meet them?"

"What are you talking about, Jan? There haven't been any Americans here."

I lay back again. Nail in mouth, my eyes catch on my bedroom curtains. I peek through the bottom to see the morning sky outside. "And you would know if there had been?"

"Yes."

"Okay…" I drop my arm over my eyes, letting it block out the world for just a little bit, hoping it might cool down the energy in my chest. It's not the excitement that usually comes with a good night, but a panic that something bigger is going on that I don't know. It's never happened before and Aleks has never called me the night after a show like this and I don't know what to do. I open my eyes again. Reaching for the curtain, I flick at its edges. "There haven't been any Russians in or around Nide."

"Hmp." Aleks sounds distracted. "Alright," he says slowly. "I'm glad I caught you at least. To confirm."

"Right. Me too, because you worry too much."

"I hope that's true," Aleks says.

I still don't think he believes me. I hear him talking to someone where he is. His voice comes through, muted and distorted, a hand over the microphone blocking out words so I can't understand him, but I still hear him. There's no other way to describe it, but like talking into a wall, staring at it, trying to see something on the other side. "Take care of yourself—And turn on the TV every once in a while. It won't kill you to know what's going on with our *neighbors*."

I wave my hand dismissively. "You should turn it off every once in a while. Things aren't as scary as they try to make it sound on TV."

There's a long pause now. I already hear him. Another lecture I've heard a million and a half times, another useless breath and words wasted, not just on me, but pushing through anxiety or tension that shouldn't even be felt. But instead of what I expect, Aleks just says, "Ignorance of war will not stop the bullet from straying into your head."

"But at least I won't be angry at the man who did it."

"And that's a positive somehow?"

I laugh. "Anger and resentment create nothing but death and destruction, Aleks."

"They create drive."

"For what? To destroy more? Eesh. No thank you." I laugh again. "I'll take boring ignorance over informed anger every day of the week, even if it means death."

Aleks chuckles low. "You're crazy."

"I'm happy."

"I guess."

A man with a deep voice says something in the background to Aleks. It's cut short by what I assume is his hand covering the microphone again. His hand draws away, the voice finishes off what it's saying. I don't know the words, but there's a stiff urgency.

"Boom, boom, boom, salute, Aleks," I say.

"Salute, Jan," he says then hangs up.

I hold the phone overhead and look over the bright screen. The backdrop's a gray mushroom cloud and the fire from its base laces around the icons on the screen. My eyes lock on the internet search bar. Even though I know better, I'm anxious and Aleks's words replay in my head: "You're going to get yourself killed, Jan. You need to keep an eye on what the neighbors are doing, even if you think you can trust them. Actually *watch* them and they'll give you a reason not to be so trusting."

It wasn't the Russians that changed the color of the sky last night, but how many people are saying that if he was calling me this morning?

My fingers trace along my phone's glass screen. Every swipe makes my fingers tingle, even as the screen goes black and there's nothing to see. I set my phone down and sit up. The sight of the chemical containers on my writing desk sends a pang of guilt through me like I should've said something to Aleks about the Americans, the sponsorship, the military-grade ingredients I have. There's no mistaking it. I go to the desk and peel the lid off one of the containers. Just that is enough to smell the material without even trying. It mixes with the scent of old gunpowder permanently stuck to my bedsheets.

Aleks isn't a liar. He's not trying to start trouble. He's only worried.

I return to my bed and pick up the phone, sending him a text that says, *It's not the Russians. Don't worry. We're safe.* I put the phone down, then pick it up again, texting him again, *I'll tell you more next time you visit. Something pretty cool happened. I want to show it to you. Everything will make sense then.*

Finally, I set my phone down and get dressed. Mama's sitting in the living room with the television on when I come out. She holds paints in one hand and a small canvas hangs on the easel in front of her. She sets down her paints to mute the TV.

"Where are you going, Jan? Are you working early today?" she says.

"No." I open the front door. "I just have an errand I want to run."

Mama stands. "Be safe," she's saying as I'm pulling the door closed.

"I will," I catch a glimpse of her as it latches.

I get on my Vespa. She's not at the door. No more questions. It's strange. She seems different today.

The roads are a little more crowded today too. Not with more cars running, but with many more cars parked along the side of the streets and roads. I pull up to Yisty's cafe downtown. A pair of men with broad shoulders, Russian fatigues, and green hats come out. They're wearing rifles strapped to their chests. They speak in Russian. They're carrying no coffee, no tea, no pastries. One of them gestures to me as I pass by. The bell over the shop door dings when I enter. The air inside the shop is hot. Too many bodies for such a small place. There are only two tables in Yisty's. One of them always homes old Bianchi and her black cat, but today, she's not sitting in her usual corner. Instead, another Russian soldier sits at her table. The cat dish underneath the table is turned over with the remains of breakfast spilled across the floor. Three more Russians stand against the wall by the table on the other side of the shop.

I order tea, but while I'm waiting, they're watching me. They're not hiding that they're watching me.

"Good morning," I say to the one. "First time here?"

None of them answer.

"The bread's very good. Really, everything is very good."

They still say nothing. Maybe they don't understand Ukrainian. Possible, but not likely. I take my cup of tea and leave without saying anything more. Russians being in Nide wouldn't normally make me uncomfortable, but Aleks's words are making me paranoid and that is exactly why I avoid watching television. If he hadn't said anything, I wouldn't think about their visiting my town as anything. "This isn't an occupation," I say to myself as I return to my Vespa. Starting it up, I see three more Russian soldiers down the street, coming out of a dress and alterations shop. Behind me, two more turn the corner at the end of the street. "It's not an occupation," I say under my breath.

I secure the cup of tea to Polina and leave. My imagination's getting the better of me. Anyone who visits Nide would visit downtown. That is where most of our commercial businesses are and without a guide, it is much easier to find than any of the smaller restaurants or shops that are spread between the trees and snow berms. My focus should be visiting the blasting spot to take pictures.

It doesn't get any better the further I get from downtown. Vehicles line the sides of the unpaved roads here and there. Three of them are parked along where I normally tuck Polina for my evening shoots. Trucks. Big. Green. Armed. A couple of soldiers stand in the snow by the edge of the trees, by the bush I hide Polina in. Closer, they're definitely military personnel, but they aren't Ukrainian. Their fatigues are adorned with a Russian flag on the arm.

A pair of soldiers stand by the street, cigarette in one hand, rifle strapped across the chest, smoke billowing from the mouth. At first, they're tense when they hear Polina's buzzing approach, but once they see me, they partially relax. I pull over to the road beside them.

"Hello—What are you doing here?" I say.

One of the men mutters something to the other. He raises his hand, looks at the man he's standing with, then comes toward me. "Name yourself," the man says in Russian.

"I live here," I say.

"Not what I asked," the man says. "Name yourself."

"Jan—"

"What business do you have here?"

I suck on my bottom lip for a moment. "I should ask you the same. There normally isn't anyone out here. It's a through-road, but…" I lean to look around him at the trees, toward the trail leading to my blasting spot. The man moves in front of me, blocking my sight. I step back. "It looks like you are loaded in there... Is something happening?"

The man takes a puff from his cigarette. When he blows out, he blows the smoke in my face. "Are you saying you did not see anything strange last night?"

"Should I have seen something last night..?"

The Russian man half turns, keeping one eye on me while looking to his partner. He mutters something too low and slurred for me to catch it. The other soldier's lips pull to one side, showing the edge of his dark teeth through his bushy beard. The other man mutters back. I clear my throat loudly. The two men focus on me. "What did you say your name was?" says the first Russian soldier.

I clear my throat. "How long will you be here, anyway?"

"Not your problem," the Russian soldier says.

"Are you looking for something? Did the president invite you? I didn't hear any announcement," I say.

"You sound defensive."

"Not defensive, curious."

"And curious people often catch bullets, you know?" the Russian soldier says. "That is not a threat, but a warning."

"I'm sorry—I'm not trying to be suspicious—"

"You are failing," the smoking soldier says.

"Is he still talking to us?" says the soldier with the beard.

"*Da.*"

"Perhaps we should do something with him," says the bearded soldier.

"I was considering it," says the smoking soldier, flicking his finished cigarette to the ground. It lands close to me. The soldier uses this as a reason to step toward me. He's only a few inches taller, but not as big as I had thought before. He is much thicker than I am, but I cannot tell if that's from military padding or muscle.

Still, I step back waving my hand dismissively saying, "Alright, alright… I'll move along." I don't turn away when stepping back, but I let my eyes drop away, partially hoping they will do the same. "I just wanted you to know that there's nothing going on here. There never is. This is Nide, after all. No one comes out here and it gets cold at night. That's about it."

"It's Russia. It's cold everywhere, all the time."

I stare at him for a long while this time, waiting to see if he corrects himself, but he doesn't, so I say, "You're in Ukraine."

"Whatever." The nearest soldier laughs. "You should be so lucky to be wards of Russia."

My laughter comes out before I can stop it. The faces of both men straighten and they stare at me. There's a soft click of the bearded man's rifle. He doesn't lift it. The click was only against his body, movement, not the trigger. "Sorry." I clear my throat quietly. "What I meant was that I wouldn't ever want to be Russian." I straighten up while I step back. The Russian soldiers do the same, the closer one looks tempted to follow me with his lean forward, but instead, he pops out a box of cigarettes, lights one, and remains still. Dry, I lick my lips and suck in a breath. The cold clogs my nose. "Do you know why? It's because we have a lot more heart than you." I tap my chest. My foot hits Polina. I grab her quickly as she threatens to fall over.

"What did you say your name was?" the smoking soldier says.

"Jan Bagan. You should remember it. I'm gonna blow up someday."

The soldier laughs into his hand something mixed with a sneer. "Go in a dick." The soldier snorts. He turns away. His Russian words mutter through his hand as poison whispered to his partner, neither of them looking at me now. I start Polina without saying anything else and we leave. I'm thinking maybe I've made a mistake, but I know I haven't done anything wrong. I wait until I'm back in town on a street with no Russians to send a text message to Aleks. Even then, my thumb hangs over 'send' for some time.

I know he's not right about his fears, but something tells me he's waiting for me to confirm his thoughts. I put my phone away without sending anything. Any confirmation of Russians in Nide would only worry him when, in fact, they're only here for a visit and they should be gone by tomorrow. This, I'm sure of and if I'm wrong, then I will text him tomorrow and he can tell me how right he was. For now, I put my phone away and return home to prepare for work. The most disappointing thing of all is that my tea is cold when I finally get the chance to drink it.

FIVE

Three soldiers come out of the small clothing shop on the corner of Boar and Black. Somehow, more soldiers are standing in the window of Yisty's. Then, at One Shop, there are four of them standing outside the entrance, smoking, talking, going quiet when I walk by just to watch me with judgmental eyes. What do they think I'm going to do to them?

I say, "Hello, gentlemen," but none of them respond, not even with a grunt. I stop in the entrance doorway and turn around to them. "Pretty quiet out here, eh?"

They smoke in synchrony. I don't know which one it is that says, "what's your name?" None of them break formation. They watch the parking lot, they don't look at me, they don't shift in position at all beyond moving their hand away from their lips to blow and suck once more. I walk away without saying anything; none of them follow me inside. Though, the smoke comes in, wrapped around my clothes, pushed by cool air.

I go to the aisle where we keep prepared meals. A handful of Russian soldiers stand there too. My fingers itch to send Aleks a message and tell him there are

Russians everywhere. I'm not suspicious, but I need this to make sense. There are just so many of them standing around, monitoring, not talking, not visiting, not doing anything, but monitoring. They peer down at me without moving. I reach between them, grabbing a sandwich from the partially empty shelf, then walk away. Their muttering makes it to the end of the aisle. If not for the soft buzzing in my ear cutting through their deep voices, I may not have heard them speaking. Still, their words are lost secrets. I try to keep moving. Laughter catches me at the end of the aisle. My foot slips.

"He looks like a problem," I think I hear, but my Russian isn't that great, so I pretend that I'm wrong or maybe the words were from the music I'm not used to hearing through the speakers since Boris turns them off at night. I quickly make my way to the register, pay for my food, and slip into the loading dock.

I enter the back room, taking off my coat as I push through the doors. It's a little cold back there, so I put it back on. My skin's sweaty. I take the coat off again and just let my shirt stick to my back while the cold seeps in.

Symon's not here yet.

I hang my coat by the lockers and stuff my lunch into my cubby. My fingers tap against the locker's metal door and my leg. Aleks's words swirl around in my head. "You should care," and "you're going to get yourself killed."

I never worried about this before and I can't understand why I'm thinking about it now. I pull out my phone with one hand. The other bangs on the lockers. I turn around, back pressing against the locker doors. Aleks's number comes up.

"Who's it?" Boris snaps from his office. The door's closed, but the light's on.

"Jan," I say.

"Who's it?" he says again.

I put my phone away and open Boris's office door.

"Jan Bagan." I lean in, holding the door open.

"Oh, good." Boris wipes his brow. He's sitting at his desk, leaning over a couple of papers. His sleeves are rolled up, revealing forearms covered in thick, dark hair. He has a couple of wide rings on his fingers. He taps a couple of them against the desk in an uneven pattern. He has a ring on his ring finger, but I've never met his wife or heard him talk about his family. "For a moment, I thought you were one of the *katsap* looking for trouble again."

"What do you mean?"

Boris leans back, crosses his arms, and looks me down. "They're looking for terrorists."

"I… don't know what you're talking about."

His eyes are tired, red underneath and veiny in the whites. He rubs at them. The red seems to turn black instead of going away. "Do you ever pay attention?"

"I don't understand why people keep asking that. I pay attention plenty," I say.

"Then you'd know they attacked us last night. The fuckers are claiming we went after them, but they couldn't strap on their boots and invade our town fast enough."

"No one attacked them—"

"I know that. You know that. They're hoping we aren't smart enough to know it was them who set off the bomb so they can stand around, looking for anyone suspicious or smelling of gunpowder and declare war." Boris growls, falling back into his chair.

"They can smell gunpowder?" I say slowly, slipping my hands into my jacket pockets.

Boris looks back at me. He chuckles, bitter, harsh, not because something's funny. "If they did, do you think you'd be standing here right now?"

I pull my hand from the doorknob like I'm shocked by electricity. "I didn't do anything."

"They don't know that—"

"What point is there to declare war?"

Boris's eyes meet mine. "It's amazing how easily the youth forget the Holodomor. Soviets not only starved us to death, but enjoyed every second of the suffering they inflicted. You're an idealist, Jan, and idealism feels nice to live by, but all it does for you is drop you in a grave thinking the guy who put you there isn't so bad."

"I haven't forgotten the Holodomor. I just don't think people are so bad they can't learn and change, see where things were wrong before—"

Boris slams his hand against the wall. My back straightens. "Humans are simple creatures. You understand what drives humanity, you understand all human motivation. There's someone out there doing something bigger than your internet videos and they won't hesitate to use you as a scapegoat if they find out you exist."

I laugh, my hand covers my mouth quickly because, for some reason, I don't think it's appropriate. Boris's eyes are sharp. He's sitting up straight. His body's tense, hands splayed on the desk in front of him. I could imagine him slapping me if he was standing beside me right then. "Sorry, Boris, but I can't think of what they would be looking for. Why they would start war—"

"Don't be stupid." Boris stands. "There's only one reason for war and everyone assumes it." He walks across the room to grab me by the shirt and pull me into his office. With one hand wrapped in my shirt, he shoves the office door closed. For how thin it is, it bounces in the frame, vibrating, almost threatening to snap. He pushes me against the closed door and pins me there. "The only reason they're in Nide right now is because nobody here wants a fight. We've got nothing to hide. They know it. The president knows it. The Russians don't care, they never have. They beg for a reason to declare us hostile so they can take everything we have. Don't give them that reason, Jan." Boris finally steps back. He paces toward his desk, grabbing his jacket off the back of his chair. He swings it on. Coming back, he pats my shoulder. "You understand? Take some time off your *projects* until they leave." When I don't respond, he gives me a squeeze. I nod. He draws his hand back and urges me aside so he can open the door.

"How long will they be here?" I say.

"God willing, not long." Boris opens the door and exits his office. He says he's going to close shop five minutes early because the Russians are scaring people off anyway, but I know that what he means by 'close shop' is turn off the music and half the lights. You might think fluorescent lights aren't so inviting until you walk into a store where half the aisles are lit by secondhand light and a quarter of the shelves are empty. I go to my locker and take out the small juice I'd purchased only a bit ago. Half of it is gone before it's away from my lips. The citrus is strong, the sweet stings the tip of my tongue where the taste buds are more sensitive. I cap it, put it back in the locker, and check the clock.

It's late when Symon finally appears. "I had to pass a bunch of fucking Russians on my way in. What the hell?" he says. He lights up a cigarette. Then, his phone's in his hand, lighting up his face. He looks over the top of it at me, then back down. His thumb flicks over the screen. "Who are they taking with 'em this time?" He spits on the ground.

"I don't think they're taking anyone with them," I say.

He grunts, waves his cigarette hand at me, and walks off toward his usual corner of the room. Already he's crouching with his eyes glued to the screen. I never know what he's so intensely looking at every day, I never want to ask.

The store shelves are more barren than normal, but there still isn't much work to do. We didn't get our usual shipment in today. When I say that to Symon, he snorts,

"Probably the damn, fucking Russians. They want us to starve, you know."

I shake my head but don't say anything to that. Symon sounds too much like Aleks, though maybe a little bit harsher. I can understand the doubt, the fear, the skepticism when approaching someone else. We don't have the greatest past with the Russians and there are tensions still lingering from other things that I try not to pay attention to. Holding onto the past only creates grudges and anger and violence and resentment and I'd rather get to know people as they are today, not who I'm told they were twenty years ago. Aleks has said to me before, "You're not that smart, Jan. There are some things you can't move beyond. There are some things you have to do for yourself to protect yourself. In this case, you should never trust a Russian."

I understand where he's coming from, but I cannot get onto the same train as him. I don't want to hate my neighbors, I don't want to hate the Russian soldiers as I see them standing in the store. Still, sometimes it doesn't seem like I have a choice. When I see them, as much as I don't want to feel anything negative, I get tense, kind of scared, I worry about what I might say to them and how they might take it, if they sound like Aleks about me the way he talks about them. I don't want to distrust them and I tell myself this regularly, but at the same time, I don't think I have much of a choice in the matter when Aleks, Boris, Symon, even Papa all say the same things. I get sweaty and scared and don't know what they're thinking when they look at me. Honestly, that would solve a lot of things, but I think if I could read minds, I could not believe in the good of people as much as I do.

For most of the night, I straighten the shelves or pace around the store. I've never been so great at sitting still and the couple of times I try, the buzzing in my ear becomes too much, I get noisy, and Symon doesn't like me making noise in the back room.

When I leave at dawn, there are still a couple of Russian soldiers standing outside the grocery store smoking. I don't know if they're the same ones from before. In the fatigues, they mostly look the same. They go quiet as I come out the door. Their heads are straight, but their eyes watch me pass and they mutter something behind my back. I turn on my heels, but keep walking backward, two, three, four steps, then stop. "The store doesn't open for a little while longer, but you don't need to stand outside and wait if you're worried about scarcity. We always have just enough at One Shop."

The Russians say nothing, though one of them grunts. I'm walking backward again, lips pursed, now looking over my shoulder for where I left Polina. My hand reaches for her before I find her. I sit down and flick her on. She purrs. "Stay warm! If you get hungry, you should try Yisty's! Good bread! Good mood! Good everything!"

Still, they say nothing, but their heads turn inward toward one another like they're talking.

I salute with a half-nod, then drive off. I'd been hoping the Russians would have cleared out by now. Though their trucks are slightly more sparse in town, they are still parked all over the streets. My blasting spot is also still being guarded well enough that I can see them from a distance and don't drive by. I stop off the side of the road. I brush my hair back. My forehead's sweaty. I should just go home, like Boris said, but I check the video I posted last night and it has over five hundred views.

My chest is tight, painfully throbbing. I'm going viral. If I want to keep interest and impress my five new subscribers, I don't have much of a choice. I must produce another video.

I return home and grab a couple of bottles from my shelf and two containers from my desk. Matches. I'm out again. I'm driving along the road, making sure no one's following me. My light's off. I'm nowhere near my usual blasting site as I look for another break in the trees and a good place to hide Polina. Nide is fortunately away from just about everything, buried in the wilderness with the only thing nearby being the Russian border.

Finding the spot, I pull off to the side of the road. I drag Polina into the snow and push her behind a bush. I look both ways down the road, looking for anyone on patrol. A pair of bright eyes comes toward me quickly. I get onto my stomach and climb into the bushes beside Polina. The truck comes close enough, the chains on the tires rattle against the ground. I hold my breath as the truck passes. It doesn't stop. The rattling disappears like a ghost in the night. I can breathe again.

I'm on my feet and hiking through the woods, fast to find a good clearing for a new, temporary blasting site. The trees are harder to go through without using a flashlight, but part of me worries if I bring out a light, someone will see me. I stop momentarily to listen to everything around me. I close my eyes. The cold winter woods make no sound out of character. The soft ringing in my right ear assures me there's nothing since nothing interrupts it. No crackling sticks, packing snow, or heavy footsteps.

After a few minutes, I'm not worried anymore and I'm moving without pause until I find a small lake hidden between the trees. There's a big rock on the other side of the lake and there's a clearing just short of that where only one tree might be a little closer than I like, but there's still room for an explosion to reach freely toward the sky. That's the most important thing to look for in a good blasting site. Every blast is one-of-a-kind and you don't want to miss any of the details once the sky lights up.

I'm moving fast, putting the tripod up, setting my bag down, getting the ingredients laid out. With the camera on, I say, "Hello, Boomer! Good to see you!" I glance toward the trees my voice is bouncing off of. I pause, listen for a moment. Nothing's there. "I almost didn't think I would be here tonight. Some crazy things have been happening around here—But I found a way to not let you down. More importantly, though, we get to keep playing… Now, today's video might be a little bit short and a little different, but you'll get to see me work, I think. Okay? So just… be patient. If I don't talk so much, I'm focusing. I have a few things today I've never seen before."

I sit down on the ground where my bag is. The bottles of ingredients come out one by one, then the vodka. I hold the vodka for a long moment, staring down at the label through the dark. Something builds inside of me I've never felt before. It's like excitement, but a little different. Tingling in my fingertips with a voice telling me to be careful that sounds much more like Aleks than me. "Maybe you shouldn't do this now," it says and I roll my eyes, laughing in contradiction while I say, "you're silly."

I take a swig from the bottle. I shake my head rapidly. Wavy strands bounce around my face. I set the bottle down and reach back into my bag for my goggles and a pair of gloves. I tuck my hair back. It falls back into my face without warning. I shake my head.

Looking up, my eyes catch on the red light shining through the darkness and the bit of phone light making it to where I'm sitting. "Sorry," I say to the camera. I slide my goggles over my eyes. "I'm just… I'm thinking a lot today… I'm not worried, it's just… people are acting kind of crazy right now. Everyone wants to hurt each other." I'm uncapping the jars, first the empty one, then four other ingredients. "People need to relax a little. Thinking too much makes you stressed out. I mean, look at me. I don't think that often, and now that I am—I almost don't think we should do this right now." I laugh, it's weaker than it should be.

I'm not sure about the combination of the four elements. I haven't had a good chance to test how they might respond to one another, but I also don't feel like I have a lot of time. With the petrol in my hand, I straighten up. I turn my head so my good ear surveys the trees around me, listening for anything in motion be it bird, bug, or man, but there's not even an echo of movement.

I pour a bit of petrol into the bottom of the empty jar, cap it, and pick up one of the new elements. I lick my finger and dip it into the substance. It's a powder. Not gunpowder. Something else that's silver-black, darker than normal gunpowder and it leaves a little sweet taste behind when rubbed onto my tongue. I sprinkle some of that into the petrol, pick up the gunpowder, pinch that in too. My fingers are trembling now. Just a little bit more gunpowder. Whatever I'm doing is going to be big.

The last ingredient is liquid, not at all gooey, but watery, bright green, it smells like something rotten. Not eggs. Worse than eggs. If I had to imagine, it's the smell of decaying flesh and it brings images of the rotten meat I cleared out from the back of the One Shop freezer some time ago. I slowly pour the rotten liquid in. Remember, pour too fast, get hot too fast, go boom too fast. I cap the smelly liquid and slip it into my bag. The mixture's already bubbling and I'm not sure about putting the lid on it. With gloved hands, I pick up the jar. It's already hot and the heat nearly sears through, making the rubber gloves stick to the glass. I get the lid on, but even after just the first turn, I know it's a bad idea.

The jar's hissing and shaking. I set it down, gloves hanging, stuck to the outside.

I'm on my feet, grabbing my bag, tossing it over my shoulder, and running. The hissing's worse, sounds like a growl, high-pitch and low-pitch at the same time. Sounds like Hell, actually. The jar I'm holding slips out of my sweaty hand. I can't waste any more time and go back for it. I grab my tripod, saying, "sorry, sorry, sorry," while I keep moving. "We need to—"

The jar explodes.

I scream.

I'm deafened by something so loud and powerful, it seems unreal.

Hot air pushes against my back. I'm flying forward. My skin burns as if I'm on fire. I slam into the ground. The air bursts from my lungs. I'm gasping for air. Blinded. Everything's black and spotty at the same time. Something in the back of my thigh stings, then I feel the same thing in my shoulder. I pull my goggles from my eyes. The dark purple sky's blotchy with bursts of red explosions that I don't think are real, but the after-effect of hitting my head too hard. My camera lays in the snow, the screen splintered with a spiderweb of cracks spread across it.

I roll onto my back. Both the pain in my shoulder and my thigh sharpen and I groan. Can't breathe. I have to focus hard to get my lungs to expand. My nose burns. I don't want to breathe. I'm going to faint. I force myself to breathe slowly, but it's not deep.

I sit up. My right leg shifts to lessen the pressure pushing into the back, creating a sharp pain. My arms shake. Something wet makes my shirt stick to my back and the morning air is cold, soothing what I know is a burn all over my skin. A thick, gray cloud hangs in the air. Trees near the blast have turned mostly into burnt stumps and fallen logs. The edges of the lake show water splashed onto the shore, carrying a couple of fish with it. Soot covers everything from rocks to what should've been snow piles, even darkening branches and trees further away. My pants, hands, and fingertips are all darkened with soot. I rub my cheek with the back of my hand. The soot there smears, but doesn't wipe away.

I reach for my tripod, but pain shoots through my arm from my shoulder. I climb to my feet. My right leg locks up from strain, searing torment burns my skin. I put my weight on the other leg. My hand reaches along the back of my leg slowly, fingers carefully probing until they find a shard of glass sticking through my pants. It's too slick, I almost can't get a grip on it. Pulling it out, blood seeps onto my thigh. I toss the glass as far as I can, lean down, and grab the tripod. My camera's still recording, the number going up in the corner by the second. I have six live viewers.

The ground is so hot, so black, the snow that had once been there is gone and beside it, a small patch of grass is on fire. Among the soot and ash is a mix of dark, dampened colors. My body locks up for a moment with my mind telling me, "you can't run from this, you have to go look," and I'm telling myself, "I'll look later. We'll have a chance later if we go now."

I look into the eye of the camera. My phone vibrates in my hand. The drop-down shows Aleks's name. I don't answer. I'm so sweaty, my hair is sticking to my head and some of the soot is running down my face, carried by sweat. In the video, my smiling, white teeth and circles around my eyes stand out against the blackened face like a Cheshire cat hiding in the night. "I told you things were crazy around here. Maybe I should explain— Meanwhile—How was the explosion?" My voice cracks.

I'm not sure if I'm hearing truck chains or that's just the ringing in my ear worse than before.

Someone yells, deep, growling, commanding. I know *that's* not in my head.

"I hope you liked the show." I grab my backpack. It slams into my spine. My shoulder throbs. I wince, grunting softly. My legs are so heavy and every step hurts. My right leg doesn't want to cooperate, but I have to move. "I'll check on you later. For now, boom, boom, boom, salute." I end the video. I'm panting from just those few words and the steps I've taken to get out of the clearing. I'm trying to move fast, trying to run, and think I'm going much faster than I am when I came in, but with the way my leg keeps seizing and the strain from the cut, I know I'm not going that fast. Liquid drips down the back of my leg.

Hostility carries through the air, echoing between the trees along with rabid, heavy footsteps. Though the words are unclear, the intention isn't: fervid Russian suspicion.

I glance behind me, panting. Bits of red speckle the snow beside my retreating footprints, but I don't see any signs of the Russians yet. I press the tripod's mount into my hip to collapse it. From the pressure, my leg stiffens and threatens to drop me. I slow down only long enough to slip the tripod into my bag. My phone vibrates. I grab it out of my bag, then toss my bag back on my shoulder.

Aleks's name flashes across the screen again. When I answer, he's already saying, "Jan—Did you see that? Where the hell have you been?"

"You mean the explosion?" I'm saying through heavy breaths.

"Yes."

"That was me."

"Where the hell are you?"

"A little bit down from my usual spot. Aleks, there have been Russians all over Nide—"

"I know—You needed to not be doing this today."

"You don't understand, Aleks. I had to do it. I had to get the views—"

"You're going to get yourself killed, Jan—"

"No, no, no, they're looking for a terrorist."

"And how do you look different than a terrorist?"

"I'm not trying to hurt people," I mutter to myself more than him. My words are all forced through panting breaths, everything about me hurts and I'm dizzy, but I can't let myself stop.

"You're out of breath," Aleks says. "Are you running?"

"Yeah."

"If you're not worried, why are you running?"

Again, I don't say anything, so Aleks says, "What you're doing is dangerous, Jan, in more ways than you realize."

"I get what you're saying, Aleks, but there's something you don't know. I have sponsors now." I reach the road I came in on. I pull at Polina to get her out of the bushes, but she's too heavy and it hurts too much to try and move her with one arm.

"What are you talking about?" Aleks says.

"You said my explosions looked military-grade. I got sponsors yesterday. They gave me these things—"

"Sponsors from where? What are they called?"

In the dark, unlit distance, a set of headlights trips through the dawn. I duck into the bushes beside Polina. I'm panting through my teeth, thinking so fast it's like I can't think at all. Can't breathe, don't even want to move again. Sweat makes my shirt cling to my back. I'm calling it all sweat so I don't have to think that it might be worse. "I have to go Aleks. I have to get home. I'll tell you later." I know what I wanted to say, but I'm not sure it's what I said.

Aleks's voice isn't making sense when it comes through the phone before the call cuts off. I slip my phone away and fight against my body to move. My shoulder screams with fire as I pull Polina upright. I grab my bag from the ground, Polina purrs, and for a while, we drive along the side of the road, going the wrong way, with the lights off.

At home, I nearly drop Polina at the front steps before going into the house. The living room lights are on. Papa and Mila are on the couch in the living room while Mama stands against the counter in the kitchen warming coffee. She runs to me when I come in. "Jani!" She's going to put her arms around me. I lift a hand and shake my head weakly.

I don't know if I can think. I've never had an explosion like this where the energy is just gone, everything hurts, and I can't think enough to talk. I can't remember much of anything at all.

"What happened to you, Jan?" Papa says. He gestures for Mama to take a step back. She does. He looks like he's going to reach for me, but he stops himself. "Did the Russians do this to you?"

"No, no, no, no. Do not worry about the Russians. Why is everyone worried about the Russians?" I mutter, walking past them. My eyes don't want to stay open, but I know the house well enough to walk to the bathroom without being able to see. Papa grabs my shoulder hard. I hold my breath as the pain builds. A dizzy spell strikes. I grab hold of the kitchen counter for balance.

"Where were you tonight, Jan?" Papa says.

I don't speak. I can't speak.

Papa says, "Jan," more sternly.

"Papa… Papa, I can't..." My voice trails off. My legs give out underneath me. I don't see her, but I hear Mama scream. Mila's saying, "Papa, what's wrong with him?" beneath the buzz in my ear and something else that's clogging them all out, making them seem distant.

I'm moving, but I'm not in control of my body. The bathroom light flickers briefly. It buzzes softly, goes away, then the light comes on strong. I sit on the toilet in the bathroom and then my shirt and pants are coming off, I'm not sure how, because I'm not doing it. Our bathroom at home isn't big, but somehow, Papa is in it with me. He says something I don't understand, then walks out of the room. My head hangs. I try to sit up. A mirror hangs over the sink across from the toilet and betrays my condition to me. So much soot turning my normally blond hair into a mix of black powder. My skin's darkened with so much ash where my goggles didn't cover, while my skin where my shirt and jacket had been is red, raw, burnt worse in some places than others. A splash of blood drips down the toilet under my leg. My pants and shirt sit in the shower, heavy with blood and sweat.

I can't pay too much attention, but I feel it as Papa takes glass shards out of my shoulder, arm, and thigh. A wet cloth washes over my skin and wipes at my hair. He bandages the wounds quickly and tightly, giving them the first bit of relief I've had since the explosion. His couple of attempts at asking questions go unanswered as I struggle to decode whatever it is he's saying through the bubbling distance muting him, the ringing, and the distortion of his words—As though he's speaking a foreign language all of the sudden.

Then I'm laying in bed with the blankets hanging over me and the smell of soot and gunpowder and antibiotic ointment and blood. The sounds of the TV make it all the way down the hall and into my room, so do Mama's and Papa's voices, getting loud, but trying to keep themselves contained. I can't hear well enough to make out any of what's being said. I notice my hands are trembling before I connect it to my whole body trembling.

The cold seeps in with the darkness. Behind my eyes are sparks of red, orange, and purple that make me uncomfortable so I open my eyes again. Then they're too heavy to keep open and I close them again. My body's weight makes me feel more at home, sinking into the mattress. My bandaged spots pulse with an intensity similar to my heart throb. Maybe I bumped my head a little bit harder than I thought. There's something I was supposed to do, but I can't think of it. I drape my arm over my face, hoping it blocks out the weird explosions behind my eyes, and some time after that, sleep comes and cuts my suffering short.

SIX

My head's throbbing when I wake up. Everything's so heavy. I'm laying on my back and my body is lead. I think about moving my arm, but it doesn't lift. I think about rolling onto my side, but the first movement pulls at something painful in my leg and sends trills of burning strain through my muscles. I hold my breath, groan softly, breathe out, and push up to sit. Blindly, I reach for my side table, groping for my phone. My eyes hurt. I rub them. Wrong arm. A stabbing pain ripples from my shoulder.

Last night is a blur of adrenaline, heat, and a big explosion I'm not sure wasn't a dream. The smell of gunpowder and iron is strong, now mixing with the smell of wet clothing. Was that blood?

I lay my phone in my lap and open up the gallery. The newest video shows a mostly quiet image. There are cracks across my screen. I close my eyes, trying to remember, but everything's just a fuzzy feeling like coming out of a dream. My voice comes from my phone, muttering against my leg as the video plays. I'm running away in the video. The jar turns into a ball of light, explodes, the same energy goes through my body and my chest hurts. My hands are shaking. From the phone, I'm grunting. The explosion fills the video. It throws the tripod back. The sky fills with fire.

"Jan?"

Mama's voice startles me. I drop my phone. She's standing at the bedroom entrance, the door barely ajar. I press the button on the side of my phone, turning it off instantly, silencing it. "Yes, Mama?"

"You're awake."

She looks like she's going to say something, but stops part way, then says, "Your sponsors are here to see you."

"The sponsors?"

Her hand tightens around the doorknob, she releases and nods. "But Papa would like to talk to you first."

"What?" A small chuckle escapes. It hurts my chest and a puncture stings in my back. That's right… The sounds from the video flood everything back into memory. Suddenly I'm aware of my burnt skin and it's annoying how much I want to rub ointment all over.

Mama turns around and waves to someone. She pushes the door open, Papa walks in past her. He closes the door, but still seems uncomfortable. He doesn't say anything for a long while. There are dark bags under his eyes and his short, brown-gray hair is messy, uncombed, sleepless. "You came in last night like a disaster."

His voice is sharp. I keep my head down like it will help me avoid him, but we're the only ones in the room and there is no escape. My body wouldn't let me if I tried. My phone buzzes against the bed. I tuck it under my leg, hoping Papa didn't notice. "I was fine, Papa. I came in quiet—"

"You were not. I carried you in here."

My shirt's sticking to my back, wet. The smell of iron is strong. Everything's sticking though, so it can't only be blood. A chill slips through my body under my skin.

Papa comes to the center of the room. His arms are crossed, legs spread for a wide stance. He waits. I say nothing. He uncrosses his arms and thrusts his hands into his pockets. Seconds later, he draws them out, paces the room, stops, looking at my shelf. "Did someone hurt you last night?" he says.

Slowly, my head shakes.

"Was it the Russians? Did they attack you, Jan?"

"No, no, no, no, Papa, nothing like that happened. I didn't even see any Russians last night—"

"Why are you covering for them?" Papa says

"I'm not, Papa. They truly had nothing to do with what happened to me last night—"

"Then, what?"

"I—" stop before I say anything. I bite my bottom lip too hard, tasting blood in my mouth, knowing that telling Papa the truth about last night would not help anything. He has never been fond of my hobbies, but he preferred them over petty crimes bred from boredom. I think the only reason I've been able to carry on for so long is because Mama convinced him to leave me alone. I don't blame him for disliking what I do. I know it's strange and when you work in mining, you don't necessarily want to think of your son using explosives for sideways fun.

Papa's pacing again. He turns away from the shelf, from the bed, he stops beside the desk. I'm not looking at him when it happens, but the energy of the room shifts. I look up, and he's standing exactly where I thought he would be. He picks up a container from the desk and turns it over in his hands. He looks at the paper, the label. He sets the container down while his fingers curl around the paper, crushing it. "Where did you get this?"

"Sponsors," I say too quickly, knowing it's the wrong thing to say just as it leaves my mouth.

"Sponsors?" Papa says. "You mean the men sitting in my living room right now, putting my family in danger?"

"They're not dangerous. They're Americans—"

Papa spits on the floor. "Are you the bomber, Jan?"

"What?" My chest hurts from the air I have to force in just to breathe.

"The bomber, Jan. We're on the brink of war and you're playing with TNT, Amatol, and God knows what else?"

"I'm not playing with it, Papa. I'm trying to make us a better life—"

"You're going to get us all killed! And for what? So someone on the other side of the planet knows your name? That one faceless idiot from nowhere, spending his time, blowing himself and his family up?" Papa spits on the floor again. His hands curl into tight fists. He's lurching toward me.

There's a knock on the door. Mama doesn't wait to push it open. Papa turns away from me. He moves back to the far side of my room, crosses his arms, and paces again, unable to remain still.

"Excuse me, sorry," Mama says, "but the guests are getting impatient. Jan, would you be able to talk to them?"

"Papa..?" I say slowly.

Papa breathes in deep. His foot beats the floor in rapid, angry bounces. The room goes quiet enough, the ring in my ear starts up. "Take care of your *pindos* and get them out of my house. The next thing to go will be all of this other shit." Papa grabs the door away from Mama and pushes past her, moving quickly down the hall until the sound of the front door slamming makes it all the way to my bedroom.

My head's throbbing, but I don't think it's from the fall last night. None of the worst pain in my body right now is from the explosion, but the fear of disappointment. Heat builds in the back of my eyes, but it doesn't get much further than that. It never does. Any desire to cry is always like an impulse in the back of my head that never comes to fruition. Sometimes I worry that I might be defective, but when I think of Aleks or Symon or Boris or even my brother Yakiv, I figure something would be wrong with me if I cried.

"I'll come out in a moment, okay? Can you tell them that?" I finally say.

She nods, saying, "alright. I'll tell them."

"Thank you, Mama."

She closes the door. Slowly, I climb out of bed. First, my legs go over the edge. They're shaking under my weight, but I don't know if it's from the cuts, leftover shock of last night, or Papa. My hands are shaking too. That's when I know it's from last night, but everything still feels like a dream. My phone falls on the floor the moment I stand. I forgot I was sitting on it.

The cracked screen lights up, telling me I have unread messages. I pick it up and sit back down. The unread messages are from Aleks. A lot of them. His most recent aren't much different from the more than two dozen of them I'd received while sleeping.

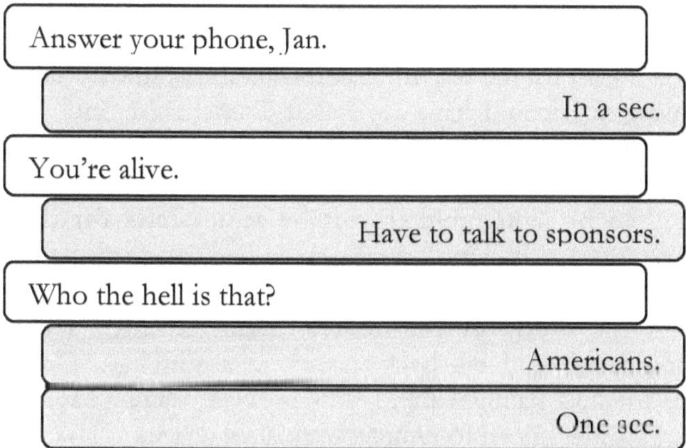

I set my phone back on the night table. It buzzes again, but I don't let myself look at it, knowing it'll slow me down. Then, when I don't answer the text message, the phone's ringing, but I still don't answer it.

Standing up, there's a bloody spot on my bed where my leg had been and a little on my pillow case. I pull the covers up to hide the stains. I'll put them in the wash as soon as the sponsors are gone.

I keep medical supplies in the bottom drawer of my desk in case of emergencies, so I change the bandages on my leg and my arm. I slip on a pair of black sweatpants. My phone goes into my pocket, then I'm on my way into the living room. My walking isn't as straight as I would have liked. My left hand pulls along the wall gently, giving sensation to my fingertips as blood races through them.

The hall smells like warm herbal tea. It's a welcome from the blood and gunpowder of my room. I close my eyes, take a deep breath, I think I'm going to fall over. I let my body drop, unable to catch it as I fall into the wall. A groan of pain comes out.

"Jan?" Mama says.

I shake my head, not sure who I'm doing it at, her or me, am I convincing anyone of anything? I'm off the wall and walking past the kitchen with my eyes only half-open. If it wasn't for the brightly colored Hawaiian shirts, I don't know if I would have registered Tom Cruise and Bob Dylan sitting in the living room. I don't think they've even changed clothes since the last time I saw them, but maybe they've brought multiples of the same shirts for their vacation. Or maybe I don't remember what color their shirts were the last time they visited.

I sit down in the nearest chair, saying, "Hello, Boomers," as I fall back. I suck in a soft hiss. Dizzy, disoriented, pain like fire. I close my eyes, waiting for it all to subside. I need to remember to slow down.

"Gen Exer, remember?" Tom says. He scoots to the end of the couch, reaching out his hand to be shaken, but I don't reach for it. Mostly because I don't think my arms would listen to me. After a moment of hanging in the air, Tom drops his hand and sits back.

Mama sets a cup of warm tea down on the coffee table. I bring it to my lips and let the warmth pass into my mouth, hoping it makes its way into my muscles. I lower the cup and look at the two men. I glance toward the door, waiting for Papa to arrive. He doesn't. "Why are you here?" I say. "I thought you were leaving. Is this because of last night's show?" I don't know what to ask first, so I ask everything.

"You're sharp," Tom says.

"Like a discounted 4k TV," Bob says. He's looking past me to what I know is Mama standing in the kitchen. His eyes say, "Get lost," but his lips say, "Can we have a bit of privacy?"

Mama doesn't move.

Bob smacks his lips, grunts, and leans back, letting his arms spill over the back of the couch. His legs spread to dominate the space.

"Now's not the greatest time to visit," I say, wiping the sleep from my eyes. It doesn't work. I yawn instead. "We have a lot of visitors right now."

"Yeah," Bob says, flat. "We noticed. Damn roaches everywhere. Did you piss someone off?" He laughs. It's stiff; it stops abruptly.

I laugh too, but it's weak. Breathing is too hard. It's not just pain. My skin's cold and sweaty. My shirt's already sticking to me again. I drink the tea hoping it helps me relax. It's hard when you don't know what's making you uncomfortable when all you know is Papa is angry, and you understand why he is angry, but you also know he is angry because he doesn't understand what is happening. With a little more information, I know he wouldn't have been so angry, but also, I know better than to try reasoning with Papa right now. When he's angry, everything he thinks is correct about the world and if you argue with him, he will just throw you outside until he's calmed down. He's not a bad person, he just gets passionate, which I understand. I'm hard to talk down when I get worked up too. I'm pretty sure I get it from him.

"They tell me something is going on," I say after finishing the cup of tea. I place the empty cup on the coffee table so I don't accidentally drop it. My hands are still shaking a little. It's like a chilly tremor in my body. "It'll pass soon, though."

Tom laughs with his teeth. He leans forward, looks at me, to Mama, back to me. "Who's telling you something's going on?"

"Pretty much everyone," I say. "But Aleks has been warning me for a while."

Bob and Tom are like a mirror. At the mention of Aleks's name, they both lean forward the same amount, they're both watching me, they look at each other for the briefest moment like exchanging a quick thought in an impossible way.

"Who's Aleks?" Bob says.

"Just a friend of mine," I say. "I've known him for a long time."

"Sounds like an interesting guy." Tom laughs.

"Does he do projects like you?"

"Aleks?" I laugh, shaking my head. "Nah. He's too practical for that. He might not like what I do, but he still supports me… Mostly through sharing his concerns—"

"So, he knows about your channel?" Tom says.

"Of course," I say. "Everyone who knows me does."

"Does he know about us?" Bob says.

I lean back. My shoulder presses into the chair. "You said not to mention you, so why would he?" My heart's racing. I'm worried they can tell I've said something to him.

Bob says, "Do you think we could meet him some time?"

"No. He's very busy studying engineering in Sumy," I say.

The sponsors exchange another glance.

"An engineer, huh?" Tom says. "That's exciting. What's coming for him after that?"

"It depends on the opportunity," I say.

"You don't know if he's going to study abroad, work for the president, any of that?"

"Like I said, it depends on the opportunity. He's very smart. Much smarter than me."

"I don't know about that," Tom says.

Bob coughs into his hand in a way that almost sounds like a laugh.

My eyes linger on him.

"We did have something fairly urgent to talk to you about," Tom says.

I try looking into his eyes, but all I see is myself reflecting in his dark sunglasses. I lick my lip. My thumb comes to my mouth. My teeth carve out any gunpowder they can find under my nail. The taste is there, but there's no dust underneath. I try another nail. This time I taste soot. "What did you have to say?" I'm saying with a finger still in my mouth.

Bob clears his throat. Both men straighten up. They sit with arms on their legs, hands folded together between their knees. "Unfortunately, urgent means private." Bob stands up. His attention is on Mama. He's not making any moves for her, but it still makes me nervous and I straighten up, inching closer to the edge of the chair, standing up on my own, using the chair's armrest to help me at first.

"What's wrong with Mama being here?" I say.

Tom stands up as well. I'm stepping back from the couch to get closer to the kitchen and Mama before they can. I don't want to assume any ill-intent, but I also don't understand why they would be standing right now. "Private unfortunately means private," Tom says.

"I don't understand what the problem is," I say

Tom sighs. He scratches the back of his head. His straw hat falls forward, knocking at the edge of his sunglasses, though his eyes don't show. "We haven't been entirely honest with you," he says.

Mama's hands are on my shoulders now.

"What do you mean?" I say.

"A little privacy?" Bob says.

I don't want Mama to go. It's not that I'm afraid, but I'm just not sure anything really good happens when you insist upon privacy. Well, there are a few good things that can happen when you insist on privacy, but intimacy is something you should only share with people you trust and I do not know the sponsors well enough to trust them in that way.

Still, these men, without even knowing me, brought me some very valuable materials and trusted me with them. Even if I can't see their faces, I feel as though I owe it to them to trust them a little. I gently pull out of Mama's hands to turn to her. "Mama, would you..?" I speak slowly, already knowing what she's thinking. It's the same thing I am, but without the benefit of the gift. She barely knows about it.

Mama looks into my eyes. She reaches for my face. Her fingers gently graze my cheek and move through my wavy hair. Her hand wraps around the back of my head. She gently pulls me to her and presses her lips to my crown. "Be careful, Jan."

"I will."

She doesn't release me immediately, but it's only a matter of seconds until she pulls back. She slowly walks down the hall, entering the office the same way she had before. The grandfather clock's ticking emphasizes her steps, punctuating with an hourly ring when she closes the door.

I'm antsy, standing still doesn't seem right and my skin's cold, so I grab the kettle from the kitchen and bring it back to my cup. Filling it, I put the kettle back and sit down. My knee bounces. I push my sweater sleeves up my arms. Shallow cuts scatter across my skin. I'm not usually self-conscious, but I don't want the sponsors to see that, so I pull the sleeves back down.

My throat's dry.

I hold the cup. Even only being lukewarm, it heats my fingers. I take a drink. Sweaty. My leg won't stop shaking. I'm worried about the next thing the sponsors are going to say. "Can you take off your sunglasses?"

"No," Bob says fast.

"Sorry," Tom says. "It's kind of a sensitive matter."

"Is it because you want your gift back?" I say. "Is that why you've come back? You saw last night's display and you want to take everything back? I understand. Papa saw some of the supplies this morning and is not happy about them being in the house."

"Oh... Is that what that was about?" Tom says.

"Just tell me, is that why you're here?" I say.

Bob's laugh catches in his nose like a sneeze.

"Actually... no," Tom says. Sunglasses reflect sunglasses. The two men share another glance. It's so strange and unnatural, but I can't place my finger on why it is so strange—Beyond that men should not look at men constantly or intimately under normal circumstances.

"If you don't want your things back, then what is it?" I say.

Bob and Tom dip their heads to the side at the same time, mirroring each other as they tip in direction of one another. Tom acts as though he's checking for Mama or anyone else who might be standing around. There's no movement in the house. The ticking corner clock covers no footsteps. "The reason we needed to talk to you alone is that... we're here on studio business. We couldn't talk with your family present because we're... scouting for talent. We don't want anyone else to know what we're looking for. You know how *competitive* the studios can be?" Tom laughs boisterously. His voice fills the house, bouncing down the hall, going into every crevice and open cupboard while Bob does little more than nod briefly with a chuckle that looks more like a sneer, but a sneer seems out of place.

"Scouting… for talent?"

"Correct," Bob says.

"That was you last night," Tom says.

It's not a question, but I say, "yes," anyway, excited, nervous, maybe for the first time that someone knows it's me without me telling them. True Boomers, and the feeling is indescribable.

"We saw it from our hotel. Incredible stuff. Earth-shattering even," Tom says.

"Almost bone-shattering." I laugh. "You should've seen how far it threw me! I almost couldn't get up!"

"We were worried you wouldn't be here this morning," Tom says.

I wave him off, trying to keep the smile from getting too big or from seeming too cocky because that doesn't look nice when anyone wears it, but humility is hard. "I'm not going to get incinerated. I know well enough what I'm doing most of the time."

"*Most* of the time?" Tom laughs.

Bob snorts.

Tom scoots to the edge of the couch cushion and leans in. His head turns a little bit to the side. "Did you upload the video to your channel already?"

Slowly, I shake my head.

"Good!"

"Good?" I say.

"Yes. You see… The studio business is very particular. Very competitive like I said and our boss… He doesn't want anyone else knowing about this deal. The industry is made up of a bunch of sharks, you know?"

I shake my head slowly, stare stuck on him.

"You find one good idea and they squeeze it for decades, long after it's stopped producing juice," Tom says with his hands in front of him, twisting like he's squeezing a towel out.

The display doesn't help. "I'm not following…" I say.

"That's fine." He waves, abandoning the charade. "All that matters is that we want to make you a TV star in America."

"A TV star?" I can't breathe, my heart throbs in my throat and the dizziness I woke up with is suddenly nothing as I'm dizzy again. I'm not even sure I'm awake or seeing right or hearing right. The ringing in my ear takes over and the room goes blurry and that ringing gets louder and louder until a tan blur waves in front of my face.

Tom's hand.

"Hey, hey, hey," he's saying. "You there, kid?"

"Did I go somewhere?" I blink a couple of times. The room comes back into focus.

"Not sure, but that's not the point. The point is an exclusive contract. NDA. Private planes. We'll get you to the ol' red, white, and blue, shooting videos in style and blowing shit up in no time. Don't worry too much about all the legal talk. It's just to protect the studio's ass, you know?" Tom says, another laugh, he elbows the air next to him like he's expecting Bob to be closer than he is, but he's not, so he misses and pretends he doesn't. He wipes the area under his eyes, careful of his sunglasses.

"And you want *nothing* for all this?" I say.

"Well… *Nothing*… in the tune of we like what you do, the boom-boom thing—And we want you to keep doing it, just on our turf," Tom says.

"Why can't I do it here?"

"Aside from all the materials being nearby, custom sets, makeup, and whatever else we want, are you telling me that you *don't* want to visit the land of the free, home of the brave, guns, hamburgers, hippies, and rednecks?" Tom says.

"It's not that I don't want to visit America. I just… I don't understand. This is happening very fast," I say.

"That's show biz, kid." I don't know if Tom winked, but if there was such a thing as winking with someone's voice, that's probably what the odd flit was at the end. "We'll get you an agent, he'll show you around, plan your events, make sure you're taken care of. The real celebrity status hits when you touch our rich, freedom-loving soil."

He says this and my mind is running a million miles a second thinking about my home, the school I grew up in, One Stop Shop and what it looked like before and after the Russians. The idea of never seeing this place again— Or at least not seeing it for a long time while I get established in the United States is frightening. I've seen the same walls, buildings, and neighborhoods all of my life. I've never been far from my family or Aleks. I had hoped someday that what I was doing in the woods would turn into a grand opportunity, I never expected it would come so fast, nothing like this, and then be left unprepared. "Can I bring my family?"

Tom and Bob lean back into the couch. Another glance to each other. I'm missing something they're saying without words or even lip movements.

"And Aleks. Can I bring him too?" I say.

"Is that your friend that works for the government?" Bob says.

"He's in school…" I say.

"Either way," Bob says.

"It doesn't matter." Tom smiles through the words. "You can't bring anyone this time around."

"Why not?" I say.

"Because," Tom clears his throat. "We have to get you set up with everything. New home, new job, new coworkers, new culture, hell, maybe even a new language.

You've never had an assistant on your show before, have you?"

"No—"

"Didn't think so. It takes some getting used to— Especially to avoid any 'sexual harassment'-type misunderstandings. But don't you worry. We'll make sure nothing like that happens—"

"What?"

"I've already talked to Bill Cosby. He's going to be your agent."

"Who?"

"When do you think you'll be ready to go?"

Everything's still spinning and really, the more Tom talks, the worse the room is spinning and the dizzier I get. Maybe I'm just bleeding out and I'm going to die soon and that's really what's throwing me off. I shouldn't have ignored the bandages for so long. How long has it even been since I've changed them? My shirt sticks to my back and I can't tell if it's from sweat or spilled blood coming through the bandages. My arms sting and itch in all the small cuts and abrasions collected in the throw. My skin's hot, burning, hoping for a shower of cold water. My phone buzzes against my thigh in my pocket, once, twice, and another time. I sit back, close my eyes, and breathe deep. I rub my face. The scent of gunpowder sticking to my hands is at least a little bit comforting.

I'm not panicking. I know I'm not panicking. This is everything I've been working toward for years. I am absolutely not panicking. I just need a second for it to process. "When did you want to go?" I say.

"As soon as possible," Bob says. "The urgency is why we're here now."

The stiffness in his voice is the first time I catch an edge of complete seriousness in his tone that had not been there before.

Bob says, "first we'll drive to Kyiv, visit the US

embassy, and from there—"

"I don't have a passport." I chew at my fingernails again. This time, it's my pinkie. "I've never needed one."

"We'll get you one," Tom says without even a bit of hesitancy. He leans forward again, his hand reaches for my knee, and he grabs it. I flatten my leg down to get it out of his hand. He notices and pulls back, then smacks the table with a sharp, hard slap. "When you're a certain kind of celebrity, you don't need to play by the same rules as everyone else. Believe me. We'll get you through customs, no problem."

"Then… You're wanting to leave now…?" I say.

"The sooner, the better," Tom says.

"What about my job? Symon and Boris?" I say.

"I don't mean to sound crass and tell me if this is going too far, but to be frank," Tom leans in. Pretending to lower his voice, but he's still loud, he says, "Who the hell needs 'em? You'll never need to step foot in that store again!"

"Unless I'm hungry when I come for a visit," I say. "That's the only grocery store in town, you know?"

"Right." Tom clears his voice. "We'll give them a call for you while you pack."

"It's fine. I can call. I think it's more proper if I tell them the news anyway," I say.

"Don't pack heavy," Bob says. The phrase gives me pause. I must be making a face, as Bob continues: "What I mean is, a man like yourself who has never traveled internationally might think you need to pack everything in your room. I'm telling you not to worry about that. We will afford you all accommodations once we land stateside."

"And that's… all there is to it? I'm going to America..?"

"That's it," Tom says, picking up one of the cups of cold tea, now raising it as if toasting.

"There is just one more requirement," Bob says. "We

will need you to sign an NDA."

"NDA?"

Bob watches something in the hallway behind me. I'm expecting to see Mama standing at the office door, but it's still closed and there is no one there. "An NDA is an industry standard nothingburger. It simply means you will not tell anyone about this deal until otherwise specified or else there will be some… very unpleasant consequences," Bob says.

"Unpleasant consequences..?" I laugh weakly. "Like… torture?"

"It might sound frightening, but it's not as bad as Bob makes it out to be," Tom says. "The entertainment industry is a very cut-throat field. You get one good idea and everyone's clamoring to make knockoffs, sequels, remakes, a hunk of trash that buries something special, pretending their shit don't stink. Even within the same companies… Everyone is desperate to put their name against the next big deal and kid, that's gonna be you. I don't think you understand just how many fans you have in the United States."

"The last time I checked, I only had twenty subscribers. How would that be so different in America?" I say.

"That's the hard thing to describe, see…" Tom trails off, scratching the back of his neck with a bit of bashfulness in his cheeks. "Once you cross the American border, you get into the American internet and once you get into the American internet, you'll be able to see just how many Americans are following you. It might sound odd, but… by watching other online creators, we've discovered this thing called a VPN and it hides your internet activity from the world. A lot of Americans are using it and that's why you can't see them in your subscriber count. Visible Person Negator—That's what it means—"

"That's not really how a VPN works," I say.

"Maybe not in a backwards country like yours, but Americans value privacy over almost *anything* else," Tom says, "I mean, what else would you call it when they let the government pass anti-privacy bills once every five, maybe ten years? Slow erosion's a pain in the ass, but it gets the job done." He laughs

Bob stands in a way that makes his foot sound like a stomp. "Do we have a deal?" He puts his hand out.

SEVEN

I'm staring at his hand for a while. My heart's throbbing again as the possibilities and opportunities fly through my mind along with the thought of never seeing my home again. I know it's irrational to think I will never be here again, but have you ever been on a hike where you walked maybe an hour or two or four away from where you've parked and when you're at the highest, most farthest point of the walk, you think about how far it is you have to go in order to reach the vehicle to take you home? It doesn't matter that the car is only maybe five or ten miles away, it feels like a universe away and your home is a universe beyond the car. America has always been the *dream*, but when I think of how far it is away from where I am now, reaching it feels not only like an impossibility, but a curse, making home and family the new impossibility I fear I'll never return to again.

It doesn't matter that this is everything I've worked toward, everything I've said I wanted, a step in the right direction to create the boom around my channel that would give my family a better life. As much as I've hoped it would happen, I don't think I ever believed someone would actually notice me and give me the opportunity to show what I can do.

"Hello?" Tom waves his hand. Suddenly, he's in front of me. Suddenly, his hand is so close and he is so close I see my reflection clearly in his glasses, but there's something about that reflection that makes me not look like me. "Anyone in there?"

"Sorry… What was the question?" I say.

"You down for the deal?" Tom says.

"Yes." I reach for the hand that is no longer waiting for me and shake it anyway. When I turn to Tom, he's waiting and I shake his too.

"Good," Tom says.

"Very good," Bob says.

"We'll deal with the paperwork in the car. Just pack your bags. We'll wait around here for you." Tom gives a dismissive nod, then sits back down on the sofa.

"You probably shouldn't do that. Papa wanted you out of the house…" I say.

"Then we'll wait in the car." Tom adjusts his tie as he stands. "It wouldn't be the first time. Just… don't keep us waiting too long, yeah? And bring the box of stuff we gave you the other day. We don't want to leave it here without your expertise overseeing it." The two men turn at the same time and in an orderly fashion, exit the house. I'm left standing in the living room by myself. The silence heralds in the ringing and I'm getting dizzy again just standing there, not sure if what happened actually happened or was all part of some fever dream from being launched in the air by a poisonous mix of chemicals that were now eating away at my brain, but I didn't know it yet. Adrenaline rushes through my body. I'm panting, slightly limping from the damage, and pushing the office door open. Mama's sitting at the desk with a book laying in front of her, closed, untouched. She stands when I enter.

"What happened, Jan? Your face is very red."

"I…" My throat tightens unexpectedly. "I'm going to America, Mama." She looks confused but saying it once makes it feel real and so I say it again. "I'm going to America!"

Her hands take my arms. I recoil from the gentle heat of the burn. She draws her hands away but doesn't step back. "What are you talking about?"

"Those two men—They work in Hollywood. They're going to make me a movie star—"

"When?" she says.

"Right now."

"What?"

"I know it's pretty drastic. I hadn't been expecting it either, but… Mama, now is my chance to achieve everything I've been working for. Maybe, yeah, I don't want to go *right away*, but… I… I must. For you. For Papa. For everyone."

Mama comes close again. She reaches. Her fingers comb through my hair. Slowly, she shakes her head and she's muttering, it might be my name, but she's not loud enough to know. "I don't know if right now is the best time to go somewhere like this."

"I don't know what you mean. This is what I've been trying to make happen for a long time." I take a staggered step back.

"Have you spoken to Papa about this?"

I shake my head. "He hasn't come back yet, but, Mama, I've already told them—I have to pack. I have to go." I turn around and leave the room. She says my name. She's following me, but by the time I reach my room, her footsteps are gone. And by the time I turn around, the hallway's empty. The front door echoes shut. In my bedroom, I flick on the light. It brings a yellow filter over everything and makes my eyes hurt. It's not because of my sleepless, difficult night. It always makes my eyes hurt. It's pretty much the reason why I almost never use the light unless I'm desperate. I flick it off again. I wipe my sweaty palms on my pants. My hand brushes against the lump that's my phone in my pocket.

I pull my phone out. The screen shows a couple of text messages and a missed call. Aleks. I open the message thread to see:

> What the hell are the sponsors?

> Jan, about last night—

> Was that you?

> We need to talk.

> Call me.

> Are you there?

> Call me.

I dial his number. It rings once before Aleks says, "Jan?"

"That's me."

Behind him are sounds of others, someone says his name, and he says, "I have to take this, sorry." He doesn't say anything for a bit, but there's a click, a door, another door, then an echo when he says, "What are you talking about, sponsors? Where have you been?"

"Fans, Aleks. I've talked to fans! Real-life Boomers! Well, one of them keeps saying he's a Gen Exer… I'm not entirely sure who that means. Do you think it's another explosives channel? Do you think they might do a collab?"

"Jan—Focus—" A door opens. In the background, it sounds like someone's urinating. Aleks doesn't say anything for a while. A toilet flushes. A sink runs. The door opens and shuts again. "Who are these fans? Where did they come from?"

"America. I've been offered a show and I'm leaving to go do it right now."

"Wait. What?" The pause in Aleks's voice gives his thoughts away clearly.

"Right now, I'm packing my bags and going to America. Which reminds me, Aleks, I can't talk right now. The Boomers are waiting in the car for me. They're taking me to Kyiv."

"Jan—"

"I'm sorry, Aleks, but I have to go. I'll call as soon as I can." It's difficult, but I hang up, knowing Aleks would want to talk me out of going in the same way he's always questioned if my hobby was a good idea or how every time he visits Nide, he tries to convince me to move to Sumy for whatever opportunities he sees there. I don't doubt there are opportunities in Sumy, but they're opportunities for someone like him, someone who was the teacher's favorite, who follows the rules, who is very smart and thoughtful and calculating in his actions. Our teachers always trusted him with responsibilities they were sure I could not uphold. I don't blame the teachers for thinking poorly of me. I wasn't interested in excelling in class. I was bored doing math problems or reading from the books and trying to figure out what deeper meaning there was to the whole of *Crime and Punishment*. Was there really anything deeper to be said than the title suggests?

While Aleks's time is better spent in a lab or a school or even working for the Ukrainian government keeping rules and peace and passing on information, that was never a life I was destined for. This is. What he sees as chaos, I see as a playground.

I toss my phone on my bed and I change into a pair of casual clothing: jeans and a sweater. There's no wet spot on the back of the shirt I'd been wearing which means it wasn't blood causing it to stick to my skin. I repackage the ingredients laid out on my desk in the box they were brought in just a couple of days ago. Then, in my backpack, now covered in soot, I place my tripod, a couple changes of clothing, my phone accessories, and my wallet. When I think I have everything, I put on my jacket. The room seems darker, but the light hasn't changed.

Morning light. A chill goes down my body with a feeling of finality. I leave the room, the door hanging open, telling it with silent, moving lips, "I'll be back soon."

My feet drag. I move through the kitchen. The weight hits me at that moment. Everything's empty. No one's waiting. No one's there for me to say goodbye to.

The front door opens. Papa comes in. The door slams shut. He's moving like he has somewhere urgent to be, but stops when he sees me. The focused expression dissolves from his face into one of confusion or surprise, but then it comes back. His lips draw back. One of his chipped teeth shows. I always wondered if I would get a chipped tooth and be like Papa. I always wanted to be like him, but I never wanted to be doomed to his work. He always comes home from the mines angry, dirty, and tired. It's a necessary evil to do your job and be in a place you don't want to be, but I never wanted to spend my life doing exactly what was necessary of me.

"What's all this?" Papa says. "Do you think you're going somewhere?"

His words hurt, squeezing my heart until it stings. I didn't know Papa could pain me with words, let alone words so simple. I nod first, unsure if my voice will work. "I'm going to America," I manage without a break.

"You're going to bomb the border and then flee the country? Do you know how this looks, Jan?" Papa says.

"I didn't bomb the border and I'm not fleeing the country—"

"Get a hold of yourself! That's not what anyone's saying—"

"What does it matter what anyone's saying if it's not

the truth?"

"Because what they're saying is what determines military actions. Ignoring what is going on does not stop the rising danger and the way your actions affect everyone."

"I'm doing the same thing I've always done, Papa! You are the one who's changed."

"I have not changed an inch, Jan. You're acting foolish and selfish—"

"*I'm* acting selfish when I'm doing all of this to benefit *you*? When I want to make you proud, Papa?"

Papa slams his hand onto the counter. "If you wanted to make me proud, then you would stop with all of this, discard this *hobby*, and get a job with value beyond the duties a secondary schooler can perform!"

"I'm going to be a television star, Papa. When everyone in the world knows my name, will you be proud of me then?"

"I will never be proud of a terrorist—"

"I am not a terrorist!"

"Tell that to every agency, media, and government, Ukrainian and Russian."

"Stop listening to lies and listen to your son!"

"With those chemicals in your room, you are no son of mine."

"Fine. Call me when you change your mind. I'll wait."

Papa doesn't stop me from walking around him, opening the door, and going down the steps. Tom is standing outside of the black Sedan, smoking a cigarette, waiting. He waves when he sees me. I don't need both hands to hold the box, but I pretend I can't wave back.

"Everything alright?" Tom tosses his cigarette to the ground. His leather shoes seem too delicate, but he presses the butt into the snow. I don't understand why he's wearing leather shoes in snow, but I don't think about it too much. Maybe he was unprepared for what spring in

Ukraine looks like. Maybe it's all he had when his plane stopped here the second time. Maybe he wasn't expecting to come out here when he got a call from his producer to put in a stop.

"I'm fine." I chuckle to push the words out, otherwise, they might've been hard to say. I smile. "I'm just going to miss my family a lot. You know, I've never been that far from any of them for very long. Maybe a weekend in Sumy with Aleks."

"Who?" Tom steps away, gesturing for me to climb inside.

"My best friend. I tell him everything." I climb into the car.

"Have you told him about this?" Tom hangs on the car door.

"A little bit," I say.

"You're not allowed to do that anymore," Bob says from the driver's seat.

I laugh a little. "You think Aleks has connections with Hollywood or some film studio in Sumy? I don't even know what the last movie he saw was. Actually—I think we were in high school and he was on a date."

"I know it might sound silly," Tom says, still leaning on the door, "but the studios are very protective of their properties. You could almost call it territorial, but motherly sounds a helluva lot nicer, doesn't it?" He laughs.

Bob snort-chuckles.

"Just… keep yourself settled," Tom says. "We'll be in the US soon and then you can tell Aleks everything there is to know about your life in tinsel town, you get me?"

I don't and I tell him that.

"You know how many people would literally kill themselves trying to get your *talent?*" Tom says.

I'm not sure if Tom is actually talking to me or someone else in the car I just haven't noticed yet, someone else worthy of receiving his compliments, of catching them in his hand and putting them in *his* pockets because they're all meant for him and not me, but there's no one else in the car beside me and Bob. "No one's ever said that to me before. You know, growing up… everyone kept telling me I'm going to kill myself. They still do it now. It's funny, because… it's not like I haven't been doing this all of my life, you know? I can tell when something's going to hurt badly or when it's going to be something amazing. This moment might not be made of chemicals and combustibles, but I can feel it right now too. This moment is going to be something amazing, even if it's scary, even if it feels wrong—"

"What?" Tom says. "What about this moment feels wrong?"

I shake my head quickly. "I didn't mean that. There's just… a lot of misunderstanding going on right now. It'll work itself out in a little while. I know it." I'm looking out. Papa's standing in the window, watching me with arms crossed and frustration etched into his brows, his lips, his entire body. The door pulls open and Mama comes out onto the step. Bob turns the car on. I push the door open saying, "one second." I'm out of the car and moving as fast as possible to reach Mama. My leg aches from where the glass shards had pierced my skin. I can't pick my feet up fully and I nearly trip on the steps when I reach them. Mama steps down and wraps her arms around me when she's close enough. Her lips press into my head. She pulls me so tight to her, my shoulder aches and the burns sear. I hold in the groan because I don't want to worry her and the pain in my body is less compared to what's in my heart.

For a while, she says nothing. We're rocking gently from side to side. Her lips flatten my hair. Then her hands release me. She leans back, cupping my face. Her eyes meet mine. "You're sure you want to do this?" The words are a mumble, our secret to anyone at any distance beyond reach.

Papa's figure in the window seems so much larger than it is. Still, I nod. "This is what I've been working for all of my life."

"Your life hasn't been that long, Jan."

A smile tugs at my lips, even when I don't feel like smiling. My eyes burn, but I will not cry. Not with Papa watching. "I'm going to build us an amazing life in America, Mama. It won't be long until I'm sending for you from our big, new house with our new green lawn and a fence and so much food in the fridge. We're going to get American fat, Mama."

Mama wraps her arms around me again. I let mine loosely hang on her. "You can call any time, alright? No matter how far away you are, do not think you are alone."

"I know, Mama." My eyes close. I rest my head on her shoulder. "I'll send pictures as soon as I land. I want you to see everything I see."

"I love you, Jan."

"I love you too, Mama."

"Papa isn't angry, he is worried."

"He doesn't need to be. It might not seem like it, but I know what I'm doing. It is only a matter of time before it all shows itself. New things are always scary until they prove themselves to be successful." I take a step back. Mama's arms drop away from her too.

"Jan?" Tom says.

I turn around. He's standing outside of the car. I imagine his sunglasses pulled up so he can look more directly at me, but that's not the case here. He's watching me with the same stiff posture, maybe from sitting in the car too long during too many long drives in such a short amount of time. Bob's arm hangs out the driver's side window with a cigar pinched between his fingers.

"You ready to go?" Tom says.

I glance back at Mama. Her face tells me she's worried and she doesn't want me to go. My legs are stiff, agreeing with her. Turning away, I'm facing Papa in the window. His arms are crossed, but he's not looking at me, he's looking at the car, at the sponsors, making a judgment on them.

"Yeah, yeah. I'm coming!" I turn around. My feet are still heavy. My leg strains against the pain from the cut. I forgot how long I'd been standing and moving and the sudden movement makes me a little dizzy and I'm worried that I might be bleeding again, but I touch the back of my leg, thinking I'm subtle. Mama puts her hands to my back like she thinks I'm falling. I laugh a little, thanking her. There's no blood on my hand. I take the first step down the stoop. Mama's fingers leave my back; she's already a million miles away.

I climb back into the backseat of the car. Closing the door, I say, "let's kick this pig."

Bob flicks some ash from his cigar. "What?" He looks in the mirror at me.

"Kick the pig," I say a little slower.

"What the hell does that mean?" Bob says.

I don't have an answer for him, so I shrug. I've never known where the term comes from. I've never thought of it before either. Maybe the best guess is that once you've kicked a pig, it will get mad and chase, so it is better to get moving, fast.

I watch the house as we pull out of the driveway, into the bumpy street, and away. I still see Polina near the side of the house. I sit up straighter, grunting as a sound tries to escape telling them to go back so I can put her away. I *need* to put her away, but if I went back, would I even be able to get into the car again? I tell myself again and again this is what I've asked for all this time and I have to follow through. I'm a man, after all, and in the face of uncertainty, I should have the bravery and the determination to push through anything that may seem too big.

Going back would make everyone happier now, but

would it make them happier later? I don't want to be angry with Papa or Aleks, but I can't stop the thoughts seeping into my mind about how none of them—Not even Mama—Can be happy for me right now. I don't want to think about it, so I push the thought back, but during the long drive, Bob and Tom just have the radio on loud and they don't talk, so I can't do anything but think and it makes everything make sense.

No one in Nide believed in me. They saw my explosive experiments as being the same thing as throwing rocks in a pond in the middle of nowhere. They figured it wasn't hurting anyone, so what was a bit of wasted time? Papa was always the least happy about it. He wanted me to be doing something he called 'more productive,' but he couldn't stop this and so long as I had a job, he couldn't complain too much beyond making a comment that maybe I'm an underachiever. I wasn't off in the city like Aleks or creating a family like Yakiv, but isn't that always how it is with a strange sort of hobby? Everyone thinks of you being all by yourself, spinning empty wheels for no benefit but to waste time into old age until one day, your spinning wheels becomes a charge of lightning that powers the house.

I think they're all angry at me because I succeeded in doing something they didn't think there was any point in. They thought maybe I'd get tired of it before I hit twenty-five and would focus on what they think is important, but they were completely wrong about it. Instead of accepting what they thought was law was wrong, they'd rather be mad at me for defying them.

I'm not mad at them, but I know that once I get to America, once I have my show with lights and makeup and authority, they will come around because neither Papa nor Aleks can argue with results.

EIGHT

My ears have been popping since the plane took off and I don't know why. Now, it's amplified to the point where my ear aches. I've asked Tom to fix the popping, but all he's done is hand me a pack of gum and tell me to get something from the bar. I ask him, "What?" and he says, "Anything. Preferably something strong. It'll get your mind off the flight."

"I'm not afraid of flying," I say and he says, "your ears will stop at some point. Just do something with yourself. Like I said, preferably a strong drink."

It's been forty-five minutes and I still can't hear very well. The popping in my ears has come with this feeling like I've gone under water and the water covers my ears, dampening sound, and giving an invisible wall for the ringing to bounce off. My head throbs with a building pressure and even when I'm laying on a couch, it's not helping my dizziness. My eyes pop open with a rushing boost of a feeling like I'm falling. I reach for the couch, but it's too smooth. I can't grip. I roll over, trying to find a spot on it which might have enough meat to grab onto. With my eyes closed, I forget the couch is small. I roll off, hitting the floor hard enough that I groan. Pain shoots through my shoulder. I roll over on the floor. The buzzing's worse. I hum to myself to give it something to compete against inside of my head.

The ringing subsides around the same time as the pain. I open my eyes and use the seat I fell off to push myself up. It becomes the thing that holds me up in a sitting position.

The body of the plane is long and slim and nothing like I'd ever seen on TV. There are no rows of tightly pushed together, gray chairs with gray luggage compartments above and rattling tables or seats that would make you question the security of the plane's engine.

Instead, the plane is a long, open space with a white couch behind me and leather recliners at either end. Red and blue pillows sit on the white leather. A big-screen television is across from the couch. The lights flash in my eyes. The sound's on, but quiet enough the plane engines growl over the drama taking place in a movie that's playing faster than time is actually going. To my left near the back of the plane is a small circular table with enough room for six, but it only has four chairs, two of which are occupied by Tom and Bob and the other two are occupied by two men I don't recognize, also wearing Hawaiian shirts, straw hats, and sunglasses. They're all smoking cigars and drinking iced bourbon or whiskey or scotch or something while dealing out cards and tossing pieces of black licorice onto the table as betting chips. That's probably the most confusing thing to me.

Just beyond the card table is a bar. A man wearing black sunglasses stands behind it, swishing a towel around the same glass he's been wiping since we boarded the plane. Every time someone asks for a drink, he sets the glass down, grabs a different one, puts the requested beverage in the new glass, then picks up his old glass to polish it with a towel again.

It's only as I watch him and look around the room and watch him again that it becomes very obvious everyone on the plane is wearing the same pair of black sunglasses. The sunglasses don't even pretend to move when the different people turn their heads. I watch the bartender closely, waiting for him to bend down so I might peek over the top of his sunglasses at his hidden eyes, but he never fully bends over. When he lowers, it's a tilt and there's a lip on the top of his glasses that stops you from peeking down them. It doesn't even matter either because when he needs to go far down, he doesn't bend over, he squats in a way that's like his knees are sinking into his ankles.

I dig my phone out of my pocket and stare it in the face.

"Ah, ah," someone says. I lower the phone. A man who introduced himself to me as Patrick Bateman sits in the recliner at the end of the couch. He's wearing a red Hawaiian shirt and has hair slicked back so tight it looks like it's made of plastic. "Maps. Remember?"

"I'm just looking," I say.

"That's what every guy says before absolutely wrecking the ass of someone who isn't his girlfriend," Patrick says. "You don't want to crash the plane, do you?"

"I'm not calling anyone." I tap the screen so it wakes up from black, then turn it around to him. "See? It's still in airplane mode. I'm not calling anyone; we're not crashing."

"You're seconds away from it every time you look at that screen." Patrick's finger flicks across his phone screen. A game of colored balls breaking reflects in his sunglasses.

I set my phone on my chest. My face is hot, my arms are cold. All the air is stuffy somehow. I lay my arm over my eyes, but without sight, the sounds become more annoying and all I have to focus on is the popping in my ears, leading to more ringing. It's been hours since we left

Nide and despite what I told Aleks, I haven't had the chance to call him yet. The sponsors wouldn't give me a moment alone, even in the bathroom at the airport. They followed me in and waited outside the stall. Well, they told me they were urinating, but they never did flush the urinals nor did they wash their hands.

My arm slides from my face and sits on the floor beside me. Even though I know the answer, I say, "What about a text message?"

Patrick laughs. "You'd be lucky if a text made it out of this tin can before we nosedived into the ocean. Do you know how to swim?"

"Yeah—"

"Doesn't matter. You hit the water going this fast from this high up? Water's pretty much concrete. You ever wonder what someone looks like splattered across the surface of the ocean? Imagine strawberry lemonade. Extra pulp… because your organs will be out to open waters."

I take my phone off my chest and slide it back into my pocket. Patrick says, "Good choice," without looking up. His phone clicks as his thumb snaps into the screen. Another line of red bubbles pop in his glasses. I use the couch to help me stand.

Something's rattling from somewhere in the room, reminding me the plane's moving—Just in case the wind turbines didn't. My soda sits on the nearest table in a small cup-shaped hole, bigger than the glass. Ice, mostly melted, makes the top layer of the drink somewhat clear and unmixed with the cola.

I walk back to the table where Bob and Tom are. Someone clears their throat like giving a signal. They stop talking before I get near. All of them straighten up just for two of them to lean over on the table, arms folded, heads down. Tom sits on the nearest edge. He turns from the table to greet me with, "What's up, my guy?"

"Where's the bathroom?" I say.

"Over there." Tom points past the bar.

"That air pressure will squeeze your goddamn colon dry," says an older man wearing sunglasses. The older man has dark brown hair, but his face is covered in wrinkles and a frown that betrays his age. No one gets that big of a frown without the misery of at least six decades. He coughs and there's phlegm in his throat. He brings his fist to his mouth and coughs in that. He reaches for his cup and uses the whiskey or bourbon or scotch like cough syrup.

It works.

"Piss isn't in your colon." Bob smacks the table like it supports his point.

"It's in the balls," Patrick says.

"Like hell it's not. When'd you become a biologist?" says the old, miserable man, smacking his hand down, mirroring Bob.

"I can be anything I wanna be, Bob," Bob Dylan says.

I stare at them both, but mostly the old man that's not Bob Dylan. He sets his cigar in the ash tray, then he's picking up his glass. The ice clatters together. He looks to the bartender, then back at me. He stares for a while. "What are you looking at, brat?" he says.

"You're both Bob?" I say.

"Yeah," the other Bob says.

"I'm Bob Dylan," Bob Dylan says. "He's Bob Arnold."

"Oh. Makes sense," I say, even though it doesn't. I thank Tom for the directions and then leave. The bathroom isn't tiny, but it's smaller than I would have thought for something on an American plane with so much room. It's not that I was imagining it would be very, very big, but big enough to accommodate regular American sizes. The room is similar to a closet with a new, polished toilet in it.

When I lift the lid, the seat's warm to touch. The sink flicks on automatically when my hand is near the faucet, and a paperless dryer clings to the wall, blowing air only when hands are between the plastic walls. Behind an accordion wall is a small standing shower—Which I also hadn't been expecting on a plane at all because where does all the water come from? Little bags of toiletries sit in a wall cubby across from the sinks. I close the accordion door and sit on the closed toilet. My hand's in my pocket, my phone's in my hand. I'm staring at the last text messages I received from Aleks before turning my phone receiver off and leaving Ukraine. Almost a dozen of them with variations of "Call me," "Don't go with the sponsors," and "Who are the sponsors. I want names."

My eyes burn with tears I'm holding back. I'm not going to let my anger get to me. I understood how much of a battle it would be to have my desires taken seriously and up to this point, I knew that Aleks was humoring me while he hoped I would come to Sumy and do something *worthwhile*. I know his desperation to get me to stay in Ukraine came in part from his ego. He's worried and I can't be mad at him for that.

The screen goes black. I tap it immediately to wake it up. Then, my finger's hanging over the airplane mode button while images of my body as lemonade float in the ocean beneath my feet. My heart's pounding so hard, it chokes me. I close my eyes. The constant ringing in my ear turns to emergency beeping, then screaming, then, right before the explosion, Tom says, "Jan! Jan! Just be honest with me! Did you try and send a text message?" and because I can't lie to Tom after everything he's done for me, I say yes and he gasps, sobbing, praying to God and his mother and the family who will never see him again, so I say, "I'm sorry, Mr. Tom Cruise. I made a promise to Aleks," and Tom says, "Aleks? Is that your friend who works for the government again?" and I say, "No, no, he doesn't work for the government. He's—" but I wouldn't get to finish that sentence because we'd crash, hitting the sheet of water that now looks like human lemonade for sharks.

Or Tom and everyone wearing glasses is lying and we won't die when we hit the water, mostly just because every plane crash I've ever seen has been through special effects and maybe no one has ever actually died from them.

I nod slowly, convinced. You can't turn people into lemonade with a plane crash. I press the airplane mode button on my phone. The circle button turns white. Seconds later, the internet bars show at the top of the screen. There's a connection to my phone network. I open the messaging app again and send a text:

> Sorry, Aleks—

> Delivery failed. Retry?

I press send again.

> Delivery failed. Retry?

I press send one more time.

The message still doesn't go.

Someone knocks on the bathroom door, then pulls at the handle. The lock stops them from opening it.

"Sorry—Occupied!"

"What?" says a voice I don't recognize on the other side.

"Occupied?" I say, slower.

"I don't know what you're saying," he says in English.

I catch my own eyes in the mirror. Red. Tired. Foreign with fear. My lips move in silence to create the sound of letters before I come up with, "Occupied?" in English. "One moment." I turn airplane mode back on and slip my phone into my back pocket. I flush the toilet even though I didn't use it, then I wash my hands. I open the door. On the other side is the younger man from the table Tom and Bob Dylan are sitting at. He's taken off his straw hat. His hair's neat and gelled back. His jaw is covered in five-o-clock shadow. He's still wearing his sunglasses.

I tip my head to him when I walk by, giving a half nod and an English, "Sorry," though I don't know if he heard me since he doesn't say anything and shuts himself into the bathroom. I edge down the hall toward the bar, but stop short in the partially dark hallway when I hear Bob Dylan's laugh rumbling in a way he never allowed back at my house. In Ukraine, his laugh was restrained, strict, more like a grunt and a snort, but here, it's an echo in a barrel with a fish slapping against the sides.

"Alright," Tom says, playing cards click, shuffling in his hands. "Everything's set up and waiting."

"The conference tomorrow will prove his place," Bob Dylan says.

"You're sure the jet lag won't be a problem?" Bob Arnold says.

"Shouldn't." Tom deals the cards. "He worked the night shift."

"How convenient," Bob Arnold says.

"Convenience is our trade secret." Tom laughs. He picks up his cup, drinks it in one go, and raises it, asking the bartender for another. The bartender brings it quickly.

"Right… You're sure he's not *connected?*" Bob Arnold says.

"I couldn't find anything on him. Bob couldn't find anything on him. The Pentagon couldn't find anything on him… Hell, even the reds weren't at his house this morning. I'd say it means we're all clear." Tom picks up the fresh glass delivered by the bartender. It's down in one go. Holding the glass up, he says, "beer." The bartender takes the glass of ice away while bringing Tom a beer. "Our only concern is that friend of his in Sumy. Aleks isn't enough to go off. Could be a nickname, a middle name, a codename if he is a sketch. Jan's said the guy's an engineer, but… without meeting him, how the hell are we supposed to know if that's the truth?"

"Don't we know that? Everyone in Rome is a goddamn fed," Bob Arnold says.

"And their moms live in Virginia," Bob Dylan says.

"Right." Bob Arnold's laugh turns into a cough.

"We've got a couple of leads, but nothing concrete," Tom says. "Might be able to get a little more info soon. A welcome party to work out some gossip. It's never *that* hard to get civs—" Tom suddenly stops. He's turned around, staring at the couch where I had been sitting. He sets his bottle down with a loud clatter and stands. "Hey." He waves at the bartender. "Hey, Patrick—" He turns to the man playing his phone game in the recliner. "Where did he go?"

Patrick waves Tom off without looking up. "Relax, Tommy. Where you think a Russians gonna go 30,000 feet in the air?"

"I'm not Russian, I'm Ukrainian." I come out of the hall. "We're brothers, yes, but we're different. Everyone will tell you. Ukrainians have bigger hearts and better vodka. Don't listen to the *Russians* that tell you otherwise."

Tom crosses the plane back to me. His hand grabs my shoulder. The squeeze agitates my wound. I grimace. He pulls his hand back, slips it down my shoulder to press into my back, and leads me toward the couch. "Where were you?" he says.

"Bathroom…" I say slow, walking slower. "You pointed me there."

"And you speak English?"

"Yes." I smile.

"How… much?" Tom stands in front of me, his eyes tight, his fingers are threatening fists.

"Enough to get by. Like you said, my biggest audience is in America, so of course, I've learned a little bit. I'm not so great at *reading* English, though. There aren't too many opportunities for reading it in Nide. But," I clear my throat, working my mouth to speak as clearly as possible. "Pretty good for someone who learned watching people play video games on YouTube, huh?" My accent's still strong, but hearing the words and seeing the reaction in Tom, Bob, Bob, and Patrick make me proud of all the time I spent alone in my room watching those channels.

Most of the people I watched had some kind of accent too, whether it was American or European or sometimes Asian—But none of them spoke as clearly as Tom or Bob Dylan. True Americans, I thought the first time I heard them and saw them. They just have that look like they *are* Americans. The comb-mustache on Tom and Bob Dylan's round face with misery darkening his eyes from all the time he's spent staring at long commercials that burn holes in your pocket. I think too much money can also burn holes in your face.

"Yeah, yeah, yeah—That's pretty good," Tom says, "but we have an important question. Do you know enough English to talk to your fans about what you do or are you going to need a translator?"

The words come fast. The question seems out of nowhere. "What do you mean?"

Tom shakes his head. "Never mind. We'll see what your agent thinks when we get to the airport—"

"Agent?"

"Yes. We talked about this at your house. Remember? Bill Cosby?"

"Right. Bill Cosby… What's he for?" I say.

"Managing your schedule, setting up meet-and-greets with your fans, event planning, project management, making sure your videos get posted on time, making sure you're fed… Pretty much making sure you have everything you need when you need it to make you successful. All great celebrities have someone like him.

Soon, you might not even have to wipe your own ass." He laughs. "I mean, once you get big enough, everything annoying about your day-to-day life doesn't even have to be a thought anymore. You'll get so used to it, you might even forget how to use the phone!" He's still laughing. The other men laugh, including the guy returning from the bathroom. He's laughing as he's walking and reaching his hand like he's blind until he grabs onto his chair at the table and he pulls it out so he can sit down again. Then *his* laughing gets harder and it's very strange. I'm watching him too close. Tom stops laughing and says, "Jan?"

I say, "Sorry," and laugh with them. "Sounds good."

"Good." Tom turns away.

I slap the side of the couch as I sit back. My hand brushes against my phone. My heart races for a moment and I glance toward the cockpit. "Hey, unrelated—I don't know how long I was in the bathroom, but did anything strange happen?"

"Happen… how?" Tom turns back around.

"I don't know how to describe it, but… something… sometimes, you know when you can get so focused on what's going on in the bathroom that you sort of *eject* from *reality* and you don't feel anything around you anymore so if there's a little shaking or the plane might be upside down or you did a cartwheel or did really hard circles, you don't know because you didn't feel anything since you were having an out-of-body experience?"

Tom is staring.

"Do you know what I mean?" I say.

Tom is quiet for a while. His tongue smacks into his lips and slowly he nods, "Yeah…" He nods a little more, smacks his lips again, swallows hard enough it's visible. "Yeah. I think I know exactly what you're talking about. No worries kid. Nothing weird happened." He gives me a thumbs up. He waits until I give him one back to turn around. "There hasn't been any turbulence since we reached altitude, but I'll check with the pilot and see if he can't keep it smooth sailing, alright? We're almost halfway over the Atlantic, so it shouldn't be much longer now. Why don't you try and relax a bit? Get some sleep?" Tom remains where he's at, watching me until I give him a nod, then he returns to his card table with the other sponsors.

I stare at the television across from me. The picture blurs from my vision, zoning out. My wounds burn and I'm smelling the smallest amount of blood now, but I don't want to change the bandages because those are the only things I have to remind me of home right now. I bring my fingers to my lips and search my nails for gunpowder. They all come up empty, sucked clean already. The weight of my sleepless night holds me to the couch and I can't resist closing my eyes.

My shoulder throbs against the hard cushion, so I roll onto my side. The cold leather's nice. My phone presses into my thigh, reminding me of what I did in the bathroom, the guilt of leaving Aleks without a word burns into my skin. I tell myself I'll call him when I land and I'll apologize for the way I left and everything will be fine again. He'll understand. He's always understood my shifting, unpredictable circumstances—Even if they've never been quite like this.

The leather surface is so cold and chilly, the hairs on my arms stick up. I reach weakly for a blanket that's usually hanging from the back of the couch back at home, but there isn't one here.

"Hey," I say.

The noise from the television distracts me; English words turn into blah blah blah because they're going too fast and I'm too tired to decode them. At some point, I catch every other word, but the soft ring in my right ear drowns them out. In a way, it's kind of comforting for how familiar it was compared to the cold, industrial smell of the leather and suits or the clean aircraft of alcohol and tobacco. I push myself up, using the side of the couch as leverage. My eyes are too heavy to keep open. I rub them hoping it'll help.

I look at Patrick through almost closed eyes. It's hard to see him, but I think his legs are kicked up and he's still tapping away at his phone. I move my lips, thinking of what I want to say, but nothing comes out. There aren't any words in my head. "Is there a blanket I may use?" I say in Ukrainian, but I'm not sure he speaks it, because he doesn't respond at all. Then, I say it again in English.

Patrick gets up without looking, he opens one of the cabinets, and he tosses a fleece blanket onto the couch near my feet.

"Thank you," I say, pulling it up over my head to block out the light of the cabin and the sight of the plane. It's soft, but it doesn't push the goosebumps back into my skin. The warmth doesn't wrap around me like it should and it smells like business. I'm not sure how else to describe it when it doesn't smell like laundry detergent, fabric, or home. There's no scent like it's ever been used and now I'm trying to remember if I heard him tearing apart a plastic bag to get to the blanket. I bring my fingers to my mouth and suck on the tips. Even though I don't find any bit of gunpowder on them, it becomes more comfortable in the cave of a blanket not made for family, but for a mission.

Utility.

That's what it reminds me of.

The military.

NINE

The plane's landed, but we haven't stopped moving yet. Tom says, "Sit back down." I don't do it until the plane goes bumpy and I lose balance. It's cloudy outside and early in the afternoon. Tom stands in front of me. He snaps his fingers to get my attention, then he sits beside me. "Alright, Jan… Glad you got some sleep, it's gonna help you a lot in the next couple of minutes, but for now, I need you to breathe and prepare yourself. Outside these walls, waiting in the airport lobby is a horde of your fans and I'm going to need you to stay focused so we can get the hell out of here before someone rips off your shirt to sell on eBay, you understand?"

"What?" I'm not sure I heard him right or maybe he used the wrong Ukrainian word.

"Have you ever dealt with fans before?" he says.

"Only you." I point at him.

"Okay. Good…" He stands up, taking a deep breath. He strokes his mustache with a couple of fingers and paces away. "This—We can do this—Don't get nervous, alright, Jan?"

"I'm not nervous— "

"I understand this is all new to you, but we can do this, alright? They've heard you're coming so they might be a little bit rambunctious on the other side of the gate, but don't let that distract you. You might see signs, you'll hear people screaming your name, you might even hear them screaming a handful of other crazy shit because they've been waiting a long time to meet you. Don't get distracted. You'll get the chance to talk to them later. Right now, the most important thing is for us to get you out of here and safely checked into your hotel, alright? Your agent should be on the other side of the gate running crowd control. Once we meet him, follow his orders and stay close. That's the only way to make sure nothing happens to you."

I nod, but pause a second after the words register. "What do you mean by that? Am I in danger?"

"You shouldn't be," Tom says. He's turned back toward me. He barely lifts his hat to run his fingers through his short hair. They then stroke his mustache again. Somehow it seems shinier. "But there have been fans who've been known to do crazy things and we—Your agent and I and all of America, really—Just want to make sure you have a *good* welcoming party and not a *traumatic* one."

I stand up. "What are you talking about? What kind of crazy things do people do?"

"Well… and I don't want this to freak you out, but there was a Stevie Nix fan—You know, Stevie Nix, yeah?"

"Who?"

"So this total freak waited to meet her outside one of her concerts. He wore a trench coat lined with her pictures and nothing else underneath. When she came over to shake his hand, he withdrew a knife and tried to stab her—"

"What? Why?"

Tom puts his hands on his hips. "Frankly, he wanted to commit a murder-suicide as he believed it would bind him and Stevie together for the rest of their afterlives. It was his obsession that did that to him. He bought into all kinds of crazy occult magic and was ready to do whatever it took to *get* with someone he *thought* was his lover. Funny thing is, they'd never exchanged a single word. This crazy-ass just listened to her music so much that he convinced himself she was singing directly to him and he deserved some claim on her soul. People are goddamn insane, you know?"

"Oh. Yeah. I don't want anything like that to happen today. Or ever—"

"There's nothing you can do to stop it. Anyone with an alluring personality risks their charm influencing those around them," Tom says.

"Social media's a trap," Patrick says. His phone's still in his hand while he stands in front of the chair he'd been sitting on before. Instead of colorful balls breaking in his glasses, it's a Sudoku board. "Trap for the feds, trap for groupies, trap for e-girls to lap up your cash in a trading card game made of their pussies. Good luck with your fame, kid." His lips pull up into a crooked smirk. The word 'kid' throws me off because this man looks like he's my age.

"What do you mean by that?" I say

"Celebrities are required to have social media. You can't keep a job without it, so… Good luck," Patrick says.

"Tom—" I say, turning to him.

"The best you can do is be aware that as a celebrity, your presence, digital or otherwise, may cause some to tremble, fall into obsession, think crazy thoughts, or develop a cult. If you wander off, we're limited in what we can do for you and it's even more dangerous now since—" Tom smiles, laughs, bumps his nose with his finger as he kicks a foot out. "You don't know Washington, do you?"

"Washington?" I say

"DC," Patrick says.

My eyes narrow. The apprehension draws me back a little. I glance toward the window and back. I'm looking at myself in the reflection of Tom's sunglasses. I'm looking hard, squinting harder, hoping to see through the black to even a faded, obstructed version of his eyes, but there's no way to see through them. "I thought LA was where the movies were made?" I say slowly.

"Tinsel town?" Tom says. "Yeah... That place died a couple years ago. High taxes, tent cities, constant hellfire storms, and the whole state smells like shit because one little town pushed all the good people out—But it's fine. Most of the people that fund the big blockbusters you're thinking of work here. They call DC the American Rome, you know?

"You have blood sports?"

Patrick laughs a stiff, "Ha!"

Tom pauses, his lips stick out and he turns his head away for just a moment before slowly coming to a nod. "You could say that, but that's not why we're here. We're here because there's a lot of big money in DC and a lot of big investment to be had in big projects like what you've been working on in your own backyard. Your TV show is exactly why the big investors picked you. Don't let 'em down, alright, kid?" Tom smacks me on the back. This time is lighter than the last. He must have remembered the wounds this time.

I nod. I hadn't been thinking of the investors until that moment. Up until even just that second, the reality of having sponsors seemed fake, even when they left a legitimate box of rare and valuable chemicals behind for me.

The plane comes to a stop. Tom grabs a small hold of me to keep me balanced. "You ready for your debut, kid?" Tom says with a toothy smile.

I smile back. My heart is thumping hard in my chest. Even my hands are trembling.

"It's gonna be okay. Enjoy the moment," Tom says. He glances toward the cockpit, he nods, and then, with his hand on my back, he gently nudges me forward, saying, "it's go time."

We cross into the terminal. Light fills the airport halls. A large dome. Lots of windows, pillars, gold. Everything about the place speaks of Roman inspiration, opulence, and royalty. I feel the presence of the other men close behind me, but it fades away in the fastness of the airport gate.

"Once we pass through those doors, you're going to see your fans," Tom says. "Just remember to breathe, yeah?"

I nod. At least, I think I nod. I can't speak, I can't say any words, ask any questions, or confirm anything Tom has said because it all seems so foreign to me. I'm floating in a dream, watching someone move my body forward while I wait to wake up from this place at any moment. A couple of people sitting by at random terminal mutter to one another. Star struck. They're talking about me. One of them points.

Then I hear the crowd before I see them. Murmurs of more than a dozen people. The doors open. My eyes are filled with a sea of faces, young and old. Men, women, children. More people than I've ever seen gathered even at Nide city events.

Someone's wearing a shirt that says BILL NYE, THE SCIENCE GUY and over the sound of chatter, someone else stutters and shouts "S S S-SCIENCE!" and someone else yells, "m-m-m-math!" and someone else yells, "ka-BOOM!" Then, without much coordination, someone starts saying, "Janananananananana," like they're singing a song and everyone else around picks up on it and starts saying it too, ending with a random person shouting, "Batman!"

A woman screams.

They start 'nananaing' again.

There's a teenage girl in the crowd with her arms crossed, looking down and away, bored. Her father elbows her, mutters something, and her face lights up with a broad smile as he points at me. On the other side of the room, people lower to bent knees and, in a wave, they straighten across the gate, hands raised. When the rise hits the other side of the room, it returns while the group continues making sounds like my name, in between saying "science," "math," and "BILL, BILL, BILL, BILL!"

"Why do they keep saying Bill?" I say to Tom, the chants from the crowd almost burying my voice.

"Because… they like science and that's what you do, right, kid?" Tom says.

"But who is Bill Nye?" I say.

"Can't you hear them?" Tom says. "He's the science guy. Think… the mascot of science."

"Oh," I say. "I don't understand."

"Don't worry about it," Tom says.

Someone bumps into me. My attention breaks. Tom grabs the offender by the arm and pulls her back saying, "watch where you're going."

"Watch the hands, glowie." She pulls her arm away; Tom lets her go. She spins on her heels, continuing to back up, shaking her head at him. She runs into another one of the sponsors. She turns around again, fast. "Holy shit. What in the hell is this? A glowie convention?" She snorts, then looks at me. Her pink lips twist into a sideways grin and a smirk. She whispers the word, "run," before speeding off.

She's the most beautiful person I've ever seen, and nothing like anyone I've ever seen before. Long, blue, almost cyan hair tumbles down her back, interrupted only by a strip of pink bangs and a couple splashes of pink strands placed throughout the rest of her hair, underneath the blue. Our eyes only meet for a moment, but it's enough to see they're dark brown embers, burnt bark, blasting spots filled with some sort of emotion that's already been released. She's wearing a soft, pink sweater dress, stockings, and blue sneakers. She has a silver ring through her nose and an expression I can't read, but it makes me want to know more about her.

"Hey," I say without thinking. I'm walking toward her. "Hey, hey, what's your name? I'm Jan—"

A hand grabs my shoulder and stops me from pushing further into the cheering fans. The grip is too hard, my burns hurt. "Remember what I told you," Tom says.

I can't take my eyes off the blue-haired girl as she pushes through the crowd. I watch her closely, not wanting her to disappear. "They won't kill me," I'm muttering, not paying attention to the wave of people. Some are still whistling and hollering, some are murmuring and checking their phones, some are talking to each other, pointing a finger up front, and turning back to holler again. The girl with blue hair pushes through the wave of people, using her shoulder as a battering ram to get through the wave too fast for me to catch up. I try, but Tom grabs me with two hands and pulls me back. The girl turns the corner and her blue hair disappears with a gust at the end of the hall.

"You don't know that," Tom says. "We never know who the crazies are."

"I need to talk to that girl," I say.

"What girl?"

"The one who just turned the corner. The one with blue hair." I point to where I last saw her.

"There will be plenty of girls with blue hair. We need to keep going, Jan. Bill's waiting for us." Tom gives a signal with his hand while whispering something to Patrick. Patrick's eyes are still on his phone, I wonder if he's reading text messages from Bill about the crowd blocking our path or if he's still playing games like on the plane. Bob Dylan and Bob Arnold step forward and wave their arms. The sea of people parts in synchrony without needing a command from the older men. Tom guides me through the group of people, but everywhere we go, around every new corner, more people are waiting with new cheers and nanananaing that are echoed by those we left behind. I'm looking at overhead signs, trying to focus enough to drown out the voices as the mixture of cawing and screaming and cheering and random words turn into a mess cramming into my head, unintelligible, waiting for me to explode. The words don't make much sense, but there are signs of cars and baggage and walking, numbers, and exits. Another one looks like a picture of the metro.

A smile comes back to my lips, fast and wide. "Do we get to ride the metro?" I say. "I've always wanted to see Grand Central Station!"

"I don't want to disappoint you, Jan," Tom says, "but we're in Washington DC. Grand Central Station is in *New York City.*"

"How far is that from here?"

"Too far to be put on our agenda."

"Isn't that something you're in charge of?"

"No. Bill's in charge of that."

"So he can change it whenever he wants?"

"No. We have schedules we have to keep. Appointments with studio executives and all that." Tom's hand presses into my back and he pushes me forward now, but my legs don't want to go. What if that girl will be at the train station? What if that's my chance to say hello? To ask her name? To see if she's a Boomer and maybe if she'd like to get married? With how many fans there are here in the states, there should be a high chance she would say yes, right?

I'm almost sure I see her blue hair flutter behind the glass door at the other end of the hall. I'm turning that way, walking that way. Tom grabs my arm and pulls me back with a tight grip. "Keep yourself focused. We have a tight schedule, Jan, and you don't want to get lost. That would throw everything off."

"Maybe that's not such a bad thing," I murmur. My smile turns into a tight frown and my shoes drag against the floor. "I'm not sure I like this very much. You know… back home, I was on my schedule mostly. Even Boris didn't treat it this tight while I was on shift. As long as I was at work on time. And if I wanted to talk to a girl, I was able to talk to a girl. The only problem was that most of the girls my age already moved out of Nide or were married so there weren't very many options…" I laugh a little. It fades fast.

"How old are you?" Tom says.

"Twenty," I say.

"And everyone in your town is married?"

"Mmm… Everyone in Nide that wanted to be. Everyone else left. Obviously, there is not much to do in Nide. Any girl who wants to be more than a housewife leaves very quickly like Aleks did," I say.

That's the first time Tom stops walking and turns his attention to me. "Oh. Is Aleks a woman?"

There's something more in his question, maybe a second question that I can't guess like, "Is she single? or "Is that why she went to Sumy?" or "how old is she?" None of those questions fill the missing part, but it's strange either way.

"Aleks is a man. I talked about him before," I say, "but he wanted the same thing the women who leave want: something beyond stocking shelves or running a bakery or taking over management next time Boris is in the hospital from smoking too much or getting in a fight at the bar—"

"Okay, good—That's what I thought, but… You had me second guessing there." Tom laughs. He's still pulling me forward with his hand on my arm, fingers tight.

Moving forward isn't a suggestion. I'm almost running, which makes a little sense with the crowds echo behind us. I look over my shoulder to see if I can spot anyone. My feet catch on something, I almost trip. Tom picks up the pace and pulls me out a set of sliding doors. At the curbside is a long, black limousine. The doors open. A man in a blue suit, slim tie, and tailored pants steps out. He's wearing thick, black sunglasses, not unlike Tom's.

"Welcome to the United States, Jan Bagan," the man says.

Everything else fades in that moment. I don't even remember why I didn't want to come outside or what I'd been looking for in the airport. My mind is completely blank but for the words he'd just said to me and the limo left open, bright upholstery inviting me in. "He knows my name." I look at Tom while pointing at the man.

"Everyone in this city does," Tom says.

"Technically, everyone in DC. Some parts of Virginia though? Sketchy as hell," the man in the blue suit says. He looks organized, sharp, has a bright smile like a Hollywood actor, slick hair, and muscles visible through his suit. He pulls his phone out of his jacket, looks over the screen, tucks it away, then reaches his hand toward me. "Everything important first: I'm Bill Cosby."

I shake his hand. Tom is looking away, covering his smile and silent laughter, shaking his head slightly.

"I'm gonna keep you out of trouble while you're here. Believe me. I've learned from the best," Bill says.

"Is it easy to get in trouble here?" I say.

Bill's head dips to the side with a half-cringing smile. "Depends on who you are."

"Or who you piss off," Tom says.

"Stay off the radar and you should be fine," Bill says.

"I'm not flying any planes, so I should be fine…" I say slowly. My hand falls back to my side. I glance toward the airport again. None of the fans are visible. Bob Dylan and

Bob Arnold must be keeping them back near the gate if they didn't follow us out here. But even with that reasoning, something is off. It's just that tickle in my chest. A tickle in my heart. "Why is everyone back there saying *Bill*?"

"I already told you," Tom says.

"It's a DC colloquialism," Bill says.

"What does that mean?"

"It's a traditional greeting here. In honor of our favorite president in recent history, Bill Clinton." Bill glances over at Tom who nods in agreement.

"Oh. That's nice," I say. "What did he do?"

"President Clinton was best known for the positions he put women in while he was in office," Tom says. Bill Cosby laughs. It's at that moment that I realize a lot of people in America have the same names. Tom licks his lips. Both Bill and Tom slowly nod their heads at the same time.

"That's a way of putting it," Bill says.

"Opportunities, you know?" Tom says.

"Is that where your name comes from?" I say. "Were you named after President Bill Clinton?" I say.

Again, Bill laughs. "No. Not quite. I'm named after a different legacy. One a little bit *darker* than our former president."

"Oh. That's interesting. You know, they say names can shape personality in the same way the stars in the sky do when you're born," I say.

"Oh," Bill laughs more openly now. "You believe in that sort of thing?"

I'm leaning back, but I don't notice it immediately. I can't tell if I'm leaning away from the car or Bill. "Not necessarily. I think it is interesting though," I say.

Something buzzes, Bill reaches into his pocket, looks at his phone, and puts it away again. "I'd love to hear more about this, but we have a schedule to keep. Are you ready to go, Jan?" Bill gestures to the open car door. Tom's hand gently presses into my back. He's holding out my backpack for me to take and I'm wondering where it came from and had he been carrying it the whole time and I didn't notice and how did I forget it while I was leaving the plane? There's so much going on, I've only been here for a little bit, but it's like there are gaps in my brain from getting off the plane to getting here, like I've missed a million years. Tom pushes the bag into my arms.

My legs are too stiff while Tom still urges me toward the car. "Wait—So, is that all President Bill Clinton is famous for? Giving opportunities to women?" I say, looking over to Bill, hoping he doesn't catch on that I'm needing a bit of time. It's nothing to do with the car and everything to do with the feeling that this vehicle will take me a million miles farther from my home as it takes me away from the airplane.

"Well…" Tom leans against the limo. "There's also his wife. No one in government has anything bad to say about her. If they do, she takes care of them *real* quick."

"Takes care of them?"

"*Philanthropy*," Bill says.

I'm not sure what the word means, but it sounds important so I nod and say, "Oh." I back up until I almost trip from not lifting my foot high enough and it catches on the sidewalk. "That sounds important."

"Hillary Clinton has lived quite the exotic life, yes," Tom says.

"With that said, why don't we go?" Bill gestures toward the cab.

"The fans won't be restrained forever," Tom says.

I nod. I throw my bag into the limo before I climb in. The seats are much more comfortable than what was on the plane, but still not as good as the couch we have back at home. Bill mutters something to Tom before he climbs in. The door closes and we're moving. "Tom Cruise isn't coming?" I say, turning around to watch him get smaller out the back window. He dips back into the airport. Through the line of windowed doors, the fans have gathered, but they're not ravenously excited like they had been before. They're idling, like someone turned off the electricity.

"Tom has some other work to get on with. I'll be taking care of you from here on out," Bill says. I sit back in my chair. Bill has his phone out, he's tapping on a couple things on the screen. His sunglasses try to hide that he's reading messages, but there are still dim shapes visible. "You'll see Tom around, but for now, it's just going to be the two of us." His screen goes dark. He looks up at me. A smile spreads across his lips. "I hope you'll trust me to take care of you."

"Of course," I say. "Tom Cruise and Bob Dylan have been very nice and if they believe you are a good man, then I believe you are a good man too." I smile back.

Bill laughs. Shakes his head. His hand covers his lips like it helps silence the laugh. "Good. Because I've just finished confirming your first major appearance tomorrow." He slips his phone into his pocket.

"First major appearance?" I say.

"Yes." He takes his phone back out, taps the screen, puts it away again. "About fifteen hours from now."

"Really?"

"Really."

"And I will get to meet Boomers? Real-life Boomers?"

Bill doesn't answer immediately. His head tilts to the side, his lips press together and flatten, but then he slowly nods. "Boomers. Gen Exers. Millennials and Zoomers even. There will be all sorts of people at the conference tomorrow."

"You know—I keep hearing talk about Gen Ex. I've never heard of him before. What type of content does he make?" I take my phone out of my pocket to search for his name on my video app. It's strange, but it doesn't look like I have service back yet. The page refuses to load.

"What?" Bill says.

I look up. "Gen Ex. He's a content creator, yeah? I want to know what type of content he makes."

"Oh." Bill's fingers tap against his leg. His heel bounces in rhythm with something not playing. He withdraws his phone again. The light doesn't reflect off his glasses like it should. Instead, the bright screen is muted and reflects only a dim, blurred square. It still doesn't seem like he's looking at much, maybe his home page. His fingers slide along the glass screen like he's doing something, but there's no app to navigate with that movement. Meanwhile, he's not even looking down at his phone as he goes through the motions of typing something in. He's just watching me. "I'm not sure. I can't say I watch *Gen Ex*."

"Oh." I slide my phone away. "I guess I can ask when I meet him tomorrow. Maybe we can do a collab. I've always wanted to do a collab."

"Yeah. Maybe…" Bill digs his phone out again. This time, he looks at the screen when he taps it. A green call sign appears. "Excuse me, but help yourself to whatever you'd like. There are drinks over there." He points to a plush console in the center of the car. I slide along the seat until I can reach it. I lift it and just as he said, there are bottles of ice-cold drinks inside, alcoholic and non-alcoholic. I grab a bottle of water as well as what looks like a mixed vodka drink. The flight left me thirsty. My skin's dry. My lips are cracking. I'm cold, but it's an under-the-skin cold that can only be helped with a warm shower or enough alcohol.

I sit back with the drinks and watch out the window. We pull off the street. Onto a bridge. Over a large body of water. A river, maybe? I'm not sure. The car comes to a stop just a couple paces onto the bridge. We're sitting there for a while. I can't see out the front. A darkened glass blocks off the driver's area. "Bill." I slip the half-empty water bottle into a cup holder and pop the cap off my vodka.

"Hm?" He turns to me.

"How long until we are at my new home?"

"Good question." He knocks on the black, tinted window between us and the driver. It rolls down. "It depends on how traffic treats us. This bridge is one helluva time."

"What do you mean?"

"It means, you know what happens when you take four hot dogs and try to force them into one bun? That's what they did to this goddamn bridge, so the only thing keeping us from getting you home is the traffic." He laughs, dropping his head back with it. He shakes his head. "This bridge can take anywhere from half a lifetime to an eternity to get over depending on how much we're smiled upon on any given day. Honestly… No one else should be using this bridge but officials like us. We shouldn't have to spend hours waiting in traffic because a bunch of random people are traveling, and for what? Shits and giggles?" Bill grunts. Where I'd thought he was laughing at first, he sounds angry now and I'm not sure why. He trails off, muttering under his breath, talking to the driver on the other side of the glass. "He can't tell us anything. We'll get there when we get there," Bill says. The window goes back up. He puts his hand to his face. "There's a goddamn train for everyone else to use for a goddamn reason. This is the kind of thing that gets people killed. Our resources, time, and patience are finite." He's muttering to himself, now reaching for the console. He pulls out a black bottle with simple gold lettering and a golden crown on it. He pops it open with a sigh.

"I don't mind if it's going to take some time—"

"You say that now, but just take a look." Bill presses a

button on the ceiling. A window in the roof slowly peels open to reveal the bright blue and white sky overhead.

"I can peek out?" I look from it to Bill back to it.

"Go ahead. Get an eyeful."

I dig out the goggles from my backpack and slide them around my head. They're over my eyes. I pick up my vodka drink and stand up. My head pops out the window instantly. In front of us is a line of cars sitting bumper to bumper in four lanes. The cars go on until I can't tell them apart. Someone honks, then someone else. We move forward, then jerk to a stop. The window's edge cuts into my stomach, but I'm laughing. It doesn't hurt. The city stands in the distance and looks huge, powerful, amazing… It's nothing like Sumy, it's not even like Kyiv. Stones and columns and glass and power.

I pinch my arm to make sure I'm not sleeping. The mild pain tells me this is real. I lift my hands into the air with a scream. "Hello, Boomers!"

The bottle's at my lips and half-empty in one go. I shout again. The river sends my voice back at me. "I hope you're ready!" The car behind us honks. I turn around and wave. The man in the car gives me the finger. I turn back around, laughing. Bill allows me to stay out the window until the traffic starts to move, so I can't watch the city approach in full view. When we get to the other side of the bridge, he says, "It's better you stay inside the car at this point. We're getting into fan-territory and once they spot you, they could swarm the car."

The streets inside DC aren't much better than the bridge. That is, they are busier than any street ever in Nide and I haven't seen Sumy this congested, even during festival season. Lights turn red and people keep driving. The cars around us thrust their way in front of other cars when there shouldn't have been enough room for them to cut in. The city is a mixture of old and new, bricks, columns, American houses, glass buildings, and embedded words I wish I could read. Even without that, there's something fantastical about this place. The air isn't cold, but refreshing and some of the trees breed pink leaves.

I don't care how long it takes to get to the hotel. I just want to look at everything I can, even if it's out a car window. Someday soon, it won't be. "Wow—Look at that!" A tall red church with a pointed, metal steeple sticks out between a couple of square, stone buildings. I turn around, looking for Aleks, but he's not there. Bill doesn't look up from his phone. "Bill, look!" I say.

"Cool, right?" he says, still not looking up.

I turn back to the window while taking my phone out. I try to take a picture, but we're past and it's blurry and I barely capture the church. Still, I think about what it would have been like if Aleks was with me and I'd say, "I told you I'd get us here, didn't I?" and he would say, "I'm sorry I doubted you." And we'd toast. "And I didn't get myself killed," I'd say, and he'd shake his head, smiling the same kind of smile he had from when we were kids where he didn't like to admit he was wrong, where he actually, secretly kind of admired what I did because he knew he couldn't do it in the same way. And he'd know what it's like because I admire him the same way. Then he'd say, "I guess not," and we'd drink until we passed out.

The car feels older and more empty than it was a couple seconds ago. The joy melts away and my smile goes with it. I slide the goggles back onto my head, pushing my bangs back. I go to my messages. There's nothing from Aleks. Nothing from Mama. Nothing from Papa. Nothing from Yakiv or Mila. There are no messages at all. My chest is tight. I'm not sure I'm breathing. My thumb slides over Papa's phone number. It hovers on the 'call' button. Bill clears his throat, reminding me he's there. My thumb moves away from 'call' and presses 'message' instead. I send Papa a message saying I've made it safely to America and I will call him when I get a chance, then I open the thread with Aleks and send the message, "Please don't be mad. I'll call you soon."

I hold onto my phone, not knowing what time it is there, but still expecting either of them to see my messages and send me something back right now. Minutes pass and I receive nothing. I slip my phone into my pocket again. The chill from the roof window creeps into the car as the sun goes down. Darkness fills the air.

My first night in America.

The sky looks so different in this city, but then, I wonder if it's America that has a different sky altogether. I can't help the feeling it's not only city lights that have removed the stars from the sky.

TEN

The hotel looks like a castle from the outside, a large stone wall of windows with statues or gargoyles at the top. Flags hang from each column, creating an image of a new Rome dressed in American flags. Red velvet canopies hang over the doors and windows on the first floor while all the others above remain uncovered. The building is accented with gold, at least the trim around the outside looks gold in the light. The lobby is red and gold, decorated with modern couches, green and gold carpet, but classic statues of Roman soldiers, beautiful maidens, and lions. Chandeliers with opaque glass look like lanterns hanging from the ceiling. Small lights line the rug edges coming in and out every door or elevator. Roses petals float in the water of a fountain in the lobby.

Bill approaches the desk. "Bill Cosby, two," he says. He's handed an envelope. We're on the fourth floor. The hall's golden when we get off the elevator. More lights line the rug leading down the hall. Pots sit on column-shaped stands on both sides, mirroring each other. In the light, white petals appear golden. Everything looks rich.

Bill unlocks a room and walks me in. The walls are

painted to look like they belong in an art museum. Blank nothing. The bed's headboard blends in against it while the mattress is bigger than anything I've ever seen. The bedroom is washed out with light coming from all the lamps. "Am I in a palace?" I say, walking in, turning around, trying to fit the whole room into my eyes, but I can't.

"It's a hotel room," Bill says.

There's a big, flat-screen television built into the wall across from the bed. On a table beneath it lays the remote. A set of large windows line the wall at the end of the room and beside it, a small writing desk nicer than the one I have at home.

"Jan," Bill says.

I turn to him, remote in hand.

"C'mere." He wiggles his finger, calling me closer. I do as he asks. He takes my hand. A card key is placed into it. "If you lose this, let me know. There'll be breakfast downstairs in the morning, but I'll come and get you so we can talk about the conference. And there's one more thing." He puts his hands on my shoulder. Guiding me back to the desk by the window, he turns me. A laptop sits squarely in front of the chair. He pulls it open. The screen immediately lights. My face reflects in the dark loading screen; Bill's face reflects behind me, his glasses seeming bigger and like small screens blurring his face. The blue loading screen devours us both and a home page turns on. "This is for you," he says.

"What do I need a computer for?"

"Vlogging. Video editing. Talking to your fans. Have you checked any of your pages since you got here?"

I shake my head slowly.

"Do it."

Though I had come to the United States entirely because of the Boomers, I hadn't thought of checking in with any of them on YouTube. Fair to say I'd been too preoccupied thinking of home and Aleks, but still. I take my phone out of my pocket and open the creator's app. I'm not sure I'm breathing. I'm not sure I'm even alive. My subscription count shows over fifteen million subscribers. Billions of views. I click to the comment section and it is person after person saying things like:

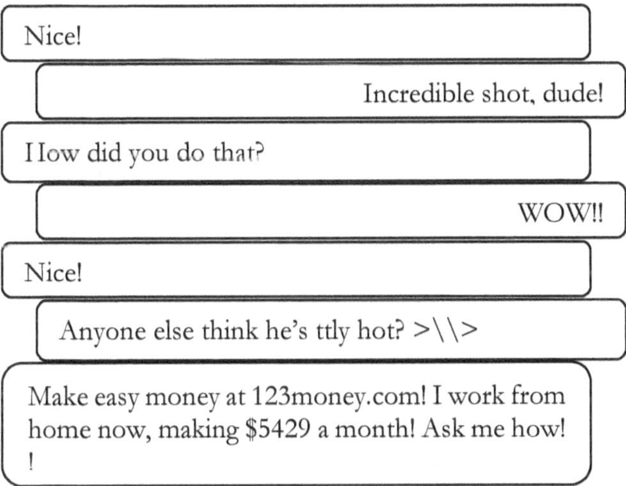

"When? How?" The words come tumbling out without me thinking them.

"I told you there's a data border or something going on. You couldn't see all the fans you had while you were in Shit-All, but now that you're here, it's going to be different. Everyone knows your name, kid."

I close the app and open it again just to see if the numbers read the same. Then I restart my phone and do the same thing, checking the numbers are still there. After my phone's done restarting, I've already gained another two hundred subscribers. "This is incredible." I take a screenshot of my creator dashboard. "I have to show Aleks!" I open our message log.

"Aleks?" Bill says.

"Yeah. He's my friend back in Sumy. We have been friends forever, even though he didn't want to live in Nide and he left a couple of years ago." I pause. "Didn't I tell you this already?" I look up from my phone.

Bill shakes his head slowly. "I don't think so. It must've been Tom or Bob."

"It could've been. We were on the plane for a very long time." I shrug.

"Oh." Bill pulls out the chair at the desk and gestures for me to sit, but I don't.

I'm clicking the messaging app and staring at the texts between us: the last ones I sent while in the car on the way here; the ones of the church; the ones of the limo; the ones saying I've landed and I missed him. He's said nothing yet. There's nothing from Mama or Papa either. There've been no calls, but I suppose they all might be sleeping or Papa is at work and unable to call now. I'll give it some time before I worry.

"If your friend doesn't respond to you, I wouldn't be surprised." Bill's looking over my shoulder. He leans back just as I catch him.

"Why?"

"Because… friends tend to get angry when they see someone else's success. They want you ruined, or at least worse off than they are. They'll call themselves your friends so long as you don't look like you're going anywhere. But the moment you find *some* success, you make them feel inferior and they don't want you around anymore."

"Maybe, but that's not Aleks—"

"I've seen it happen a lot. Probably more than you might think." Bill's hands slip into his pockets. He nods for me to sit down at the computer again, but I still don't.

"Maybe you have, but Aleks isn't like that. He's a real friend."

"We'll see." He turns away. I follow him toward the

door. He takes a hand out of his pocket only to wave and put it back in. I follow Bill halfway to the door, but my feet are dragging and hard to lift. My muscles are stiff and don't want to move. Throbbing pain pulses in my shoulder, my thighs, and my back. It's like I've been running all day, even though I've only been on a plane. It's strange to think about how long it had been since I was last in Ukraine.

It was only yesterday when I was stocking shelves at One Stop and walking past Symon smoking in the loading room and thinking about how to use the chemicals my sponsors had just given me. Then, I had been thinking about whether I'd skip making a video or if there was a way to avoid the Russians around my blasting site and what's the worst that could happen even if they found me. I was talking to Aleks and still tasted the last thing Mama made me for supper. Now, I didn't even know when I'd get to eat Mama's cooking again or when I'd hear Aleks's voice since I thought that would've happened already by now.

I swallow hard. The weight presses into my shoulders and I'm not following Bill anymore. I'm standing in the middle of the hotel room and my feet are welded to the floor. There's silence. Bill isn't moving either. My eyes trace the shapes in the carpet. "No..." I mutter in Ukrainian. My head's shaking. "I... Aleks *is* a good friend. He wouldn't get mad over this, just like I didn't get mad when he went to Sumy. We're still friends. You can be friends through that."

"Says the friend with less value," Bill says.

"I'm not the friend with less value." I look up at him.

"No, you're not, but the person who thinks he has a better future by more traditional means would think that. Then they dispose of the less traditional." His hand's on the door, but he makes no move to open it. He smiles in a way his lips press flat and it's melancholy. "But you're not a nobody, Jan. You may be one of the most consequential individuals in modern US history."

I chuckle a little and turn away. It's hard to believe he means that. Flattery. They say it comes with becoming a celebrity, but I didn't think my agent would be like the Boomers, feeding nitrate to my combustible ego. I stare at him, desperate to see his eyes and connect with a person, not a screen, not his sunglasses which act like a screen outside of my phone, making him anonymous like the avatars leaving nonstop comments on my videos now. "I'm not *that* special," I say. "I make explosions on YouTube."

Turning back to the door, Bill laughs to himself. "You do much more than that. Believe me." He pulls the door open this time. "Check out your room. Take a shower. Get some rest. There are a couple pieces of clothing for you to try on, different sizes, colors, styles. See what fits you, then we'll get you some more."

"What about a home? When do I get a home?"

"Soon," Bill says. "For now, relax. Shower. Sleep. Vlog. You've got a big day tomorrow. Your *premiere* as an American star. Don't think too much about anything else, alright? You might freak yourself out. Good night." He doesn't pause before leaving the room.

I think to chase him, but I can't will my legs to carry me over. The room's so quiet, it's unnerving. A soft *bump, bump, bump* precedes the ringing in my ear becoming so intense, it aches. I press my palm to my ear, holding it hard against my head in hopes to stop the vibrations. I sit on the edge of my bed. The ringing softens, but doesn't go away. I hold my phone with the messages to Aleks pulled up. He still hasn't responded. I write him a quick message:

I'm not trying to brag or anything

> But isn't it cool?

> Did you know there were borders that block subscribers from other countries?

> I didn't.

I wait for a message to come in, but Aleks sends nothing. I toss the phone to the foot of my bed with a grunt. The remote's in my hand now. The TV's on, volume low enough it's not overpowering, but loud enough I can hear it in the bathroom.

The bathroom is strange. There's a tub behind a glass wall, separating it from the toilet. The sink is shaped like a long bowl, but it's dark and marble with black streaks running through it. There's also a separate standing shower with a glass box around it. I turn on the water and fill the tub. The only soap they've given me is in small bottles and one piece of wrapped bar soap that I throw into the bottom of the tub, hoping it makes it smell better.

I make the water hot enough, my skin turns red when I get in and I'm reminded of the open cuts left all over my body. Arm, leg, my upper back... Everything's burning. I take a deep breath and exhale to get through the pain. Yet, it's not the worst thing I've ever felt.

The mirror fogs. The water's still running, but I'm so hot, I need cold water. I'm dripping wet. Naked, I check the small fridge in the main room. Bottles of water stand beside each other. I'm disappointed there's no alcohol. I bring some water back with me and drink it before I'm even in the tub again. With my phone, I take pictures of the bathroom to send to Aleks too, captioning them, "not bragging, I just want to share it with someone," hoping that he'll respond to something. So far, that hope has meant nothing. "You can't be mad at me, Aleks," I say, setting the phone down near the toilet. "I know you better than Bill and I know you're not angry at me for this… It was always the plan. You *knew* it was the plan."

I don't know how long I'm in the bathroom, but when I come out, my face is so red, I almost look like I've been burned from an explosion that went off while I was too close. The pajamas left in the drawer are silk, soft, nicer than anything I've ever owned. The water in the fridge isn't cold enough for me, so I pick up the ice bucket and key card Bill gave me to find the ice machine somewhere.

A man stands on the other side of the hall outside my bedroom door. He's wearing slacks, a flowery polo with the hotel emblem on the heart, and black, square glasses.

He points to himself. "I am room service. Can I help you?"

I glance down the hall. Another room service person stands one door down and another two doors down in each direction. "I was…" I glance at the empty ice bucket in my hand. "Just going to get ice—"

"I'll get that for you. Stay here." He takes the ice bucket from me and makes his way down the hall, fast and even-stepped. The other room service person watches me. I wave. He turns away. I don't understand American customs as much as I thought I did, I guess. The room service man doesn't take long. He thrusts the ice bucket into my hands. "Did you need anything else?"

"I sort of wanted to ask Bill about some things for tomorrow—"

"You can talk to him in the morning. Go to bed," the room service man says, giving me a nudge back into the room.

I stumble. The door hangs open. The service man now stands where I had been. "You work for the hotel, don't you?"

The man doesn't answer immediately. "Yes. I do work for the hotel. Why do you ask that? I am wearing the uniform, am I not? Why else would I be dressed like this if I didn't work here?"

"I'm not saying you don't work here—"

"Then what is your question?"

"Because… You work for the hotel. I want to talk to my agent. Why should you get to tell me when I can talk to *my* agent? That just… doesn't seem right to me, you know?" I'm clutching the bucket of ice.

The room service man stares at me from the doorway without moving until he reaches in to grab the doorknob. "Mr. Cosby said do not disturb for the night. Stay in here and don't cause trouble." The room service man closes the door with a loud slam I feel through the floor. I'm stepping back from the door slowly, keeping an eye on it, like someone is going to fly through and surprise me with something.

A gun.

A machine gun.

A Russian with a machine gun.

No. That's crazy.

I'm not in Russia.

They aren't here.

And I didn't do anything wrong to get their attention either.

I set the bucket of ice down and try the door again, but it won't open. Something is blocking it from the other side. I didn't know there were locks on the outside of hotel room doors. I go to the desk and pick up the pen and notepad sitting beside my laptop, I write a note to ask Bill about the door locking from the outside in the morning. I also want to ask him about bringing vodka to the video conference we're going to because it is sort of necessary for my videos. Even if he doesn't think it might be, it is. It's part of my process.

I sit on the edge of the bed. Stand up again. Get a bottle of water. Go back to the desk and chair and sit in that. Open the laptop. My YouTube page fills the screen, I still can't believe the numbers. I take a picture of the laptop screen and send that to Aleks with the caption: "See? I'm not lying," and "they also gave me a laptop. That's pretty cool, right?"

I go to the window and pull back the curtains. Cars line the sidewalks, parked against them all up and down the street except for right in front of the hotel where the red canopy and a small podium sit. Lights on the buildings across the street illuminate old-looking stone. An obelisk reaches up in the distance. I take a picture of it and send that to both Aleks and my parents.

I lay back on the bed, then crawl under the covers. They are so thin and smell like nothing. I turn the lights off, but leave the TV flashing for a little bit of sound. Come morning, it would be the only thing to make me think of home. Instead of hearing Mama, Papa, and Mila getting ready for their days, a TV would substitute. I yawn, pull the covers closer, and wipe my eyes with the back of my hand. I tap my phone's screen one more time, looking for messages. Nothing.

"He's not mad…" I plug my phone in and set it down. Surely, Aleks is only tired and sleeping, just like me, and tomorrow when both of us wake, there'll be a message from him and my family and everything will be exactly as it should.

ELEVEN

We're sitting in the limo outside of the convention center in Washington DC. The building is large. The walls are made of glass and we passed a Hilton not that long ago. A short trail of people comes from multiple directions. Some must be coming from hotels. Others come out of cars. Others come from the stairs leading to the metro. Bill says to me, "I talked with events. They said they've gathered your requested items."

"It's not Smirnoff, right?" I say.

"You're really leaning into this celebrity demand thing fast, aren't you, kid?" Bill says. "Maybe slow it down. Gotta make us like you before you get on our nerves."

"I don't normally drink Smirnoff though?" I say.

"It's fine. We got something that should work." He pats my leg. The limo door opens, the driver stands on the other side, holding it for us. I'm climbing out, but Bill grabs my arm and stops me. "Stay close, Jan. I know you'll want to meet the fans. I know you'll want to talk to a lot of people, but keep close. You won't know who is dangerous, alright? Promise me."

"Alright. I promise." I give him a thumbs-up before

climbing out of the car.

Bill's behind me. I look around the convention center. There are no signs or tables for registration or workshops and panels. There aren't as many people as I thought there would be and many of them are older than I would have imagined for my fans. In fact, most of the VidCon videos I'd seen online had more young people in them. Most of the people I see now are well into adulthood, closer to Papa's age or even older than that. Some have graying hair, many wear what look like military uniforms. Maybe it's for a specific panel. A costume contest. A specific fandom I don't know about. I had seen plenty of costumes in videos of VidCon, so that makes the most sense. The one thing they have in common though is they're all wearing thick, square sunglasses.

A pressure suddenly falls onto my shoulder. Another presses into my back. A squeeze, a push, Bill guides me forward. "We have to keep moving," he keeps his voice low. "We have places to be." We go through the main hall. A wide room with high walls, a walkway, an elevator, a closed shop that looks like it sells coffee or candy outside of the other rooms. The carpet is bright, red, and wild. At the front of the workshop room is a movable platform stage with a podium, a metal table, and a brown box. A bottle of vodka hides behind the podium. Rows and rows of chairs fill the room, many of which have Boomers already sitting in them. Again, I'm surprised by the reality of my American fanbase. I didn't imagine my viewers would be very young, but I thought many would have been around my age at least by a couple of years, one way or another.

Bill leads me to the bottom of the stage, but doesn't take me onto it. "Everyone's here for a small sample of your talents. Do you understand?" He pauses. He doesn't say anything else until I nod. "There are a handful of ingredients up there like what you brought from home, but nothing that should create the kind of visual you made with your last video. All the studio wants you to do is make something small, but impressive. These are studio investors and if you want your projects to be well-funded, you need to show them your talents aren't fake. Do you understand?"

I don't think I'm hearing him right. "You want me to make an explosion inside a building?"

Bill licks his lips. "A small one, maybe. And speak English while you do it."

"I don't think hotels usually like that. I've heard some horror stories about people getting whole conventions banned for bad behavior. Hair dye. Destroyed linens. Filthy messes and urine in the elevators. I don't want to do that to this convention. I don't want to be known as the VidCon wrecker."

"This isn't VidCon."

"Then... what is it?"

"New... National Technology."

I bite at my thumbnail. "What does national technology have to do with making YouTube videos about explosions? It almost sounds militaristic." I laugh.

Bill doesn't. "It's a feature on just how far video streaming and human outreach has come in a few years. What you do out in the woods isn't the only thing that's amazing, but the fact you *can* record, upload, and meet people of similar interests through the internet with whatever cheap electronics you have in Shit-All is something to be admired."

"So, you want me to talk about creating videos out in Nide?"

"Yes. And how exactly you do it. The bomb making."

"Not bombs. Explosions—"

"Whatever."

"I've always wanted to create something with a live audience, but Aleks would never come more than a couple of times. He claimed work or lack of interest, but I think he was afraid after the one time he got hit by a—"

"That's not a problem here, kid. Everyone's come to see *you*. Listen to *you*. See *your* natural talent. Do tell your stories, but mostly give them the show they came for, you got it?" He pats me on the shoulder, then gives it a squeeze. I nod.

My lips curl into a wide smile. The room had a lot of people in it when I entered, but it's only gotten fuller since. The energy of their conversation buzzes through my body. My heart's pounding in a good way that's like the preparations I make for an explosion. I'm licking my lips, eyeing the bottle of vodka on the stage.

Cîroc.

I look over the room of Boomers. Not a single one even *looks* younger than me. You would think at least a couple of Boomers might be in university.

I shake my head. The energy's turning from excitement to nerves as I'm not sure how to approach a group of people so much older than me, their misery bleeds through their invisible eyes, down their necks, and into the collars of their military cosplays. I repeat to myself it shouldn't be that hard, it wouldn't be that hard—They all came to see me. They know who I am; that would have been half of the battle.

My signature goggles hang around my neck. I pull them over my head and stick them to my forehead, pushing my wavy bangs back. Bill says, "It's go time. Any questions?"

"Can I take a drink before I get started?" I say.

"Hm?" Bill says. He's pulling me toward the stage by the front of my shirt. He stops at the foot of the stairs. "Don't move." He has a small microphone in his hand which he clips to my shirt. He tells me to pull at the collar, then he drops the box down the neck hole. I mutter a sound from the feeling of cold plastic against my skin. He catches the box near my hips and slides it into one of the pockets on my jeans.

Bill takes the stage. He approaches the podium. The microphone screams with feedback. The chatter in the room quiets down. "Good morning, everyone. Today, I have a very special surprise. I hope you won't be alarmed by his age. It can be a little surprising. But this is the Eurasia's leading expert on experimental explosive technology. Please join me in welcoming this explosives specialist, Jan Bagan from Russia."

Everyone's clapping. Bill's waving his fingers for me to come up the stage. "Ukraine," I'm muttering to him. "I'm from Ukraine."

"That's what I said," Bill says, but he's not listening. He picks up the bottle of vodka from under the podium and puts it into my hand. I'm led to the table. Everything around me is in slow motion. My head's spinning. The soft whistle from the usual ringing slices through my thoughts. My shirt clings to my back. My feet tap and roll and I'm breathing so hard I'm a little dizzy. I already smell the gunpowder, even with the lid closed on the box in front of me. I twist the lid off the vodka and toss back two shots worth. My arm runs over my mouth to wipe away excess liquid. "Hello, Boomers!" I say.

My voice echoes through the speakers above the stage, accompanied by squeaking feedback. I've imagined this moment so many times—The first conference I'd ever speak at—The first time addressing my subscribers in person—The first time looking people in the face who are here because they want to talk to me about the same sorts of hobbies I enjoy too. I'd imagined saying those same words and the phrase flying right back at me with enthusiastic hands thrown into the air and laughing. Instead of receiving this greeting though, there's murmuring passing between the seats. Deep, questioning confusion sweeps. I lean back, letting my hand drop to the table. They're still talking. I look down the steps at Bill.

He's slicing his hand across his neck. I squint, turn to him, and walk to the edge of the stage to get closer. "What?" I say.

He points back to the table. "Go." He rolls his hand in the air. "Just work. They're fine."

I'm not so sure they are when they're unresponsive or even appear like they don't know where they are or if they should even be here. I pick up the bottle of vodka again. It's this time I notice my hand's shaking.

It's not excitement.

"Just a little palate cleanser before we start, eh?" The shake's in my voice too. "That's weird," I say, putting the bottle aside. "Usually I'm shaking for a different reason." I laugh, but the trembling chokes it.

I've never shaken like this before. I've never felt nervous. Even when making videos for the first time. Even when working at the grocery store and running into my first customer after night shift ended. Even when going to Sumy with Aleks and being around all the people there who seemed stressed out that were driven by anxiety and fear and worry. Yet now, the trembling is burrowed under my skin. My foot bounces. My heart rattles. It's almost hard to breathe. I laugh to try and push a lump out of my throat, but it just makes a disrupted laugh. "Sorry. This is strange for me too. I've never talked in front of people like this before." I laugh again. Swallow. Part of it gets stuck in my tight throat. I take another drink of vodka. "I didn't need that one for my palate." I laugh a third time. This one comes out easier. "You know, talking to a camera and a bunch of trees is very different from looking over the edge of a stage and seeing a bunch of eyes—Er— Sunglasses and suits staring back. You really can't tell how many people ten or five hundred or ten thousand are there when you're looking at the number on a screen. Virtually, we just know it is a lot. Anyway… You came here for something specific, didn't you?" I reach into the box, twisting the lid off the jar of gunpowder first. I don't know what I'm going to make next, but I'm a little desperate for the smell and the smell makes me hunger for the taste. "I don't even know what's been prepared for me. They didn't tell me." I tap my fingers to my tongue. Next, they scoop through the gunpowder. Gray dust paints my fingertips. I press it to my tongue. The familiar taste is comforting. There's a small spark of heat in my nose. There's a collective, scattered gasp in the audience. I look up, searching for the sources, the faces watch me intensely, but the sunglasses turn their eyes into meaningless black voids, blurring one head into the next. It's worse than looking at a stream of anonymous avatars.

I clear my throat. I knew there would be people here who weren't familiar with me. Those were the gasps. "If you don't know me, do not worry. I do this all the time." I dig my tooth under my nail, grabbing at whatever little gunpowder's still under it until the last clump comes out. "Okay, okay, okay, sorry. I'm a little nervous and it feels like I haven't set something off in a long time." I take each substance container out of the box and lay them out in a line on the table, all by color since the containers are all the same. The empty container is on my left.

I pick up the gunpowder and pour some of it into the empty jar until it reaches almost two centimeters. "You know why you should use glass for this type of procedure? It is because hot solutions can melt through plastic or chemicals in plastic may cause an adverse effect in the solutions. It depends on what the plastic is made of. Glass does not have the same effect in most cases. These containers are plastic. I hope they are high quality." I press the gunpowder into the bottom of the jar. My fingers are on my tongue again, wiping off excess dust. Murmuring continues in the audience. I stare up at them. I've never had a hard time coming up with words to say to the camera, but an audience is different. They're immediate.

Their energy shifts the room. "One thing I can tell you is that this is not the highest quality… Where did you get it from?" I look back at Bill offstage. He doesn't move from where he stands. He's not even looking at me. His fingers press into his ear and it looks like he's muttering to someone. I take a bit of vodka and move on to the next jar. I alternate, drink, taste, collecting information on the possible solutions.

I could never explain it to someone else. I've tried with Aleks, but he's only ever called me crazy. I understand his hesitancy. It's not like I've never heard the warnings, but the worst reactions I've ever received from consuming anything was a burned tongue and a burp that may have felt like acid spray a couple hours later.

I taste the last of the chemicals. My lips purse. "When Bill said he wanted something small… He wasn't lying…" A laugh slips out. Nervous. I haven't done something this small for an audience in years and I'm sweaty thinking they're going to be disappointed by all I can do with this after the video that brought me here.

Of five ingredients, four of them are pretty basic, the other is a little less common and you have to put some work into refining it back in Nide. I don't know if they made it straight here. A liquid, a goo, and two other powders. I don't need a lot of them to create the picture in my head. I place a copper powder in the jar with the gunpowder and stir them. The goo comes next, creating a layer between the base. The next layer is pale, silver powder, before I pour a little liquid on top. I cut a line of twine and stick it through the bottle lid. My wounds ache in remembrance of the glass that perforated them not long ago. The goo's keeping the solutions from mixing too quickly, but still, the liquid on top is making it down the edges. The jar's already warm. I light a match and strike the fire to the short fuse. "It won't be bad, just… take a step back." I do as I say, but stop.

I forgot something.

I grab the vodka, and then I'm moving back a little further. "Maybe find cover. I'm not *totally* sure *all* that will happen, but that's pretty typical, yeah?" I'm standing behind the podium now, my knees are bent to give me a little more cover, I'm thinking of getting down. But I have my phone out and the camera running. I bring the bottle's lips to mine and drink. "You see, I've never used blue gin, that's what I call that blue stuff. Not the appropriate name, but in certain places like back home, you have to make sure certain people don't hear you saying certain words or you'll get in trouble, right?" I set the vodka down on the floor by the podium. I grab the box of extra chemicals from the counter and set it under the table. "The top layer, call it silver dust, has a strange metal component to it. When exposed to heat, it will dissolve rapidly."

I move back behind the podium and grab the bottle of vodka from the floor. "If you're sitting in…" I eye the trajectory of the bottle and where it sits, rattling on top of the table. It's gonna go. We don't have more than a few seconds. Checking the crowd two, three, four more times. I point again. "If you're in this area… maybe move. Prepare yourself because if it hits you—"

The jar hisses.

"It's gonna hurt." My skin's clammy, and I have a dry throat. A couple of people in the audience stand. Muttering overtakes the hissing, but not for long. I duck behind the podium, but I must keep standing to keep my phone trained on the bottle. The hiss turns to a howl, then it flies into the air.

Instantly, rows of people clear out, separating to the sides so they aren't under where the bottle goes. The plastic disappears. Lights flicker. The container pops, while the walls echo its blast and a flicker of light turns to smoke. Anything heavier falls on the seats below. Plastic bits hit the floor; hot goo burns seat fabric. I can't see it, but I can smell it.

The room settles down; no one moves. Looking out at the audience, eyes return to me. I bring the vodka to my lips. A drink. A burp. "What was *that*?" a man approaches the stage fast. He's wearing a dark suit with some badges pinned to his chest. A pair of men with sunglasses and black suits stand between me and the approaching man.

"Were you trying to kill us?" The man's not angry, but his voice is stiff, demanding, and harsh. It reminds me too much of someone in the military.

I never liked the military for how stiff they are. A human in a military uniform is trained to forget their name and act like a weapon. It's why you couldn't get Russian soldiers to laugh. I had never met an American soldier before, but I couldn't imagine them much different. Soldiers have the same purposes across the world, regardless of what they say they're fighting for; they do not choose what to fight for, the people above them do.

It's the reason the Soviet Union was able to last as long as it did.

I only ever hope to bring the military out of the soldier when I speak with them, but it hasn't worked so far.

I drink the vodka, letting the blueberry alcohol fill my throat. The bottle's slipping in my sweaty hands.

"What are you doing bringing a terrorist in here, Cosby?" The military cosplayer now faces my agent.

"I'm not a terrorist," I say. "I make videos."

The military cosplayer walks past the stage, brushing aside the two security men to step up to Bill. "What the hell was that?" He points an accusatory finger at me.

"I think you should sit back down. The presentation isn't over, Colonel," Bill says.

"Like hell it's not—I want to know what the hell that was!"

"Natural talent." Bill's sunglasses slide down his nose. For a moment, I catch a glimpse of his eyes paired with his grin. Devilish.

"It was a child ingesting chemicals and trying to blow us up. You've lost your mind!" The cosplayer's hands shake at his sides.

"You should see what he can do with napalm, uranium, lithium. Imagine what he could do with plutonium. Imagine what he could make for us—"

"I want the name of your supervisor," the cosplayer says.

"Watch." Bill's glasses are covering his eyes again. He points to a large, pale screen hanging behind the stage. The lights are mostly dim. The man in the military costume is stiff, hesitant to turn, but at least half turns to the projection screen. A video starts playing. The trees in it are familiar.

"You'd think something strange was going on," my voice comes through the speakers. The video centers on a jar sitting in the middle of a new blasting spot, not yet blackened by soot and experimentation. I only barely recognize it as the new spot I picked out a couple of days ago. The jar's hissing, glowing now against the dark and snow. My skin's hot, tingling and energized as physical memories from that night flood my body.

"Sorry, sorry, sorry—"

Had that panic always been in my voice? I don't remember hearing it before.

I'm not saying much, the room illuminates with the blast from the screen, my biggest explosion yet. It's so much more amazing on a large screen than on my phone. The camera smacks into the ground just as my body goes flying. The screen is a picture of the sky. Purple mixes into red, orange, yellow, and white. It's fine, like embers at the bottom of a pit of fire. The explosion shoots thick smoke into the air and blossoms into round, puffy clouds.

"I hope you liked the show. I'll have to check it out later. For now, boom, boom, boom, salute!" the video says.

"Boom, boom, boom, salute," I say back, giving a lazy salute. I bring the bottle of vodka to my lips and toast the work with my other hand.

My ear's ringing so I can't hear anything, but the military cosplayer's talking to Bill. Not angry this time. I put the vodka down and press my palms to my ears, both sides, dampening the sound. I close my eyes and focus on nothing. The ringing gets so loud, it hurts, but then it passes. I lower my hands. The voices are there. A bunch of people talking. It's all English, but it's too much for me to pick up on what any of them are saying as they mix to make whispered, breathy gibberish.

"Just *who* the hell is *he*?" the military cosplayer says.

I sip at the vodka. Then, between sips, my teeth are digging at the gunpowder under my nails. I'm not looking at them anymore, but around the room, at the seat where my bomb mostly landed, then back at Bill. The military cosplayer's staring at me now.

"I told you, he's a one-of-a-kind explosives specialist," Bill says.

"I make videos," I say.

"Where did you find him?"

"Russia," Bill says.

I point at Bill. "Ukraine." I point at myself. "I'm Ukrainian."

"Do they all do that?" says the military cosplayer.

"What?" Bill looks at me. "Drink excessively?

"Eat chemicals."

"No," I say. "That's just me. I'm strange back home too."

"What sort of training do you have?" the military cosplayer says.

"I don't…" I look at Bill.

I take a drink and wipe my lips with the back of my arm. The nerves shake my voice. The small shake is still visible in my hand as I lower it to my side. "I don't have any training. I just sort of… have always done this. I sort of started with eating rocks I found in my yard. You know, I lost all of my baby teeth very early. Mama told me I'd lose all my teeth forever if I didn't stop eating rocks." I laugh. "I wasn't eating rocks though. I was just chewing on them. I was figuring out the composites, you know?" I watch the military cosplayer, but it's more like I'm watching myself as I follow my reflection in his sunglasses. "You know?" I say slow. "Sucking on rocks is not the same as eating rocks—But she didn't like it any better—"

"Then how do you know what to mix?" the military cosplayer says. "Or was that all a hoax on screen?"

I shake my head. "The taste." I walk to the edge of the stage and sit on it. The vodka sits between my legs. "I don't know if you've ever tasted explosives, but when you do, you can see what they—Or, I guess, you can *feel* what they do. It's the same reason I licked rocks. I was finding the composites and compositions in them. You could say I have very good taste buds, but I don't like to think I'm the only one that does this. No one in the world is *that* special." I laugh.

The bottle's back at my lips, but I'm not taking a drink. They're all looking at me like I'm crazy. Maybe I just look a little crazy with my goggles on and my curly hair a little messy and my face red and I can see what they're looking at, but I don't want to think I'm looking crazy. Yet security stares at me. So does the military cosplayer and Bill and the people standing right behind the cosplayer, also cosplaying.

I take a sip, holding the vodka in my mouth for just a bit before swallowing. I push my goggles away from my eyes. "Did you think I faked tasting materials in my videos?"

"I've never seen your videos before," the military cosplayer says.

"Oh." I sit straighter. "You're a new Boomer?"

The military cosplayer looks at Bill, though his expression is flat and unreadable to me. I'm not even sure if he's making an expression, actually. "What are your plans with this?" he says to Bill.

"He will continue what he was doing at home, but in one of our *studios*. If you'd like more information on the project going forward, contact my office. Everything's currently under a very strict, private contract and we can't talk about it so openly. Competitors and enemies to the state," Bill says.

"The State?" I say. "What's that?

"The name of our studio," Bill says.

I don't like to think this about people, but I know Bill's not telling me something.

"After what you just showed me, I don't think your biggest concern should be someone overhearing you *speaking* about this *project*," the military cosplayer says, followed by a brief, deep chuckle. He turns back to me, watching me through his sunglasses. I slowly reach for him, for them. He pulls back as my fingers come close to his face. His smile's wiped away, but once he plants his feet again, he smiles again. It's stiff, cold, I don't want to say human. It's just… there's something off about him. He reaches his hand out. I don't take it. "What? Don't you shake hands in Russia?"

"Ukraine." I take his hand. He grips mine, hard. The shake is even harder, flinging my hand up and down.

"It's been a pleasure. I look forward to seeing more of your work." He lets me go. My hand throbs from his tight grip. He gives me a look down then back up, laughs in his chest, and turns away. He makes his way to the back of the room where he talks to another military cosplayer. They whisper. He points. He makes a motion with his hands that I imagine is something exploding, then points to me again. I smile and salute with the bottle I'm holding.

The two of them leave the room.

"Good Job." Bill's voice startles me.

I turn to him, still mid-drink. Half of the bottle's already gone. I'm not trying to set an example. I'm not trying to be a stereotype. I don't normally drink this much. I'm trying to think if I've had too much. I press the back of my palm to my forehead. It's warm. I push my sleeves up. My skin's red. I'm not that drunk, I've only been drinking a bit.

"Another new fan," Bill says.

"Yeah," the word falls out of my mouth like a sigh. "That's great." I look over the room, the few people left mingling around are either security in black suits or convention center staff. I'm not sure when the room emptied. No one came up to say hi. "They're all so different than I imagined." I turn back to Bill. "What kind of convention did you say this was?"

"Video re-enactors, history buffs, people who enjoy battle field games and new technology—"

"Oh. A video game conference." I glance back at the stage. Standing in the door at the back of the room is an old man. White hair, balding head, glasses, and a weird-shaped chin. I purse my lips. "I didn't know so many Boomers played video games."

"Right…"

"When do I get to meet Gen Ex?"

Bill's holding a finger to his ear. He draws his phone out with his free hand. The screen light reflects on his glasses. A calendar. A text message. I check my phone for messages from Aleks or my parents. There's nothing.

"I'll see if he has room in his schedule to meet," Bill says.

We go to the next meeting. There is no presentation of my YouTube channel. No one is there to see me. I am supposed to listen and I didn't listen very well. Something about central planning. Something about nuclear power.

Something about the Russia and Israel and China. Most of it I can't follow, but Bill leans over and says, "I hope you're ready to make an impression. You're in the big leagues now, kid, and these are not the kind of investors you want to disappoint."

When we leave, it's without meeting Gen Ex.

TWELVE

I'm sitting in the back of a black sedan with my phone out scrolling through my videos and pictures looking for the one I took at the conference a couple of days ago. I want to upload it to my channel for other Boomers who hadn't been at the convention, but every time I scroll through the camera roll, I can't find it. There's a blurry picture of the floor with one of my shoes in the shot. There's a picture of the blurry projection, there's a picture from outside the convention center, but the picture I took from inside and the video of my explosion are gone.

I know I didn't forget. If I close my eyes, I can even see myself standing behind the podium with my phone in my hand, watching the bottle. As much as everything else from yesterday is a blur and the little bit of a headache I have isn't making it easier to stay focused, I'm sure I videoed my event. I always film them.

I give up looking for the video and post one of the blurry images and an exterior shot of the conference center to my social media page. "Sorry, this is the most exciting thing I have for now." Then, I go to the messages where Aleks should be. It's been three days and I haven't heard anything. I think three days. They're sort of blurring together a little bit since I left Ukraine. While there, I had a regular schedule, so it was easy to tell when time passed and what day it was and what came next. Here, it's been the hotel room and conference and random place and hotel room or sometimes hotel room for a whole day. I'm sure of it. I flick the screen with my thumb, sending the messages down, then up. I don't know why he hasn't responded yet. Maybe he's not mad at my success, but maybe he's mad because he thinks I'm lying to him. I send him a blurry picture of the convention center carpet and the projector screen saying:

> I was at this conference yesterday.

> Tech-Con or something.

> Washington DC.

> Call me.

> I wanna tell you about it.

Send. Then I add:

> Some cosplayer almost beat me up.

I'm hoping that gets his attention.

The car comes to a stop, bouncing me against the seat. Bill shows his ID to a man in a booth. He gives me a look. They mutter something to each other. Bill says, "new explosives specialist."

I smile, salute.

The man in the box has the same kind of sunglasses Bill's wearing, that everyone at the airport was wearing, that the cosplayers at the conference were wearing. Black, square, defensive. I'm starting to think it's an American thing.

Bill rolls the window up. The steel gate in front of us rolls open. We drive inside.

"Am I going to get sunglasses soon?" I finally say. "Everyone has them except for me."

Bill's quiet until he parks the car. The engine shuts off, but it's so quiet, that the real signifier is the radio going silent. He turns to me, one arm on the steering wheel. "If you really want a pair, we can probably find you some."

"I'm not saying I want the same sunglasses," I say.

"Then why are you asking about them?" His voice is sharper than I expected it to be.

"I don't know... I guess... I thought it was kind of weird that everyone has them, but if I'm going to be American now, I might want some American glasses, you know? It's like everyone here is tuned into the same fashion—" Except that girl with the blue hair. I saw *her* eyes. I need to find her. "It's kind of cool, I guess, but it's also kind of strange, isn't it?"

"Maybe, but who are you to label what's strange?" Bill laughs. The tone of his voice is confusing, trying to be a joke, but it's not. There's something else in there. "Look, isn't there something where you're from that everyone seems to be on the same page about? A piece of clothing everyone wears or at least enjoys?"

"We all wear coats outside because it's cold...?" I say. Bill says nothing, though his lips flatten. "But I understand what you're saying. It's an American thing, yeah?"

"Yes. Very American. Patriotic. Strong." Bill clears his throat. He grips the edge of his glasses, adjusting them without showing his eyes. He smiles, showing his teeth. "Don't they speak of secrets, debonair, authority?"

"I'm not sure if that's how I would describe them..."

"America has been a global superpower for almost the entirety of our existence. What you should take away from this— " He barely wiggles his sunglasses, "is the thought of superpowers, Superman, James Bond—"

"Isn't James Bond British?"

"We popularized him, though. Did you know that? Probably not. What I'm talking about here are hidden identities. We're not hiding anything because we're doing wrong, but Clark Kent is a symbol of the average American, hiding his ability to go above and beyond to protect those he loves. Superman is a symbol of what every American has within: the fight for the freedom and safety of others, worldwide. By wearing the sunglasses, we align ourselves with…"

He's still talking, but following what he's saying is more effort than I want to put in. All I understand from what he's said is that every American likes sunglasses the same way they like freedom and guns. The door locks click open. Bill smacks his hand on the dash. I jump, turn around, and wait for him to say something—To notice I wasn't paying that much attention. He claps his hands together. "Are you ready to see your new movie studio?"

I smile so big, my face hurts. "Yes."

"Alright then." He looks away, thinking for a moment. "Let's… kick this pig."

"Yeah, let's kick it."

We get out of the car. The building in front of us is huge. Three, four, maybe five stories tall and made of tan brick. It has evenly placed windows around it on all levels. A half-wall of marble stone surrounds the building along with an iron fence and about every two meters, there's a darker line of gray-blue marble with numbers on them. 1964, 1965, 1966, and so on.

"Where are we?" I say.

"The State Studios. Some call it the Pentagon for its shape. Ever heard of it?"

I shake my head slowly.

"Not surprising. We're more of a producer than a direct studio most of the time. We partner with Disney,

Sony, Warner Media, Universal, Lion's Gate… Maybe you recognize those names."

I nod slowly.

"We might not fund all the operations in those films, but we work closely with each studio on most projects. If you watch the credits carefully, you may spot our influence in there, somewhere."

"That's cool." I keep my eyes on the building, taking in as much of it as I can. I look back to the parking lot, but I try to keep it limited so Bill doesn't think I'm looking for other celebrities to talk to. I'm one of them now, so I shouldn't be so excited to spot anyone I might recognize. Still, I can't help but think how incredible it would be.

Men and women move through the parking lot, all in suits and wearing sunglasses similar to Bill's. "There — There—There!" I say, pointing to what looks like Daniel Craig and Scarlet Johansson on the other side of a car five meters away. "Daniel! Scarlet! Hello!" I wave. "I'm looking forward to working with you on a project!"

Daniel stands still. The only thing that moves is his head as I walk by. He steals a glance at Bill, then, slowly he lifts his hand, but puts it down before waving. He presses a finger to his ear. Probably calling his agent.

"I know that life." The words are strange in my mouth, but I have an agent now, just like Daniel Craig. I'm a movie star, *just like* Daniel Craig.

I'm walking ahead of Bill now. He puts a hand on my shoulder and pulls me back when we're closer to the studio's front doors. "This place is big. You could get lost in it. Stay close, alright?"

"That would be crazy though, wouldn't it? If I walked onto someone else's set. What are they shooting today? Jurassic Park 7? Fast and Furious 20? A new Disney remake of Tarzan?"

"I'm not sure. I'll check once we get you settled in for your shoot." Bill gives my shoulder a hard squeeze. The studio doors are long, stacked two by each other in pairs. He runs his card over a mechanical box on the wall. It clicks. He pulls the metal door open. The immediate inside hall is off-white linoleum. It looks yellow in the odd fluorescent lighting. There are no windows, but the halls look like they go on forever. Wood paneling accents the doors and runs a trim near the hallway ceiling. Against one of the walls is a big USA statue. The U is red, the S is white, and the A is dark blue. A golden eagle spreads its wings while standing on top of the S. A shield presses to its chest and underneath the letters are a couple of metals and plaques. Bill puts a hand on my back and pushes me forward. I didn't realize I was walking slowly. "Sorry," he says. "There's not much time to dawdle. We've got a schedule to keep."

"What's that statue for?"

"Excellence. Studio excellence. You've heard of the Golden Globes?"

"Yeah—That wasn't a globe though—"

"No, it's better."

I'm looking around as we walk, moving from one hall to the next and all I see around me are men and women in suits, some in suits with skirts, all of them wearing sunglasses. Some are bald, some have long hair in tight ponytails, some have short hair, but they all have cards clipped to their lapels. They all have to be working on the same set or they must be set assistants. I'm waiting to see someone wearing something different, who looks like they might be an actor in costume, going from makeup to set. "Are they shooting a James Bond movie today?" I finally say.

"Why do you ask that?"

"Because everyone around here looks like a secret agent—If I had to imagine what a secret agent in a movie would look like. But I've seen enough movies to know what American agents look like. That, and I saw Daniel

Craig coming inside. Didn't you see him too?"

"I guess I missed that… But you're probably right."

"You guys like your secret agents here."

"Heroes," Bill says. "We call them heroes. Defenders of democracy. All that and then some. They protect a hellova lot more than you probably realize and they don't get enough recognition for it." His voice sinks a bit as he looks down the hall. His hand, again, presses into my back, and we turn, going down another hall. American flags hang on the walls all over the place, adding the only bit of color to the otherwise sad-looking space. I had imagined a movie studio would be large and fairly dull if you're not on set—Because they need wide, open spaces to move around set pieces, costumes, mechanical things, and electronics—But none of this reads like a movie studio. If I didn't know better, I'd think this was a government building.

We slip past another blank wall, then a podium in front of blue curtains with an American flag hanging off the side. Ahead of us, large golden words spread across the wall from a number of framed photographs. Bill pushes me by too quickly, I can't even pretend to read it. He uses the card clipped to his shirt to unlock another door. He leads me through a pair of thick, white, double doors. I know they're metal without touching them. "Jan, let me introduce you to your new studio." Bill grabs each looped handle and pulls them toward us. They're barely open before they continue on their own once he releases them. Before us is a white room with a wall of metal shelves stacked side-by-side. Square, metal boxes sit on each shelf, labeled with different chemical compositions and their names. Many are familiar, but many more I've never seen before. My nose tickles from the sweet sting coming through one of them. I nip at the skin on the tip of my thumb as I walk down the line of shelves.

One after another.

All in alphabetical order.

At the end of the line is a fridge that has more containers inside, some of them liquid. In the freezer: blueberry vodka. On the other side of the fridge are two more shelves containing only liquid materials. At the far end of the room is a clear box the size of a room. A camera's pointed at the glass. Holes in the wall allow for microphones to pick up the sound. The background where the camera is pointed reads the words BOOM, BOOM, BOOM, SALUTE in thick, red lettering.

Then, on a desk across from the back end of the camera is a computer, connected to a cord that crawls down the side of the desk and disappears into the ground. My eyes blur with a build of tears, but I wipe them quickly. While Papa has said there are some circumstances in which it is alright for men to cry, this is neither a family member's death nor the absolute annihilation of my homeland.

"This… is for me?" I walk toward the glass room.

"Of course." Bill nods.

I pull open the clear door. It's heavy, but not glass. I don't know what it is, but I can only assume it's not glass due to how many glass bottles I've personally destroyed through experiments. Plus, the right kind of pressure in a bomb can shatter glass with ease.

The room's huge, the size of half a stadium, and the smallest part is the setup with the chemicals, fridge, and computer. I stand in the middle of the clear box. You can't even see the walls. The only thing that gives it away is the bit of light reflecting from above and the metal, loop handle on the door to the side.

I smile at the camera. I salute. "Hello, Boomers! This is amazing, isn't it?"

"The camera's not running," Bill says.

"I know, I know—But I'm practicing." I slip my phone out of my pocket and snap a picture of myself in the box where the wall says BOOM, BOOM, BOOM, SALUTE behind me. I send it to Aleks. Then, I open my video app and start a live stream. "Hello, Boomers!"

I wait a moment to see if anyone joins, greeting people as they make themselves known in the chat and the number on the screen under "concurrent viewers" climbs. Unlike back home, thousands of people log into the stream almost immediately and before thirty seconds is up, I'm over ninety-thousand viewers. The chat fills with people saying, "hello," "hi," "wow dude, where are you?" "hello from Paris," and they just keep going so fast, I can't keep up.

"I have some exciting news. We just got our own studio! Check this out!" I tilt the camera around the studio as I walk. It is so strange that the first people I'm telling about this directly are not Aleks or my parents, but a bunch of strangers. I have nothing against any of them, but all of my life, I thought I would be speaking with Aleks when this moment came and he would be saying, *"Well, I'll be, hell… You actually did it."*

"And for the record, we have a large *blasting site* separate from the rest of this," Bill says. "So… If you get ideas for something very different like what you did in your last video, let me know and the studio will take care of all proper preparations."

"That's so awesome…" I mutter to myself. The camera in my hands disappears for a moment until chats flicker rapidly across the screen. "Right. You heard that, yeah?" The chat floods. I can't read them fast enough. I can't read them at all. I peek toward the shelves stacked with chemicals. "It feels like forever since we've had a little fun. I don't even know where to start, you know?"

I exit the clear box. My phone's placed on one of the shelves, propped up by leaning on something else. I open one of the containers, giving it a short, careful sniff. There's only a little heat in the dust. I sneeze. It smells somewhat like dried water. I place it back and grab another. This smell is so much stronger and sticks to my nose before I even inhale. I cough, close the lid, and cover my nose with my arm.

The heat crawls down the back of my throat like I've ingested a bunch of hot powder. I go to the fridge and take one of the vodka bottles. I'm not sure where the cap lands, but cool blueberry quiets the building burn in my mouth. I cough into my arm again, lowering the bottle. The alcohol burns my nose a little. "Sorry," I say through my arm at the camera. "I wasn't expecting that."

"Maybe you should slow down on the ingesting part of this?" Bill says.

"How else will I know what I have to work with?" I cough again, this time a little milder than the last.

I pick up the phone and turn away. Bill watches from beside the set camera. I've never felt self-conscious before, but apprehension takes hold of me and I slow my walk from looking over the ingredients waiting for me. My heart's suddenly racing and pounding in my ears. My skin's hot. It's not from the powder. The thrumming goes down my arms and I catch myself in the camera facing me. The expression doesn't look like me at all. Bill's over my shoulder, his face obscured by sunglasses. "What are you doing today, Bill?" I turn around.

"Seeing what my favorite client is doing." Crossing his arms, he leans against the clear room wall.

My chest is tight. I never minded when Aleks watched me work. Though, he never tagged along that often and every time he did, he said *that's dangerous* and *you should go to the hospital* when it was only a small gash in my arm. Since he came so few times, he never saw anything I wasn't proud of and I trusted him not to laugh at me for being weird, but I don't know that about Bill. There's even more of a strange feeling because I can't see his eyes. I've never seen his eyes and it's kind of a big deal. It shouldn't mean anything. Superstitions are just that, but Mama always stressed speaking to someone while looking into their eyes. That is how you know they are honest. If they desperately hide their eyes, they're desperately hiding the truth.

"You can't lie while looking someone in the eyes, Jan," Mama said. "Even when false words come out, your soul will betray you. Your soul wants to betray bad intentions."

"What if a lie is better than the truth?" I asked.

"A lie might be better than the truth in a moment, but the consequences of the lie will never supersede the outcome of the truth."

"What if you want to marry this woman and you have to lie to get her to look at you even just once?"

Mama laughed that time. I feel her thumb stroking my cheek. "Jani, a relationship built on lies will never grow fruit that is not poisonous. Pain begets pain. Lies beget lies. If you want to be a man of your word, look people in the eyes when you make promises and never trust those who won't do the same."

I meander to the center of the room. My hands drop to my sides. My phone's screen taps against my thigh while I look around. A moment of surrealism passes and I'm not sure where I'm standing. I don't know if I exist. Everything's too much like a dream or a thought someone else is having. All of the sudden, there's pressure in my head and I'm dizzy and I'm not sure what's going on or where I am or how I got here, but I feel the distance between Ukraine and my family and me.

I'm staring at my own words through the clear wall, but they're foreign and unreadable, no matter how many times I try. I feel sick, like I'm never going to see my family or Aleks ever again.

"Something wrong?" Bill says.

I'm walking toward him without thinking. I place the vodka on the computer desk and continue until I'm standing right in front of Bill, looking up at him. He's not that much taller than me, maybe close to ten centimeters, if that, but his boxy uniform and glasses make him different, inhuman, monster-sized. It's not the same as the Russian soldiers who come in and around Nide sometimes. At least they don't shield their eyes. Some of them laugh, some of them look like they want to laugh, but none of them hide their intentions.

I squint, trying to see through Bill's glasses, but all I see is my face, my own disheveled hair, my own tiredness in somewhat red, puffy eyes. I reach for the glasses. Bill grabs my wrists just as my fingers graze the frames.

"Ah!" he says like he's correcting a dog. "Jan… What are you doing?" He steps back, but he's still holding my hands, lowering them now.

"I—Sorry. I wanted to see your eyes."

"Why?" He chuckles in a way that says it's not because I said something funny.

"I… don't know." My eyes trace the wall behind his shoulder. There are small cameras in all the corners of the room and one above the desk. "I've been working with you for a week at least and I still haven't seen your face. You're my agent, yeah? I should be able to recognize you." I don't look at him while I speak. When I step back, he releases my hands and I keep going backward, getting faster and moving with a sway until my back bumps the desk. I swipe the bottle off it.

"Are you nervous about something?" he says.

The bottle presses to my lips. I laugh into it, choking on alcohol. Some of it spills down my chin. I wipe it with the back of my arm. "No, no, no." I wipe my lips a second time. "Nervous about what? I've done this a million times before."

"But has it ever been *this* real?"

"It's always been *real*, Bill. I have the burns to prove it." I laugh. "That's always what made it so… exciting, but…" I turn around, spinning, looking at the room, humming as I walk. My heart is telling me something is off. I want to call it a liar, it's the nervous one, not me, but I can't quiet its constant whisper. "It's never been like this before. Do you think I could get to know the studio and do my first show with just the Boomers?"

"I am a Boomer," Bill says.

"Yeah, but I mean up until the conference, every show I've done has been through the camera and I don't think I was prepared to have people watching me the other day. I should have known what was going to happen with that solution, but I didn't. I got distracted by all the people watching me—So I watched them instead."

"You've got a bunch of them watching you now, don't you?" He gestures to my phone with a nod.

"Yeah, but they aren't standing here, watching me like you." I glance down at the phone. The chat is filled with emojis of rockets, faces, fireworks, and fire. People are asking when we're gonna start while others are still coming in to say hi. "It's different when it's you and me because we are… more intimate. You know, Aleks is the only person who has ever watched me do a show in person like the one the other day. I used to do small stuff outside of my house until Papa got worried I might break the windows on the house. Papa was never a big fan of the show because it could cause trouble. 'Don't bring attention to yourself,' he'd say. I don't think he understands what I've been doing, but I want to succeed here. I want him to know it wasn't a waste of time. I want him to be proud of me."

Bill closes the space between us. He places his hands on my shoulders and gives them a squeeze like he's a family friend going back. "Whatever you do here, your father will be proud. You're changing the world, kid."

A laugh bubbles up in my throat. Turning away, I pull out of Bill's grasp. My shoulders are heavy where he touched them. "I'm making videos on the internet."

"Look over your comments and tell me you're not changing the world," Bill says. "From your little house in Shit-All, Russia to this monster of a room in the capital of the free world. Believe me when I tell you that you're going to have an even bigger impact than you know. From here, you're going to change more lives than you may ever realize. I get it." His smile is compassionate, gentle, and friendly. He slides his hands into his pockets. His lips flatten. "If you want your first show to be *traditional*, I won't stand in the way of that. I'll come back when you end transmission. Deal?"

"Deal."

Bill slowly makes his way toward the door. He keeps watching me all the while and I'm not sure why, maybe he's waiting for me to say something, object, change my mind, but whatever it is doesn't come. His hand rests on the knob before he pulls the door open. He turns around to look at me and then, with a sigh and a brief smile, he says, "have a good stream." He's out the door. His phone's in his hand before he closes himself outside of the studio.

I take a deep breath. Turning back to the camera, I sigh with pursed lips and a shaking head. "I'm not Russian."

The room falls into a silence that's both familiar and foreign. A reminder of what the forest felt like when I sat on my blasting spot, preparing for my shoot. I walk around the room like I'm stepping through thick layers of snow, finding a patch of ice underneath everything that fell the night before.

The phone slips from my hand. I forgot I was even holding it until it clattered on the floor. The camera points up at me. Comments from viewers stream across the screen. I pick up the phone and smile, blowing a speck off the camera. Cracks web from the bottom of the screen. "I'll be right back, guys… I'm going to set something up."

I shut the stream down.

I hope Bill doesn't think this means he can come in yet.

I return to the computer desk. I don't remember putting the vodka down, but it's next to the keyboard. I'm forgetting a lot of things. I take a drink to calm my nerves. It doesn't really work. There's just something I want to check on. I scroll through my files, looking over the last week worth of photos and videos since I got to America. There are pictures of the plane, of the hotel I had been staying in and the new home I'd been moved to. Bill says I can't get a house for a while and will have to live in studio housing for a bit. I have pictures of the yard and street outside of my room, but Bill says I can't go out there because it would be too easy to spot me from the sidewalk and that could put me in danger.

He says we have to wait until my first video goes live before I can go out on the yard. Last time, he said it was only until I signed the contract. Before that, he didn't say there were any restrictions like this.

I don't think any of it makes much sense when I've already been seen in public at the convention center and the airport, but I haven't been asking that many questions since every time I try, he says all these things about legalities and appearance fees and broken contracts and exportation and paying them back.

I'm checking my reel one more time for the video from the convention center, not only to upload to my channel, but also to send to Aleks, like it could be some kind of explanation for my leaving that might satisfy him like nothing else I've done. Looking at the text messages he hasn't responded to makes me depressed. We haven't fought like this before. I got angry when he moved to Sumy, he got angry when he saw my blasting site the first time. But we moved on.

There's no reason he should be giving me the silent treatment unless he thinks I am lying to him.

There are no videos of the convention center on my phone. The videos from the limo when I arrived are also gone. The crowd at the airport is gone too. I take a sip from the bottle and keep it pressed to my lips, even when I scroll through my social media feed without drinking. The couple of posts I made about arriving, showing off my hotel room, or my new room are all gone. At least, I thought I'd posted about them.

Maybe I've just been tired.

I lay the phone down on the desk. I'm at the shelves of ingredients, grabbing a handful of liquids and powders and whatever I can and stack them on the desk next to my phone. It's hard to smile when it shouldn't be. Once I've gotten maybe a dozen items together, I turn the phone camera back on, now pointing it at me from a close distance. "Hello, Boomers! Sorry about the interruption." I wave a lazy salute. "I thought I'd surprise you—" I pause, thinking better than to say what I was going to, knowing that Bill is watching from another, nearby room. "I wanted to pick some surprises from the shelf so we can try them together. Let's get set up to make something nice, eh?"

I watch the phone as people filter in and more chats fill the screen. Filter in? That's a weird way to say it. Filter usually means pulling things out, not dropping a bunch of something in. The bold number telling me how many viewers are watching seems consistent, even when a couple drop in or off at the end. It's not enough to matter. It's not enough to make them a real number.

Nothing real like Bill walking out of the room or Aleks standing in the forest with me or knowing my room back at studio lodgings will be empty when I get there except for a paper-wrapped sandwich waiting for me to eat it.

There's a user at the end of every one of these numbers, but they're not the same thing as a person standing in front of me.

I open the first canister. The smell hits my nose immediately and my fingers tingle with the familiar excitement of coming sensations. I'm a little buzzed from the alcohol, and honestly, I think by the end of today, I just might be drunk.

I'll do it on purpose. At least then I might feel like someone is keeping me company when I get home.

THIRTEEN

I'm staring out the window from my bedroom. It's not a hotel, they've told me, but it still feels like one.

Hotel. Lodgings. Gulag.

I shouldn't call it that. It's an insult to everyone who died in a gulag and was not lying on a pillow-top mattress with a wide, flat-screen TV playing HBO Max all day. The sun shines through windows I can't open. Even if I wanted fresh air, they're sealed. I've tried them every day since I was moved here, so I know they won't open, but I try opening them again just to see if, somehow, today they're different. They don't move. I've tried asking Bill if I can go for a walk for some fresh air. He laughs, tells me I'm funny, then gets all serious when he says, "Nnnng… too risky. Did you forget what *celebrity status* means already? You've seen the movies, haven't you, Jan? If not, you have a TV now. *Watch them.* Get informed."

I never know what movies he's talking about. I was also under the impression that movies were not real life, even when they pretended to be.

My new bedroom is bigger than it was in the hotel. Now I have a small kitchenette along with a small fridge.

It holds mostly vodka and water and there are bags of jerky on the counter. I don't know why they keep bringing me jerky.

A couple of empty bottles of blueberry vodka and jerky wrappers stuff the trashcan. The room smells sterile; the spilled alcohol in the sheets doesn't help. My phone's in my palm and I'm still waiting for it to buzz with a message from Aleks. I can't help but check it every thirty seconds. Maybe more often than that. I'm not keeping track.

Every day I've been waiting for him to send me a message saying, "Sorry, I've been busy. You worried I was mad at you? Ha. How's America? This looks expensive," and we'd slide into our normal back and forth like nothing happened.

I bring the phone to my ear. No one's on the line, but I say, "I wouldn't know. Bill Cosby is my agent. Have you heard of him? He's the one in charge of my life now and he is *more* demanding than Boris ever was. He won't let me leave the house. I haven't seen much of America yet…"

I hear Aleks chuckle and say, "get to the point, Jan."

I smile wide, but it fades fast. "I was saying I wouldn't know if America is expensive. I'm not buying anything. Everything's just brought to me. It's like being royalty. Bill calls it *celebrity status*. It's horrible."

And Aleks wouldn't say anything for a while, but then, because he's the pragmatic and thoughtful one, because he's an engineer and lives in Sumy with a job that isn't stocking shelves, he would say, "Do you feel like a celebrity?"

I'm always surprised by how much better Aleks knows me than I know me. My heart's racing again. It's been doing that a lot recently. My hand falls from my ear so my phone taps against my thigh. My throat's dry and my eyes go blurry, but I close them so nothing escapes. I go to my bed, falling onto it when I finally get there. My voice muffles in the sheets. "I'm bored, Aleks. It's not much fun around here when you can't do as you want."

"Why can't you do what you want?" Aleks says to me.

"Because Bill won't let me."

"Since when do you care what other people say you can do?"

I roll onto my back. The television across from my bed is huge, but that doesn't stop it from blurring while I stare at it. "This is different. My agent has security stationed everywhere—"

"And yet you still made a video in the middle of the woods while Nide was crawling with *katsap*."

"And I didn't get caught by any of them."

"Yeah… What happened to that guy?" Aleks says. His voice continues in my head, but it grows distant and static breaks it up until he's missing.

"Aleks?" I say. "Aleks? Are you there?" I bring the phone back to my ear, pull it away, look at the screen. It's black. It's been black. My call history is empty except for all the times I've tried to call Aleks since I left Ukraine. I put the phone back to my ear saying his name again, waiting for him to say, "Sorry, I got busy for a second, someone came in, I tapped mute by accident—" *Anything.* I just want to hear his voice, but for real. I pull the phone away from my ear and tap the screen with my finger. The broken glass disrupts the image of my blasting site back home. Green trees from summer surround the black spot in the dirt where I used to run my activities.

The screen reminds me I wasn't talking to Aleks and I stare at it until it assures me no one's coming by turning black again.

I get up and go to the freezer. I toss my phone onto the counter. I'm taking out a bottle of vodka and it's half gone the moment I take the cap off. A burp pushes a burn of spiked blueberry into my nose. I wipe my mouth with the back of my arm. I stare down at my phone.

Another drink.

"You're right." I put the bottle down, grab the phone, and stuff it into my pocket. "This isn't anything like I'd ever do. Since when do I hide like this?" My Ukrainian's slurring a little bit, but it's not the vodka's fault. It couldn't be. I haven't even drank that much.

I grab the bottle again and drink another half of what's left. My head's bobbing to music that's not there while HBO plays in the background. "Ba ba, ba ba, ba ba, ba!" My shoulders sway and lips mutter, though I'm not sure what I'm saying, I open the door to my room and look down the hall. First left, then right. I jump from just how close a man in a suit is. He's been there every day, I don't know why it startles me every time.

"Is something wrong?" he says.

"No." I slowly push the door closed and back away again. I'm sucking the residue of gunpowder out from my nails as I walk back across my room toward the window. A desk sits near it. I'm on the third-story by a street. Across the street is a small park, a fountain of a man surrounded by a lot of cement and streets filled with cars almost all the time.

My fingers curl around the back of the desk chair. My foot bounces. I shift my weight. My other foot bounces. The traffic lights outside change. I count the seconds between each direction change from red to green back to red. My head drops forward, my forehead presses to the glass.

"What'chu'do'in?" I say, pronouncing each sound hard. I clear my throat. "What'chu'do'in?" I say harder. I grab the chair with both hands. Dragging it away from the desk on two legs, a couple paces away, I swing it and toss it into the window. The legs slap into the glass—Not glass—It thuds. The chair flies back at me. I duck. The chair smacks into a lamp and a side table and crashes. I run across the room, tripping over my feet. One of my socks is half hanging off my foot and I'm thinking since when did that happen or am I just noticing it now because it's hindering me? I slip into the bathroom, turn on the light, and toss my phone into the sink. I'm in the shower. The water's running. The shower doesn't have a curtain, though. It's a big, glass box. I rip my clothing off and toss them on the floor outside of the shower door. My foot slides on the linoleum.

The bathroom door flies open. The man in the suit from outside the door comes in.

"Ah!" I say, my voice shakes with uncertainty. "Please don't hurt me—I'm naked!" My arms cover my face. The water's steaming the glass and quickly turning my skin red. It's probably too hot.

"There was a sound," the man in the suit says. "A lamp in your bedroom is knocked over."

I gasp. "Really? Was it the kidnappers I've been told about?" I peek over my arm.

The man in the suit is looking around the bathroom. He stares at the pile of wet clothing. There's a flicker of something on his lips. Irritation? He doesn't move. I hear my heart over the rushing water. The man turns back to the bedroom, says something to someone in there, then turns back to me. "You didn't hear anything?"

I'm shaking my head before he's done talking. "No," I say. "I don't think so."

"How long have you been in the shower?" he says.

"I don't know. Am I supposed to keep track of that kind of thing? Sorry."

The man in the suit looks back at the wet clothes again, then the mirror, then the sink. "Why is your phone in the sink?"

I shrug slowly. "It must have fallen off when the earthquake hit?" I say.

"Earthquake?"

"I don't know. You heard a sound. I'm just guessing."

Another man comes into the bathroom and whispers

something into the other man's ear. They both look at me. I stare back at them. They look at my clothing. The one points at me. I say, "I'm naked, sorry." The hot water steams the glass. It steams their sunglasses. I'd think they'd take those off, but they don't. They watch me for a long while, whispering, I can't read their lips. I turn my back to them and run my fingers through my hair, getting it thoroughly wet and pretending I don't notice them anymore or I don't care.

I hear something.

They're leaving. I give it a couple more minutes before I turn off the water. I hang my wet clothing in the shower to dry. My wavy hair is weighed down by water which drips down my neck. I peek out the bathroom door. No one's there. The chair's pushed back under the desk. I keep going into the room. The air's freezing.

"You need to be more careful," a voice says.

I turn around. Bill is standing against the door to my room. "Why?"

"You could get hurt."

"How could kidnappers have found me? I haven't done much of anything—"

"I didn't say kidnappers, Jan. There's more going on than you're aware of." He looks at the empty bedside table where the lamp used to sit. There's nothing there now to match the lamp on the opposite side of the bed. "Stay away from the windows. Keep your lights at a minimum—"

"I can't sit in the dark—"

"If it's not something you think you can do on your own, then we'll be happy to move you to a room where windows won't be a problem. We might set that up anyway—"

"A room with no windows? Now you're starting to sound like this is prison." I laugh, then swallow.

"Don't think like that. You'll make yourself crazy."

"But why is this necessary?"

"You're too important for us to lose, Jan. Do you understand that?" Bill's standing in front of me. He places a hand on my shoulders. Goosebumps form down my arms.

"I don't understand. I just make YouTube videos. No matter what the numbers say, I'm a nobody from Nowhere that could be replaced by someone else with something more interesting going on."

"Jan…" Bill squeezes my shoulders hard. "You might not see it, but you need to believe me when I say we need you and we need you focused and safe, alright? We've got a couple of big meetings coming up in the next few days. International investors. Studios from all over want you at the lab trying things out and thinking of how to make things bigger and better every damn day you're at work. We need to impress these guys—"

"But what will it do?"

"Hm?" Bill pretends he didn't hear me. His hands draw back like he was touching fire. He's looking away.

"What will it do if I impress these executives with my videos?"

Bill chuckles and nods. He's responding to someone that isn't there. His lips curl into a smile. "You don't need to worry about that, kid."

I stare into my reflection. My body repulses looking at him. His smile is stone, his face is that of a monster with a snake for a tongue. The lenses of his sunglasses are black holes pretending to be eyes, trying to suck me in by using my face as bait. I reach for the sunglasses. Bill grabs my hand before I'm anywhere close enough to touch him.

"We talked about this," he says.

"Yeah, but I don't get why you wear them inside. I don't get how you can see in a dark room like this." I draw my hands back. He lets me go. I'm stepping back slowly, arms falling to my sides.

"It's an American thing. Don't worry about it." He steps back, making his way toward the room door. "But Jan? Get dressed. You hungry? I'll call you something to eat."

"Or we could go out to eat—"

"I'll call you something. How's a cheesesteak sound? Great." He doesn't let me answer. He's talking to himself still as he steps out the door and I hear him in the hall, muttering to one of the men out there. Maybe there's only one of them out there.

I open the door. The hallway's colder than my room and I feel it immediately on my lower half. The man in the suit looks at me, brows furrowed and lips offended, but trying to stay straight. Bill's halfway down the hallway, turning on his heels he sees me and yells, "I told you to get dressed! Dinner's coming!"

I close the door. I put on a pair of bleached jeans and a Hawaiian shirt Bill gave me when I got here. I look through everything searching for a pair of sunglasses because maybe if I put on all the right gear, I could walk right past everyone in the hall without them knowing it's me. They never gave me sunglasses. I think they took away the ones I had. My goggles don't blend in well enough, but I let them sit on my head after I put them on.

The bedroom curtains are closed now.

I finish the bottle of vodka I left on the counter then toss the empty bottle in the garbage with the others. My tongue runs over my lower lip. I can't take my eyes off the one lamp beside my bed. I go to the freezer and open another bottle of vodka. My foot slips, but I don't fall. I lean on the counter, drinking. I can't stop looking at the lamp. Then, I'm running across the room, legs tangling and untangling as I go. I jump onto the bed, turn the light off. All the lights are off now, but the TV provides constant illumination.

My goggles are over my eyes. I pull the lamp's plug

from the wall. One of the few things I've brought from home is my pocket knife. I sit on the bed, pulling the lamp into my lap. I unscrew the panel covering the lamp's circuitry. I don't have a lot of experience with electronic bombs, but I know enough to cross wires, make something hot, and add a little fluid to make something spark. I use the tip of the knife like a pair of tweezers to pull loose different wires. A spark of residiual energy makes my fingertips warm. I lick the burn, but don't let myself slow down. I cross a couple of box wires, connecting the ground and neutral and live to all the wrong places. Maybe random places. I don't know. I close the lamp case back up and place it on the nightstand. I smell heat and warm melting plastic. My fingers tingle with the familiarity that comes with anticipating an explosion. I plug the lamp back into the wall. There's a buzz. I press the switch to turn the lamp on.

Boom.

Electric fire catches on the blanket.

I guess I didn't need the sparker fluid after all.

I pull my goggles down my neck. The bedroom door flies open. I didn't even hear them run the card to unlock it, but, to be fair, my ears are buzzing a little from the explosion and the ringing in my right ear is the worst. I climb off the bed, staggering, just as one of the polo men is grabbing my arm and pulling me away.

Bill runs in the door next, turning on the light just as he does so. The bedside table lays on its side, the top burned from electric heat. The lamp's busted. A small fire crawls across the bedsheets. One of the men in suits is putting it out. Bill says something, looking from the fire to me. His voice is harsh, demanding, suspicious, but I'm having trouble translating. Maybe I drank a little more than I thought. The TV isn't making sense either.

"Answer me, Jan," Bill says. "What the hell happened in here?"

"I don't know…?" I say first in Ukrainian, then realize it and repeat myself in sloppy English. "I was watching that." I point to the TV. HBO has been playing for hours and I don't know what's even been on it since I haven't been paying attention, but right now there's someone not wearing a shirt on top of someone else and it sounds a lot like they're having sex and I'm not looking at it. My face burns, hearing the moans coming from the speakers.

"Did you do this?" Bill says.

I'm shaking my head before he's even done asking the question. "I'm just a chemicals guy. I don't know about anything else and all I did was turn on the lamp. Maybe it's faulty?"

Bill looks me down. His eyes catch on the goggles around my neck. "What are you doing wearing those, then?"

I look down, then back up. "I was having a good time? Vodka, ladies, shower, you know?"

"Is something wrong, Jan?" Bill says.

I'm still shaking my head. I don't know if I ever stopped.

"Are you lying to me, Jan?" he says.

"Lie? I don't even know what that means."

Bill grabs my arm hard. He's pulling me out of the room while muttering something to I don't know who, but he's obviously talking to someone and his voice is so low, I can't hear the words.

"What is it, Billy?" I say and he doesn't say anything back. He's pulling me and my feet are tripping over themselves since I can't move fast enough or in the way he wants me to go. "Where are we going, Billy?" I'm pulling a little, but he's pulling back harder every time I try. "Billy?" And he's still saying nothing so I keep saying his name. We're walking down the hall fast. The carpet's red with diamond blue shapes in it and white lines crossing through it at different angles and it's making me dizzy when I look at it. My mind's tricking me that the floor's moving, a conveyor belt more persuasive than Bill's pull. My eyes cross, so I look up at the ceiling instead. White doors pass. No windows. I'm still saying, "Billy, Billy, Billy, Billy," waiting for him to say something back. We're going down the stairs, we're in the lobby. There's a black car outside waiting and Bill pushes me in. "Bill!" I'm scooting to the other side of the car.

"What?" He answers only after he's in the car, door shut behind him, and we're moving.

"Where are we going, Billy?"

"Somewhere more secure. Somewhere that will keep you safe."

"Is this about the kidnappers?"

"What else could it be about? Something slammed into your window, a bomb went off in your room—If it wasn't you, then what else could it be, Jan?" He speaks through his teeth. His voice goes low and there's something in there that sounds so much worse than before when he says, "It wasn't you, right?"

I'm touching for the door behind me, looking for the handle. The car's spinning, we're going fast, but then I bounce against the seat. We've come to a stop. The door handle slips into my finger. "You're speaking Russian!" I pull on the handle and force the door open. Bill lunges at me. I'm running into the street, across a concrete roundabout, behind a statue, between some buildings, I'm not looking back even as Bill yells at me. "Don't do this!" Bill's voice echoes, though it's not getting farther away. His shoes slap against the concrete. "You're going to get yourself killed!"

"That's what they all say!" I yell. I run across the street. Down an alleyway. More buildings. Then trees. I don't know how long I'm running or where I'm going before I'm jumping over someone else's fence. The darkness. Another fence. A potted plant. I dodge right and keep going.

I can't breathe anymore and I can't think, but I don't stop running. If I stop, they'll find me. If they find me, I'm going back to a quiet room where I sit by myself until they decide to take me out again, and this time, it'll be one with no windows. It doesn't matter what they say, no matter how many times they say it, doing a live stream with all these people doesn't make you stop feeling alone. It doesn't matter how many people there are.

Who's talking to me?

None of them have real faces.

The cool night air feels nice. My feet slap against the concrete. Dirt and rocks lodge themselves between the surfaces of my shoe soles. I'm feeling the sting and wetness in my arms now and it's not until I pass by a lamp on the backside of someone's house that I see cuts on my exposed arms left behind by the lamp's explosion.

I'm surrounded by concrete homes stacked on top of each other. They look American, but also like they belong in another time.

I'm lightheaded. I breathe deep, but I don't think I can stop just yet. I look back over my shoulder. Grass crackles under the foot of something unseen. I run between buildings. I'm through an alley, over a chain-link fence, going between cars, across the street, and another car. I duck behind a car in a parking garage and press my back to the driver's door. I hold my breath, listening for any passing cars, watching for any light, but there's nothing and I think I might have finally lost them.

FOURTEEN

I'm laying on my stomach under a car, but no one's driven down the street for a while so I climb out to keep going. I'm still not sure if I've lost Bill and the others, but it seems okay for now and there are plenty of places to hide if I see anyone again. The quick walking turns to running. The cold air invigorates me and I'm trying to go faster. Everything's tingling in the chilly air and freedom. I turn on my heels and keep walking backward. The city lights brighten the horizon. I turn forward. My fists raise into the air. I can't help the scream. I'm running so fast and so far and so hard, everything hurts and I can't breathe, but I'm smiling and gasping and the crisp, fresh air pushes me harder. I check back over my shoulder.

A street light flickers.

I'm not seeing totally straight, but part of me knows the buzz is helping me keep going. I'm not sure how Bill hasn't caught up yet.

A chuckle builds in my stomach and comes out of my throat. It turns into a laugh that threatens the buildings in the neighborhood I'm walking through. I duck between yards, run across the street, jump a fence. I've left the area of townhouses and entered a neighborhood of single-family homes.

The cement looks nice, the yards are perfect, close together, and lit with warm light behind curtains. Red trim. Blue trim. American flag. So many American flags. Nice, big cars in driveways with garages made for two or three cars. They look so huge. They look so rich. They must be so happy with one of the houses I've always wanted and one of the big fridges that never runs out of food. My legs finally slow. My chest rises and falls with rapid breath. A relaxed smile comes to my resting lips.

I turn around completely, letting my arms fly out as I do a 360. I yell into the air. I turn around, walk backwards, watch the street while walking down the middle of it. There's no one there.

Then, the harsh sound of something cracking, splatting, a grunt.

Muscles stiffen, my heart races again. I turn around, waiting to see a black car with headlights pointed at me and Bill standing outside the car saying, "get in, you massive disappointment," in Russian.

He's not there, but my feet become welded to the ground while my legs threaten to give out. They're shaking, weak from running, weak from nerves.

Five meters away. It's her. The girl from the airport with the bright blue hair, the sporadic pink streaks, and the cocky smile on her plush, punk lips. She has a half-empty carton of eggs on the ground at her feet. Her hand pulls back. She throws. An egg crashed into the home of her focus. I can't look at anything, but her.

"Hey." My voice shakes a bit, surprising me. I swallow hard. I'm walking toward her; I stumble on the edge of the yard she's in. My throat's tight and it's suddenly so hot outside. My shirt sticks to my skin, especially under my arms. When did it get this warm out?

She leans down, grabs another egg, and throws it at the

house.

"Hey," I say, a little more stable this time. I step through the barrier of grass, reaching for her. "Remember me?"

She grabs another egg and throws it.

"Hello? Can you hear me? I've been looking for you—"

She turns to me. Her face isn't as happy as mine. She looks me down, then up. There's a pause on my shirt, then my face. I look down just to remember what I'm wearing. A Hawaiian shirt. My goggles.

"*You've* been looking for *me*?" She picks up the carton of eggs. "What did I do?"

"I guess... not really *looking*, but I wanted to meet you—"

"Oh, really? And what the hell did I do to earn your attention?"

"I don't know what you mean—"

"Which website flagged me?"

"I'm... sorry? I think you have me confused for someone else. I don't know you from a website. I saw you at the airport a couple weeks ago. You told me to run then ran yourself. I think you might have laughed. I don't think you were laughing at me though. It felt nicer than that?" I'm replaying the scene in my head.

"Wait..." She puts her finger up. "You're the dude who was surrounded by glowies, aren't you?"

"Glowies?"

She nods.

"You mean the Boomers?"

She stares at me for a moment longer, then she covers a laugh. "Yes." She picks up the egg carton from the ground. She flips it closed. Her eyes trail from it to me. I'm trying to see the color, but there's not enough light to expose it. "So, then..." She clears her throat. "You're a glowie too?"

"No." I chuckle.

"Then what are you exactly?"

"Jan Bagan."

Her eyebrows raise. She covers her lips, her crooked smile, her laugh. "I don't know what that means, dude." Her smile peeks through her fingers.

"I'm a famous YouTuber. Over fifteen million subscribers."

"Famous for what?" Her hand falls from her face. Her laugh says she doesn't believe me.

I raise my hands slowly. My fingers spring into open palms and fly away from my face. She blinks a couple of times. Her head cocks to the side. She looks over my shoulder one way, then the other, then over her shoulder. I look over my shoulder with a sudden panic that maybe she saw my agent, but no one's there. When I turn back, she's watching me, unimpressed. "Explosions," I say.

"Explosions?"

"Yeah!"

"Right…"

"I'm telling the truth."

"Then show me."

I reach for my phone, but it's not there. I check all my pockets; I come back empty. "I'm sorry. I must have left my phone at the hotel."

"Right…" She takes her phone out of her pocket, looking over her screen at me. "What's the name?" she mutters to herself.

"JanananaXD."

The refreshed page lights up on her face. She laughs again.

"What?"

"22 subscribers is *not* famous. You really think you could trick me with that?"

"I don't have 22 subscribers." I lean over to look at her screen. Under my name it says exactly what she said. "I have a bunch of subscribers. I don't know why your account says that. Maybe you have the firewall problem I had—"

"Or maybe it's because your subs aren't real." Her lips flatten. She slides her phone back into her pocket.

"They are real. They've talked to me—"

"You're lying to me and you're an agent—"

"*I'm* not an agent, I *have* an agent!"

She crosses her arms. "And what's your *agent's* name?"

"Bill Cosby." I smile with my teeth.

"Bill Cosby?" A snort catches in her laugh. "Like *that* Bill Cosby? Are you fucking serious right now?"

"What?" My smile fades.

"This is the glowiest glow shit I've ever heard in my life… and I live in DC."

"What does that mean?" My fingers come to my lips, giving my teeth a chance to dig under the nail and suck at the gunpowder residue still there. Not much is left but the ghost of experiments caught from years of staining. "Why do you have different numbers than me?"

"Are you new or something?" she says.

"New to what?"

"God… You can stop playing dumb already. Your accent might be better than most—I'll give you that—But you're not *that* good. Like who the hell wears the standard-issue *vacation look* in the middle of March?"

"Standard issue vacation…?"

"The Hawaiian shirt, jackass."

I glance down at my shirt. "You have a problem with my shirt? I'm sorry, I'm new—"

"Yeah, I can see that."

"I mean to America. I'm from Ukraine."

"Really now?" She tucks the egg carton under her arm. She doesn't look like she wants to hold it, but she doesn't want to put it down either.

"Yeah."

For the first time, she comes closer to me instead of stepping away. My heart jumps into my throat. My skin's hotter than it had been. She looks me in the eyes, down my neck, back to my face. She's so close, she smells like fruit. Peaches. Mango. A hint of vanilla. She looks so soft and pretty, even up close. Long lashes and dark eyeliner spike off the edges of her eyes, making them look more diamond shaped. Her cheeks sparkle in the moon and lamp light. I'm not sure if she's wearing something or if that's just her skin glowing, but I could believe it either way.

The pink in her hair is almost purple and mostly in the bangs, swept to the side and melting into the waterfall of blue that is the rest of her hair. Peaks of the same color mix in the bottom layer of her hair. She has a silver ring in her right nostril and a star-shaped pendent with diamonds at each point on a silver chain. Her sweater modestly shows her collar bone and goes down to her thighs. I'm not sure if she's wearing shorts, but stockings stick to her legs, and on her feet are a pair of dark pink skater shoes that match her hair. Her glance comes back up to meet mine. I wipe my sweaty palms on my shirt.

Finally, she leans back and smiles. "At least you've got one thing going for you." She points to her own eyes with her index and middle fingers, then mine. "Unlike 99% of the glowies, I can see your eyes and you know what they say about the eyes being windows to the soul or whatever," she mutters the last part.

My hands are so, so sweaty I have to wipe them off again. I'm sort of forgetting English and as quickly as I try to form a response, my tongue wraps around itself. I'm smiling, but my lips twitch. I don't know if I have full control, but I know I can't lose it or I'll look silly in front of the woman I'm going to marry.

Knowing that's who she is, everything leading up to this moment makes more sense.

Mama always said I would know when I met her—I wouldn't know when or where or what her name would be, but she would understand me and I would *know* when I was around her and this… this is that feeling.

The lightness in my stomach makes me sick. I'm sure it's not the vodka.

She's looking past me down the street then behind her shoulder in the other direction. Her eyes land on me again and she says, "You really don't have your phone?" She sets the egg carton on the ground.

I shake my head.

She looks me down, staring at the pockets in my jeans for a long while. In her eyes, I'm sure I see her thinking of checking my pockets herself and I'm not sure I'd mind if she did. "What kind of YouTuber doesn't carry around his phone?"

"I forgot it in the shower." I touch my pockets again, coming up with nothing. "Today has been kind of strange. Actually, the last while has been kind of strange."

"Okay," she says.

"Why does it matter?"

"Well, if you were *with* the glowies and now you're *not*… and you aren't one of them. They're probably looking for you, tracking your phone, and if you're carrying it, they'll be here soon if they're not already waiting for you to get out of the burbs first so there's no media shitstorm to explain." Looking around me, she glances down the street again. "You know how many stupid fucking media shitheads live in this neighborhood?" Her hand closes around mine. She picks up the eggs and pulls me toward the house. "One even lives in this house." She gestures to the one she was throwing eggs at.

"What happens if they find me?"

"You probably don't want to know."

"Then what do we do?"

"*We* can *start* with *you* telling me who the hell you are if you're *not* a glowstick and we'll go from there." We're on the stoop of the house she was throwing eggs at, then she lets me go, opens the door, and we're inside. She grabs my hand and pulls me in. My fingers curl around hers. She looks back only briefly. "Lock the door," she says.

I do it.

"Are you sure we can be here?" I say.

"Yeah. We're fine." She's pulling me, setting the eggs down in the kitchen, my legs stiffen. "I live here."

"Are you a media shithead?"

She laughs, though her hand tries to catch it. She fails. "No. God no. That's my loser dad." She cups her mouth to amplify her voice. "He thinks he's part of 'the resistance,' but you're not the resistance if you're getting paid six figures to rant about your feelings on cable TV!" Her voice echoes off the walls.

I don't know what about it makes me so uncomfortable. Maybe it's because I would never talk to Papa like that. I'm waiting for her father to come out of his room and lecture, but instead, all I hear is a television I didn't hear before getting louder. I look at the dark walls in the house as she pulls me upstairs. Framed portraits of a family, a baby, it must be her.

We're upstairs, in her room, she closes the door. It's mostly neat with a bed for one person, but the cover's pushed back and messy, one pillow, and a bunch of stuffed animals pushed to the floor beside it. Most of them are tigers. She goes to the closet and pushes back a pair of accordion doors. "Take off your shirt."

"What—?"

"The glowies know what you're wearing. I assume they know. Even if they don't, there's no blending in if you look just like them." She turns around holding a pink sweater in her hands. She looks me down again and then at the sweater she's holding. "Take off the goggles too."

She snorts another laugh on the word *goggles*.

"What's wrong with my goggles?"

"We'll talk about it later if you don't want a trip to the gulag."

"You *do* have gulags here—?"

"Okay, guy—Listen, I'm happy to talk to you, but we need to get shit done and get out of here before your friends decide it's time they pick you up. So… if you could change real quick, that'd be *great*." She crosses the room, standing in front of me now with the pink sweater. I nod. My shirt comes off, dropped onto the bed. I reach for the shirt. The blue-haired girl pulls back. "Wait." She tosses the shirt to the foot of her bed. She opens the top drawer of her desk. From the inside, she retrieves a small makeup bag. Unzipped, she pulls out a couple of bandages. She gestures to my arm with a nod. "Don't need you bleeding on my shirt. Let me fix you first, alright?"

I'm not sure what she's talking about. I don't feel any pain, but I listen to her anyway. She's got a cloth dampened with alcohol and dabs around the cuts left behind by the hotel lamp explosion. When my arms are cleaned and stinging, she wraps the cuts in bandages. She picks up the sweater again, handing it to me. It's pastel pink. A white skull head is on the front with metallic stars glittering along its crown and at the tips of the sleeves. I look at her.

She shrugs. "I like pink. So, what?"

I'm not sure what question she's answering. I'm not sure what question she's asking either.

"Hurry up," she says with her hands.

I pull the sweater on. It fits fine, but is probably oversized on her. I'm not a very big person, but I'm bigger in comparison. She ties her blue hair up in a messy bun. She pulls on a beanie that says LOSER on the front and tosses me a newsboy cap. I put it on. She grabs my hand and a bag from the desk, then we're in the garage, out the door, and driving down the street in a white Tesla. I don't know where we're going and I don't know if I care. The car smells like her fruity soap and my heart is racing, trying to find the words to say to make the moment with my future wife more perfect.

It all sinks in. I turn to say something to her or to ask how she knows what's going on. The realization strikes. I don't even know her name, so instead of the thing I was going to say, I ask, "What's your name?"

She chuckles. Switches gears. "You ask that *now*?"

"I don't know what you mean by that," I say.

"They're gonna need to do better with you, newbie."

"I don't know what that means—"

"Blake," she says. "My name's Blake."

"Blake." Her name is nice to say. I reach for her hand. She doesn't pull it away. "Where are we going?"

"Well… if you're evading glowies, the best thing I can think of right now is anonymity. How's a dance floor sound?"

I nod to her. The houses turn into city, homes to towers and columns and buildings like coliseums and obelisks lit in the distance. The car's quiet. Blake's got the radio on low, she's humming to the music while her head bobs. She's pretending to pay me no mind, but since I can't stop looking at her, I notice every time she glances toward me and I smile.

FIFTEEN

We're sitting in the parking lot of some place called *Continental Hush Hush*. Colored lights spill into the streets and sidewalks from the high windows and opening warehouse doors. A line of people file onto the sidewalk. A couple of them sit on car hoods, smoking, chatting, swaying to the bass that bleeds out of the club and rattles our car windows. Blake gets out of the car first and gestures for me to follow. I've never even been to a club in Ukraine. We don't have them in Nide and Aleks was never interested when I visited Sumy. I pause outside the car. My hand's searching my pocket for my phone, but it's not there. "Can I use your phone?"

Blake looks at me over the top of the car with a look that says she doesn't believe I'm asking for something like that.

"I'll give it back," I say.

"Sorry—Left it at home."

"What?"

"Let's get inside. Then we can talk." She closes the driver's side door. She doesn't wait for me to come around before she's walking fast toward the club's entrance, but she doesn't have to. I'm running to catch up.

Outside, the music's already so loud, I can't imagine much talking happening on the inside. I follow her past the line of people standing outside the doors. I'm not entirely sure what they're standing in line for if we can just walk forward.

At the front of the line is a man wearing a vest, a black, neon-paint speckled t-shirt, and black pants. He puts his hand up saying, "IDs."

Blake pats her pockets, then shrugs. "Looks like we don't need 'em," she says.

"Then you don't get in," the bouncer says.

Blake steps closer so the tips of her shoes are touching the tips of his. She looks up. He's at least fifteen centimeters taller than her. She beckons him with her finger to lean down. He doesn't do much but turn his head to hear her better through the music. "See that guy?" She points at me. The bouncer follows the gesture. "You're gonna let us in because he works for the government."

"Yeah?" The bouncer sneers, straightening up. "So does everyone in this godforsaken city. No ID? No entry."

Blake takes a step back. Her tongue flicks across her lips. Turning to me, she shrugs. "Fine." Her hand runs along my shoulder as she passes. I hold my breath. Dizziness comes fast. "If you really wanna mess with the IRS, enjoy getting *audited* tomorrow, dude." She winks at the bouncer, a brief smile, then she keeps walking.

"Wait!" The bouncer steps aside. Blake turns around. "If you're with *them*, you should've just said so."

"Thanks. I'll remember that next time." Blake takes my hand. My heart races from the touch and my fingers tighten around hers. She's ahead, pulling me into the club, pulling me through dancing bodies as multi-color lights flash across her and change the color of her hair from green to blue to red to purple. The music is only a little more than throbbing booms as the bass almost drowns out any speaking, and even the speaking is so distorted, I can't follow whatever the singer might be trying to say. The air's thick and sweaty.

The soft ringing builds in my right ear. I tilt my head to the side, hoping to snuff it out. It doesn't work. I stick my finger in my ear and pick at it. Blake stops suddenly and I run into her. "Sorry," I say.

She stands on her toes, looks around, and continues toward the bar. She waves the bartender over. Her voice is lost to the disco noise.

She exchanges a few words with the bartender. While she waits, she turns away from the bar and leans against it instead. Her head bobs to the music. She looks around the room, looking past me, it's almost like she's looking for something. I come to stand beside her, but face the bar. She doesn't shift. "What does audit mean?" I say to her.

She looks at me. "Huh?" She leans in.

"What does *audit* mean?" I try to say clearer and louder.

She laughs. Her mouth says, "oh," even though I didn't hear her voice. She leans in. Her hand wraps around the back of my neck and she pulls me in close. Her breath tickles my ear; the hair on my arms stands up. "A good, hard *fucking*," she says.

I pull back with heat trapped in my cheeks. Everything in me is on fire. I pull at my sweater's collar, but the club air doesn't allow anything to cool. The dancing bodies around it just make more heat, thrusting it our way. "Oh— You know him?"

She laughs, but her expression tells me I need to repeat myself because the words didn't come out in a way she could understand.

"Are you close with that man? Are you dating? You want to, uh, audit him?"

"Oh. That." She turns back to the bar. Her elbow bumps mine. "Don't worry about it."

The bartender comes back and sets a couple of drinks down on the counter. First, a pair of shots. Blue and clear. They remind me a little of lighter fluid.

"Drink," Blake says, putting one of them into my hand.

I tip the shot glass to her. "Salute." I throw it back. The burn outweighs the slight hint of fruit. There's something trying to be coconut in there.

Blake takes the shot glass from me and exchanges mine and hers for a pair of mixed drinks the bartender set down. She nods her head away from the bar. There's a new drink in my hand. I smell vodka among the contents. Her hand goes around my bicep and she's leading me. We sit at a booth off to the side of the dance floor and near the back of the room. She points for me to sit while she slides into the booth and up against the wall. I mirror her. She scans the room one more time, her head bobbing, her teeth biting at her bottom lip, her feet bouncing under the table in the same rhythm. Finally, she relaxes. Her eyes fall on me again. Leaning against the table, she brings her drink close. "Now, spill." She grabs her straw with her teeth.

"What?"

"If you're not a glowstick," she places her hand on top of mine. Her thumb strokes the back of my hand. "Tell me who you are."

I'm not sure where to start, so I begin back in Nide. I'm describing the town and telling her about Aleks when she rolls her hand in the air. The tip of her straw's crunched up from her chewing on it, so she stops drinking through it. "Get to the important parts. Tell me about the sponsors," she says, so I do. And I tell her about the Russians, the explosions, the plane, the hotels and laboratories, the blasting sites, conventions, and military cosplayers, then the kidnappers that Bill Cosby kept mentioning. Every time I say a sponsor's name, she nearly chokes on her drink laughing and says, "Really?" or "Are you serious? That's what passes as a cover now? How did you not get suspicious about *Tom Cruise?*"

I shrug. "I don't know who that is."

"C'mon. Really? *Mission Impossible? Top Gun? Jack Reacher?*"

"I don't know. I've never heard of those. Maybe they were never relevant?"

Blake laughs with a snort. "Ouch."

I finish telling her everything I know. Her glass is empty. She leans back, shaking her head, saying, "I'm gonna need another drink for this. You want?" She doesn't wait for an answer before getting up.

She's across the room at the bar.

I shouldn't be sitting in the booth alone. I push my hair back. My neck's sweaty, my hair's moist. She's staring at me through the dancing people. She has drinks in her hands fast. Her lips are moving, but she's not talking to anyone I can see.

The same could be said for my agent and his many associates these last couple of weeks though.

Blake sets down another drink that smells the same as the last one, but stronger, then slides into her side of the booth. She stirs her glass with her straw. Her finger wipes up some of the sugar from the glass's rim. She licks it off, then looks at me.

"Okay… Jan… Let me get this straight: you're a *literal who* the United States government kidnapped after trying to use Ukraine to start a proxy war with Russia, then they discovered that you're not *just* a useful idiot, but you're a *brilliant* useful idiot, so they brought you back to create bombs under the guise of making YouTube videos?"

"That sounds accurate, yes."

"Holy shit." She covers her mouth. "I mean, that's pretty cool for you, but holy shit US government. They were really wearing Hawaiian shirts?"

I nod.

"Holy shit." She's laughing.

"Why would America want to start a war with Russia?"

"It's not America; it's the war machine in the White House. Believe me: most Americans don't give a shit about what other countries are doing and we definitely don't want to be at war with random people." Blake leans in; her voice lowers. "The thing is: the government here isn't really American. Hell, the freaks running DC are hardly even human."

"What are they then?"

"Fucking lizard brains."

"I don't know what that means."

"Some people are better than others." Blake glances out to the dancers in the club. She watches the patrons, the door, the bar. She's tense, not just looking, but looking for something. She leans in again. Her foot bumps mine under the table. "Now, I don't know how true this is scientifically, but there's something psychs call 'the reptilian brain.' It's less evolved, managing only the basic needs for survival in the animal kingdom and apparently, some *humans* never evolved to have the mammal part of the brain that makes you give a shit about other people. The evidence? Most politicians only give 3 Fs: finances, feeding, and fornication. Thus, I'm inclined to believe most of them are a bunch of fucking lizard brains trying to take everything they can from the rest of us."

"But why?"

"Because they don't care? Because they feel inferior? Because they're all a bunch of psychopaths that would make Patrick Bateman blush? I don't know. I'm not a fucking lizard."

"I met Patrick Bateman. He didn't seem crazy."

"What?"

"On the plane here, I met Patrick Bateman. He seemed nice."

"No, Jan… Patrick Bateman isn't real."

"But I met him—"

"No, you met some edgy boy pretending to be Patrick Bateman. God—I bet he was a glowie too, wasn't he?"

"Look—I don't want to be involved with the government." I'm pushing away from the table, shaking my head.

"You could try to go home, I guess. Do you have a passport?" She leans back, purses her lips, and shrugs.

I shake my head. "I don't have any IDs. They told me I didn't need them at the embassy in Kyiv and then took everything I had while doing paperwork."

"Of course, they did." Blake rolls her eyes. Her smile isn't so much from happiness as it is from a kind of smugness of something she thought being confirmed. "It looks like the people who would've given you a passport decided to stop short of throwing you in a burlap sack and dragging you here blindfolded."

"Then how do I get home?"

Blake's lips part like she's going to say something, but she doesn't. She's watching the dance floor again, unmoving, focused on something. I start to turn. Her hand jumps to mine and squeezes while she says, "Don't," at the same time. My throat goes dry. I'm holding my breath, waiting for her next words to bring me comfort and promise. Her eyes finally meet mine again. It's brief, only long enough for her to say, "I don't think you can," and then she's watching the dance floor again.

"I thought America was land of the free?" I try to see what she's looking at, but she gives my hand another squeeze and I stop. Instead, I take a drink of the vodka beverage she brought me. "But it's not the land of the free to leave when you would like?"

Blake chuckles. "I think *land of the free* is a bit of a misnomer in the *current year.*"

"But all over the world—That's what they tell us America is about—"

"Yeah, sure, but the problem is DC is hardly America.

In fact, it's where the worst people in America come to vacay from freedom, and while here, they try their *damnest* to turn the rest of the country into the same kind of shithole DC is."

"But everything looks so nice here—"

"It's not the buildings that make this place shitty. It's the assortment of people." Blake's eyes shift to me for only a second. She squeezes my hand before I even try turning.

"What do you mean?"

Her hand leaves mine and exchanges it for her vodka drink. She leans back again, bringing the straw to her lips. She sucks what's left down fast, puts the glass down, and scoots to the edge of the booth, getting out. "How about I tell you later? I think we have company…" She's reaching for me, pulling me out of the booth by the front of my sweater. On my feet, one of her hands slips around my neck. Mine go around her waist, she's stepping back onto the dance floor, holding me close, swaying, our chests touch. I'm tripping, she's saying, "You okay?" and "You're not drunk are you?" and I say, "No, I'm fine. I don't get drunk."

She laughs, then says, "Do you trust me?"

"*Tak.*" I don't know if she hears me. She doesn't pull away and we're swaying to the music as she leads with the beats, showing me which foot we should step on and guiding me on how to turn her. She's urging me back. Her hand slides up my chest. I can't look at anything but her. She moves a little faster. Fingers hold my chin. Then she presses her lips to mine and I'm tripping, slipping on my own feet at the rush of weakness in my legs.

Blake releases my shirt to grab my arm, stabilizing me. She breaks the kiss, but doesn't pull back. "You sure you're not drunk?"

"Ukrainians don't get drunk."

"Oh, please…" She strokes the back of my neck.

"How much have you been drinking, Jan?"

I laugh softly, nervous, my sweater's sticking to my back. "Maybe… only a little before setting off a bomb at the hotel."

"You set off a bomb on the glowsticks?" She licks the corner of her mouth.

"Yeah."

"That's so badass." Laughter laces her words. The hand on my arm tightens, stabilizing me. "But Jan, I'm gonna need you to hold onto me if you lose balance, alright? We need to get to the other side of the room without drawing attention, got it?"

"Where are they?"

"I'm not sure, but we're not the only one's hiding. Just… be chill."

Something comes over me in that moment and my hand's grabbing hers. Even as I want to keep close, I also want to be safe, I want to be alone. I want to be somewhere cool and less busy and away from the throbbing music that wraps around the dancers. For the last few nights, being in a club was all I wanted, but now all I can think of is a desperate escape. At the same time Blake is saying, "Jan, what are you doing—" I'm running, pulling her along behind me. I don't know where I'm going, but there are signs for the bathroom hanging on the wall and I follow them until I'm running down a hall, past the bathrooms, and into a set of swinging doors with white words on them I can't read.

A storage closet

Blake's no longer holding me close, but she's holding my hand tight. I'm pulling her past shelves and boxes of decorations, alcohol, unmarked cases, and trash bins. Somewhere passing us, someone says something, Blake says something. I don't hear words, only voices. A glowing red sign illuminates the way to go. I press into the door's bar with my back. The cool air's colder against my sweaty skin and now it's only more obvious how my shirt clings uncomfortably to me. I slow down, trying to think of where to go next, though my legs never stop moving. I'm going slow enough that Blake takes the lead again and pulls me behind her. I speed up to walk alongside her instead.

"What happened to *be chill?*" she says.

"Sorry. I didn't want to ruin the moment, but I needed to get out of there." We round the street corner, leaving her car in the parking lot at the club. I look back, slow down, her pull makes me stumble back to attention. "Where are we going?"

"With any luck, somewhere private."

"I don't know if I'm ready to be audited," I say.

"What?"

"Um…" I glance over my shoulder briefly. "A good, hard *loving*, right? I don't think I'm ready."

Blake's laughter echoes down the street. She quickly covers her mouth. "No, not that." The words come through her fingers muffled. "Right now… the only people who'll be auditing you are your friends from the club if they spot us."

"I'm not into that."

"I don't know too many people that are. You don't have like, anyone else that might be after you, right?"

"Not that I know." I'm still having a hard time grasping that Bill Cosby is not my agent and the Boomers I've met while being here were not really fans. Blake's hand holding mine is the only thing keeping me moving as everything from the last few weeks replays in my head. We reach a hotel lobby. It's alright, but it's not as nice as what I had been staying at. The green couches look lackluster from age, dust, or both. The TV on the wall is pretty big, but the picture isn't great and the color is also lackluster. The gold trim doesn't so much break up the monotony of green, but make everything look dingier and dirtier. Blake tells me to keep my head down and go watch the TV. I do what she says.

Wherever she went, she's laughing now and leaning on the counter while she gives the hotel attendant a bit of cash, then she comes back with a key card and a room for two.

She opens the room door. I wait for her to enter first. She tosses her bag onto the bed.

The single bed.

I stand at the room door. I hope Blake isn't saying anything to me because my heart's pounding so loudly, I couldn't hear her anyway. I slip my hand into my pocket, looking for my phone so I can text Aleks and ask his advice for what I should be doing, but my phone's not there. I'm on my own.

Blake sits on the edge of the bed with a sigh. She uses her feet to slip her shoes off, toes to heel, then she kicks them under the night table beside the bed. She grabs her bag, shuffles through it, and pulls away, taking nothing out. She sits, then drops the bag on the floor beside her shoes. Her eyes find me standing in the entry. "You know you can come in, right? Or do you need an invitation? Were vampires a Ukrainian thing?"

"You're thinking of Transylvania and Vladislav Dracula. That legend was not created by us. The invitation thing wasn't us either."

"Let me guess: more lies invented by the government?"

"I'm not sure." I step in, closing the door behind me. "What do we do now?"

"I haven't gotten that far yet." She pulls her legs onto the bed and crosses them. Remote on the nightstand, she turns the TV on. The volume stays low as she flips through channels. "Assuming everything you've said checks out and the sketch lord I saw at the club was there for you and not some toilet stall quickie… What is there even to do when a foreign government has taken you captive? You'd think I'd have that all figured out after living in this hellhole for twenty-two years, but…" She purses her lips. Delicate fingers comb her hair back. She rubs her eyes. "I guess we could go get some burners…"

I slowly enter the room, leaving the entry hall behind. My movements are stiff as I walk to the other side of the bed. I'm at the edge. My knees touch the mattress, then I back away and move toward the window. I peel back the curtains a little, but only enough that I might see the view outside. A third-floor view of the street below with cars passing intermittently. How many of them are holding people that want to keep me here? How many of them are looking for me?

I release the curtain and step back. A phone sits on the room desk. Quickly, I pull the chair out and pick up the phone. I punch in Aleks's number, but a robotic voice on the other side tells me the call cannot be completed as dialed. I hang up and try again, getting the same result. Blake's watching me.

"What are you doing?" she says.

"I wanted to call my friend."

"You probably have to dial out first."

"What does that mean?"

"I wouldn't recommend it right now anyway. Glowies've probably got it monitored."

"How do they know? Wouldn't they be knocking on the door if they knew we were here?" I'm standing at the side of the bed, looking down at her where she lays.

Blake's arms are folded under her head. She rolls onto her side. "They don't know *yet*, but if you made a call to Ukraine, assuming that's where your friend is, you don't think that might be something they're keeping an eye out for?" She pauses, maybe waiting for me to say something, but I don't have an answer. "They'll trace the phone signals back to where they came from and bam—Suddenly you're back in Gitmo… or wherever they were keeping you.”

I sit on the edge of the bed, holding my breath until I'm forced to breathe. I don't want her to hear me breathing. I don't want her to know my concern by looking at my face. I don't think there's a way around it. "What do we do?"

"Sleep for now… and figure it out tomorrow." Her voice is a mutter, her lips barely moving, and it breaks off into a yawn at the end. She shuts the TV off.

The night's wearing on me too, but at the same time, I don't want to stop moving. My legs are restless and I pace the room a couple of times in order to satisfy them. The universe is telling me I need to be doing something, but I have nowhere to go, no one to call, and no one to talk to but Blake who is done talking for now.

Without sitting up, Blake lifts her hips to pull the blanket from underneath her. She folds her legs to pull the blanket over her, and then rolls over so her back is to me. She flicks the light off on the nightstand. The blanket's curled around her neck. I pace again. I bring my thumb to my lips, looking for gunpowder. When I don't find it, I switch to another finger. I smell of alcohol and sweat. I go to the bathroom and wipe my chest and face with a towel, some warm water, and a little bit of soap.

I come back to the bed where Blake is laying. I stare at her back. I wipe my sweaty palms on my pants again. Step forward. Step back. Can't sit down yet. I'm too close maybe? I hold my breath, then sit on the edge. I wait to see if she moves or says anything. She doesn't.

I kick off my shoes next, then wait again.

Nothing.

Lamp off, I lay back, but stay on top of the sheets and stare at the ceiling for a while. The cool hotel air and groaning air conditioner are far from the way my bedroom at home feels. I close my eyes, trying to imagine it's more like the night air, but even night in Nide isn't this loud as the trees rustle and whisper or when snow crushes under a boot. The familiar ring in my right ear cuts through the noise.

With everything going on, I think it's going to be hard to fall asleep, but the moment I think of home and I see my room, my bookshelf, and the hall that leads to my family on the other side, I'm no longer in Washington DC and I'm not a guest in America anymore.

SIXTEEN

There's no alarm, but the bathroom fan's running. I'm not sure where I am. The left side of the bed has covers peeled back and shoes on the floor. It looks like America, but it doesn't feel like the America I've been living in for the last few weeks. I throw my legs over the bed's edge. My head's throbbing a little in the front. My throat's dry, lips cracked. I need water. The night comes back to me as soon as I'm standing.

The bathroom door opens. Blake comes out, running her fingers through her mostly dry hair while her bag hangs on her arm. "You're awake," she says. "Good. I didn't want to try and wake you up. You know how insane some people can get when you do that?" She snorts a laugh.

I nod, smiling. She's really, really cute.

Blake grabs the remote off the nightstand and turns the TV on. She flips to a specific channel. An anchorman speaks. The man on the screen says, "You're watching S-T-R-8 F-A-Q-S."

"I've got an idea." Blake's tying her bright blue hair back into a messy bun. "The biggest problem we have is that no one knows you're here, right?"

"My family knows I'm here—"

"But they probably don't know you've been *burlapped*."

I nod, though I'm not entirely sure what she means.

"I said it last night—Washington DC isn't the United States. Glowies get away with shit here that they couldn't get away with anywhere else because of *their* population density. Lizard brains outnumber regular people here. For quick math, being a lizard brain equals being a psychopath, and do you know how many psychopaths live in DC? It's nearly equal to the number of people who work for the government. That's not a coincidence." Her finger is in the air, one of her dark eyebrows raises.

Her expression makes me feel like I should know something that I don't, so instead of looking stupid, I nod and mutter, "right, yes. That makes sense."

A man with smooth brown hair is centered on the screen. Shiny, slicked back, he smiles with his teeth and waves his hands when he talks. The dark hair is straight beside his ears and curls into a tip on top, peppered with silver. He speaks with a mild lisp. He's talking about decency and slamming his fist into the counter. "We need to do something. We're losing what it means to be American!" He wipes his hair back. He's speaking too fast, I'm missing the exact meaning in his words.

"Real piece of work, right?" Blake says.

"What's he trying to say?"

"Nothing. He's just filling the air between commercial breaks, hoping to get eyes to stay on him so he's paid more. The worst part is knowing he's *my* dad."

I hold my breath while looking back at the TV slowly. It's so early, too early for my heart to race like this. I know he's not standing *right* in front of me, but she's introducing me to her father.

The man on the screen says, "I'm Brian Beck." The bottom corner of the screen reads the same.

"Your name is Blake Beck?" I say.

"Gross, isn't it?" Her lips draw back when she speaks, even though a small laugh comes out. It's more disgusted amusement than anything. "Anyway, obviously he's kind of a sellout, but we can use that to our advantage and there's a positive he made it into work today."

"I'm not sure I understand."

"It means the glowsticks didn't grab him last night, maybe they didn't even know you were in my neighborhood." Blake comes toward me. Her arm slips around my shoulder. A playful smile pulls on her pink lips. They're shiny. Did she recently apply lipgloss? Her hair doesn't smell the same as it did yesterday and she doesn't smell like alcohol, but bamboo and flowers from whatever soap the hotel keeps in the shower. I don't like it as much. "Anyway… You came to America to get on TV, so I'm thinking that's exactly what we'll do. We'll head over to the station and broadcast your story to every home in America."

"Am I going to meet your Papa?" I look from her to the screen, watching him like I'm studying the cloud of an explosion, trying to read the colors for its ingredients.

"Mmm… Maybe. We'll see if we're that unlucky." She pulls away. "Did you want to shower before we go?"

I would have said no, but if I'm going to meet her Papa, then it is probably a better thing if I don't skip. I don't take long. Most of the soap is already gone and I avoid using the small bar soap Blake left behind because it feels wrong to share a bar soap that has touched her naked body. Even though we shared a bed last night, this is too intimate, too soon, too much to not ask for her permission to use it and I am too nervous to ask for permission right now. I'm out of the shower and pulling my jeans back on while staring at the pink, skull sweater Blake loaned me. It's the first time I have worn any kind of clothing that belongs to a girl.

"You ready in there?" Blake's knuckles knock against the bathroom door. She pushes it open. Pause. Our eyes meet in the mirror first. I turn around. She looks me down, then back up to my face. Her smile widens. Her face looks a little pink. "You're not looking as bad as I thought you might," she says.

"What do you mean?" I pull the sweater on.

"After last night, I thought you might've been a little more out of it than you wanted to admit."

"I told you, Ukrainians don't get drunk."

"Yeah… That's not how it looked yesterday. I mean, setting off an IED and running from the feds? How you even managed to get away from them on foot, I don't know—"

"Fences, mostly."

"Well, Mr. Fugitive, if you're ready, let's go." Turning away, she knocks on the door frame. "I'm starving and we need to get to the station before two. My dad disappears after that and we'll lose our opportunity."

Blake doesn't have to say more. She has her bag over her shoulder. Her shoes are already on. My hair's still wet and the longer part sticks to the back of my neck, though the slight curls already have their shape again. She slips on her hat and sunglasses, waits for me to do the same, then we leave.

I'm happy to follow.

"I know it's pretty much obvious at this point, but stay close," she mutters. "Glowies are hiding everywhere. Listening, waiting to violate you every way to Sunday. They legalized every bit of that shit before I was even born, you know?"

"Who did what?"

"I'm just saying… Yesterday you asked if America was the *land of the free*, but as far as I can tell, it hasn't been that way for a while. They wrap this shithole in a flag of red, white, and blue like a cannibal wearing the corpse of his victim, expecting no one will say he's a freak in a meat suit that doesn't connect to his face and we can see the fake hands slapping on top of his real ones, trying to hide the knife he's gonna kill us with—"

"You talk so strangely…"

"What I'm *trying* to say is America isn't the picture of barbecues, guns, freedom, and hot girls eating hamburgers you probably saw on TV. That's the old America and one I'm not even sure ever existed. The glowies parade that picture around every time they want to put people at ease and push them back into place. DC is especially made of glowies. You can't talk to anyone because maybe they're gonna send you to the dungeon or maybe they know someone who can. Four out of five people in any given situation involving politics are probably rats waiting to harass you into a bad decision so they can lock you away forever—Even though the whole thing was their idea. Or if you're lucky, they'll take you into a backroom and beat what they want out of you, threaten your family until they find your weak link, you know? But I guess, at least the glowsticks have the courtesy to out themselves with how obvious they are—"

"You keep saying that, but I don't understand what you mean. You didn't like my Hawaiian shirt, I know, but are the glow people as obvious as someone wearing fatigues?"

Blake tugs my arm. "Duh. Only worse." A grin pulls at the edge of her lips. "You see that hotdog guy on the corner over there?" She points with a nod. On the street corner stands a man with a hot dog cart reading GRAB A WIENER TODAY on the side. He has a tall, multi-colored hat, an apron over a colorful shirt, and a pair of square, black sunglasses. "That's a glowie. And that homeless guy sleeping on the park bench?" She nods across the street. There, a man with ragged hair and a smelly-looking blue shirt covered in fire lays on the park bench with a splotchy, brown paper bag in his hand. He also has dark, square sunglasses. "Glowie. And that pigeon?" She nods to the bird sitting on a stoop two meters in front of us. "It's a glowie too. They're all freaking glowies. They brag about this shit at the Spy Museum on L'En. I mean, it's only made worse by the fact they do it in broad daylight, lie to your face, and think they're getting away with something. It's like a dude whipping his dick out at a party because everyone's drunk, but he's not and since he knows he's gonna get away with it, he jacks off too."

I'm not really following what she says, but I like listening to her talk, she has a nice voice and she's very expressive. I glance between the bird, the hot dog man, and the homeless guy trying to analyze what makes them stand out against any of the other morning commuters we pass, but I'm not even sure what I should be looking for. "What do you mean by glowies?"

"Feds." She pauses. "Federal agents." She pauses again. "The bad guys and don't let anyone convince you otherwise, got it?"

"How do you know they're feds? They look pretty normal to me."

"Well, start with the stiff posture, the complete inability to blend in, and the copy/paste black square sunglasses they all have. Pretty sure the government's got a deal with Hugo Boss and everyone receives a pair during orientation."

"How do sunglasses make someone a federal agent?"

"Look—I'll just show you." Blake pulls me toward the hot dog man, but once we're within a meter of him, she releases my hand and continues forward. She mutters, 'stay here,' leaving me behind. Upon approach, the man turns stiffly with mannerisms that remind me of a robot. His neck doesn't turn. His smile twitches up all at once. His hand raises to greet Blake in a stiff wave. "Hello, fellow American citizen," his voice goes artificially high-pitched and perky like a commercial against doing drugs. "Would you like a hot dog? For I am selling hot dogs. They are approximately 131 degrees so they will not burn your tongue immediately when placed inside your mouth. They are consistently six inches long and you are allowed to choose two toppings at no extra charge—"

"Yeah… No thanks." Blake's words come easy, like a sigh she's said by default many times before. She gestures for me to follow her. We go across the street without looking both ways, without waiting for the light, and without a car hitting us. None of the cars in the street are moving, though they honk at us anyway until we're out of the street. At the edge of the park, she puts a hand up, gesturing for me to wait again. She pushes her fingers to her lips. A soft 'shhh,' then she approaches the sleeping homeless guy. "Hey, old man—"

The homeless man instantly sits up. Much like the hot dog vendor, he's stiff, almost as though his elbows don't bend. His knees don't bend naturally either. His hair's gray, but shines silver in the morning light. He doesn't smell like trash and body odor, but more like alcohol he's poured on himself, expensive cologne hiding underneath.

"Hello, young woman," the homeless man says. His voice is a failed attempt at hoarseness, scratching higher and squeaking more like a boy going through puberty. "Yes. I am a homeless man. You are correct, indeed. I am starving. I would like some money. Do you have any change for me? Maybe a bottle of alcohol would be better for I have an alcohol problem which stems from the corporal punishment my father used on me as a child and the abandonment issues I developed when he walked out on me and my mother—"

"Oh my god, get bent." Blake quickly returns to me. She walks past. I don't follow, so she comes back to grab my arm and pull me, but I don't want to go. I want to observe. I want to see more of these weird creatures that look like people but there's something horribly defective about them. I mean, I had never even seen a Russian soldier act so inhumanly. "We need to go," Blake says.

A sense of dread and disgust go through me when I look at either the homeless man or the hot dog vendor. My face crumbles a bit, with lips pulling back. I turn away and my muscles relax. I look at them, and my entire body stresses again. "What is wrong with them? They don't sound like they know what they're doing?"

"That's because they don't." Blake leans in a little. She's watching the hot dog vendor, the homeless man, and the pigeon. "They just hope you're too freaked out at the prospect of a bullet finding its way into your brain that you won't call them out on it."

My eyes are wide. I'm stiff and suck in a deep breath. The idea of getting shot for saying the wrong thing to the wrong person isn't new to me, but I didn't imagine Americans might be so casual about their government shooting them too. "Why would they do that?"

"To maintain control."

"There's more to life than dictating how everyone else lives." I turn back around to look at the homeless glow man. A woman in a pencil-skirt suit is walking away from him, bag hanging off to one side, phone in her hand, though she's wearing earbuds. The homeless man fingers through a bit of cash. "That person just gave the glow person money."

Blake looks back in the direction of the homeless man. "Oh... Yeah... Don't worry about it. That's a congressman. They can never tell the difference between the scammers, glowies, and actual homeless people." She pats me on the shoulder, giving it a squeeze to get my attention, then she continues on her way. After a couple of steps, she turns around and nods her head for me to follow. I do.

We go a couple of blocks. Down the street is a cement

staircase disappearing into the ground. The metro. An *authentic* American metro. It's only more exciting knowing Bill Cosby didn't want me to get on it. She glances around the gate, leaning forward to see if anyone's in the nearby booth, watching. There is someone, but she's on her cell phone, fingers tapping rapidly at the screen. Blake braces herself and leaps over the barricade. "You coming?" She spins on her heels now walking backward without pause.

"Without paying the fee?"

She snorts, a chuckle, then a shrug. A playful smile tugs at her lips. She doesn't stop walking. Her eyes lock on me, daring me to jump as if I've never done anything crazy before.

I'm smiling back. No one else around us exists anymore. I grab the gate and jump. Her smile turns toothy. She turns around and speeds up. It makes me run to chase her. Hitting the stairs, she slides down the rail like riding a slide. Further underground, she hits the platform and runs, ducking around people standing and waiting until we're by an orange and blue line. She's panting softly when I catch up, trying to hide the exertion, but she's smiling and my smile's big, getting bigger when I look sidelong at her. Slowly, I reach for her hand. She slips it into the shallow pocket of her jeans. I don't know if it's in response to me, but I'm going to convince her to hold my hand again today. I promise that.

Pulling into the station, the incoming train echoes a high-pitched squeal. People line up on both sides of the platform before it even comes to a full stop. There are more people waiting to get off. As soon as the doors open, the ones getting off the train look like fish swimming upstream, pushing past the rush of passengers boarding. The number thins fast. Blake heads over.

It hasn't been long, but by the way everyone moves, something tells me we don't have a lot of time before the train leaves again.

The inside of the train is dark, yellow, looks stained, but it has to be the lighting. There's a musty, moldy smell and a mild scent of soiled underwear. None of it seems strong enough for anyone else to notice. That or they've all become used to it. The worst of it is the tinge of rotten lemon that stings the inside of my nose with the same sort of feeling of rawness you get from blowing your nose too many times when you're sick. I don't mind that the seats look dirty enough to puff dust when you sit on them. Blake sits down and gestures for me to take the bench behind her. She kicks her feet up on the seat. She faces the other side of the train, making it easier to look over her shoulder at me.

I watch her posture, pulling my feet onto the seat. My back presses uncomfortably into the wall, but I'm used to it quickly. The train squeals into action, picking up speed fast. The inside of the cab echoes with metal sliding against metal. Someone coughs into their hand. Someone else is yelling into a phone. The beats of someone's music bleeds into the air, quieter than anything else. Blake's head bobs slowly to some rhythm that's not the hushed music. She gropes her thighs for something, but her hand comes up empty and she sighs, dropping her head back against the window.

For the first time, there isn't a man wearing a Hawaiian shirt in sight. For the first time, even under threat of being *found* by the United States government, I'm free, like I've actually made it to America. Under normal circumstances, is this what it would feel like to explore this country? I want to hold Blake's hand, but her seat acts as a separator, so I can't. I'm going to ask for her hand, but when the words come out, I say, "Why do you call them glowies?" instead.

Blake lifts her head from the window. A smile pulls at the edges of her lips then flattens into something more thoughtful and muted. My skin dots with goosebumps.

She smiles again, but it's different this time; I'm not sure how to describe it. "Because they *glow in the fucking dark*, don't they?"

"What does that mean?"

"They stand out so much—You couldn't miss them in a pitch-black room."

"That's the same for you, though."

Blake blinks a couple of times. The smile drops from her face and her eyes squint. It's not so much a neutral face as one that looks like she's maybe slightly offended. "Excuse me?"

"You glow in the dark too."

"You think I'm a glowstick?"

"Well, no… but you light up the room and you're hard to overlook."

A laugh catches in her breath while her cheeks turn pink and the smile comes back. She turns away. Her face looks darker from this angle. "What—Is that supposed to be some kind of cheesy line?"

"No." My feet hit the ground. I slide to the edge of my seat to get closer to the back of hers. I fold my arms over the top of her seat. "I just wanted to tell you that."

"Whatever, weirdo." Her lips are pursed and she's trying to hide the smile. She drops her feet to the floor so she can turn her back to me. Her shoulders relax. I can't see it, but I'm sure she's still smiling. Aftef

r a moment, I lean back into my seat again. She remains facing forward. I look out the window instead of at her.

Most of the ride is the dark underground of the train tunnel. We go through a couple of stops. I'm not counting. When Blake stands up, I follow. We get to the surface again, but stop at the top of the stairs. Pulling her sunglasses down her nose, she looks in both directions then puts them back on.

Someone bumps into me coming from underground. I stumble forward. "Dammit. Sorry—" says a man's voice.

Instantly, it's familiar. I'm hearing him again. I've been hearing him for weeks on a phone that has yet to send me any texts or calls from Aleks Diduch or anyone back home. I know I've been desperate to hear from him, but I've never heard his voice when I wasn't carrying my phone. I turn around to excuse the passerby, but I lose my voice. I'm not only hearing him now. I'm seeing him. His clean-cut hair, longer on the top, the serious face on his squarish jaw, the tan pants and green button-down shirt, always looking like some kind of official. "Aleks?" I say, approaching him, expecting his face to melt into someone else's if not disappear altogether. I lower my glasses in case his identification is a sun glare.

The man turns to me. His serious expression breaks into surprise. "Jan?" My name is a relieved sigh. "Is that really you?"

I reach for Aleks. He grabs my biceps to look me in the eye. I nod. My visions going blurry and my eyes burn. I blink several times to fight back the tears. He pulls me to him. "How did you find me?" My arms wrap around him just a second after his wrap around me. The hug hurts, it's so tight, but for the first time, I don't feel like home is impossibly far away; I don't feel like my family and life don't exist; I don't feel like I'm an observer living on another planet anymore. I'm not stranded and alone.

Aleks pulls back. "Luck, mostly." His arms drop to his sides, mine match. "I can't believe you're actually—" he says. "I—" He glances down my body and back up. "What are you wearing?"

I have to check myself to remember it's the pink skull sweater Blake gave me to wear. The metallic stars around the skull's crown reflect in the morning light. "Oh. My girlfriend's shirt—"

"Girlfriend?" Blake and Aleks say at the same time.

"Sorry—Fiancée?" I slowly look at Blake.

"Fiancée?!" they both say.

"Sorry—I didn't know what I should call you," I say.

"Friend is more than enough," Blake says.

"What is going on here?" Aleks says. "And who are you?" He crosses his arms, assessing Blake with another look-over.

"Funny. I was going to ask you the same question. Jan?" Blake says.

"Ah, ah. It's my turn for questions. Jan, where have you been, who is this, and what does she want with you?"

"Whoa, whoa, whoa," Blake says. "You're *not* about to assume I'm some kind of *bad guy* in this situation."

"I'm not assuming you're a *bad guy*, I'm assuming you're a *federal agent*," Aleks says.

"That's the same thing here, Aleks," I mutter, keeping my head down like it will hide my words from any glowing passersby.

"Oh my god," Blake bites her lip. She reaches into her bag for something, comes out with nothing, then grabs me by the arm. "We don't have time for this. We need to go, Jan."

"*Nii.*" Aleks's voice is stiff. He grabs my other arm and pulls me back, not allowing Blake to take me. "You're going nowhere until you explain why I haven't heard a damn thing from you in a month."

"We. Don't. Have. Time," Blake says.

"Make it or we're not moving." Aleks stares at Blake while still not letting go of me.

"Oh my god, fine." Blake thrusts her hands into her pockets. "But let's at least get off the street corner where every glowie in the damn city can pick us off."

SEVENTEEN

We're sitting in the corner of a small coffee shop that looks a little bit like a cabin. There are three people behind the counter. The one behind the espresso machine is a very tall man with wide shoulders, a short, black beard, and hair like Aleks's. I don't think he's wearing a shirt under the green apron. There's also a girl with brown hair and a pink streak in her bangs and a man with a red beard and thick glasses. I'm having a hard time taking my eyes off the espresso machine man. He doesn't seem like he should be there and every time I look at him, he's staring over the espresso machine at us. I'm sure I'm crazy though. Aleks is tense and keeps shifting, looking toward the glass windows that surround the store front and Blake keeps checking her pocket for her phone before her glance sweeps around the coffee shop. Every time the shop door opens, Aleks and Blake look at whoever entered and I think it's getting to me.

The door opens again. They both sit up, look past me, a moment later, they relax, though Blake leans back and Aleks sits straight. Someone doesn't even have to walk in to make them tense, they straighten when someone walks by the window too. I'm not allowed to turn around. Though they haven't agreed on much, they have agreed I can't look for whatever they're looking for. My tea's half gone and cold. The paper cup didn't do much to keep it warm.

Aleks rubs the bridge of his nose. His shoulders relax again as another person he's watching goes beyond the coffee shop without stopping. "Jan… I told you that you needed to watch the news more," he says.

"I don't know how the news could have prepared me for this," I say.

"You would have at least thought your sponsors suspicious," Aleks says.

"How?"

"No visitors to Ukraine wear Hawaiian shirts in March," Aleks says.

"Only March?" Blake says.

"Or ever is also an appropriate answer," Aleks says.

"It should've been a dead giveaway they were freaks when you talked to them," Blake says. "I mean, seriously, Tom Cruise and Bob Dylan? It's like they wanted to be caught."

"I just thought they were weird. Americans are weird. Rich people are weird. I've never been one to judge eccentrics though." I wrap my hands around the paper coffee cup.

"At least you've got that right…" Aleks sighs again. His harsh eyes turn to Blake only briefly, then back out the window. His lips are straight, his body still stiff, focused, observing something hard. "Meanwhile, your government has gone so insane that they've stolen and imprisoned a Ukrainian national, yet your only plan is to put him on television? Like painting a bullseye for collection, eh? Tell me again how you're an independent operative."

"I'm not an *independent operative*, I'm a *nobody* who hates my government probably more than you do, alright? But if you've got a better idea, let me know, because I highly doubt the people that brought him here like they did are just going to let him board a plane and head back. He'll be lucky if they don't use their next interaction as a reason to imprison him for real as an illegal—"

"And what will they do then? Export him?" Aleks snorts.

"Detainment, you dolt." Blake shakes her head; a snarky frown comes to her lips. "They open the floodgates for power. They only export if they catch too much heat, but otherwise they will use every string they have to keep a hold on the people they think will give them power."

"Jan has nothing to give your people—"

"Wanna bet?" Blake's tongue whips across her lips. "How are the tensions over there with Russia?"

"Whatever you think you know, you do not," Aleks says to Blake. Then, he switches to Ukrainian when he says, "Jan, where did you find this girl?"

"What does it matter?" I respond in Ukrainian.

"You need to marry someone who is more homey, less eccentric, and preferably not American."

"What's wrong with Americans?"

"Have you looked at her?" Aleks gestures toward Blake.

"Excuse me, rude ass—" Blake says.

"Aleks," Aleks corrects.

"I'm sitting right here," Blake says.

"You speak Ukrainian?" I say.

"No," her voice pitches up. "But I know you're talking about *me* when he's literally pointing."

"No one at this table was pointing," Aleks says.

"Get out of here with your goddamn semantics," Blake says.

A chair creaks. Attention is brought to the large man wearing the coffee shop apron as he approaches our table. Now that he's closer, the differences stand out more. He's older, maybe in his thirties. He has a scar near his right eyebrow and thick, muscular biceps that look like they belong to a soldier, not a coffee maker.

"Do you want something, dude?" Blake crosses her arms, looking up to the barista. First, she's at his waist, then trailing up his body to his face, then back down, stopping on his thick arms. He is definitely not wearing a shirt under the apron.

I lean into her. "He doesn't look like he belongs here," I mutter.

"No kidding." She tries to laugh, but it catches in her throat.

"Do you think he's a glow person?" I say.

"What's a *glow person*?" Aleks says.

"I'm going to need you to stand up and come with me," the barista says in a thick, Russian accent.

Blake bites her lip and leans back, shaking her head slowly. "Yeah… I don't think he's a glowie. The accent's too good."

"You don't think he's suspicious?" I say.

"I didn't say that—"

Aleks shoves the table over so the flat side smashes against the Russian barista. "Jan, run!" He grabs my arm and pulls me, then we're running out of the coffee shop. A black sedan with two men in tailored suits sits in the traffic, parked three cars down. Aleks mutters, "Shit," and pulls me in the opposite direction. His hand releases my arm once we're running.

"What about—" I'm looking over my shoulder when I catch a flick of her blue hair in the sun and Blake says, "I'm here!"

"Doesn't matter—We need to split up," Aleks says.

"But how will we find each other again?" I say. "We don't have phones."

"Once we're free of pursuers—Back where we found each other," Aleks says. He keeps it short and waits for a nod. I give it to him. He doesn't wait for Blake before he's running across the street in another direction and weaving through cars mostly paused in the street from the overwhelming city traffic. I'm too busy watching Aleks that I don't notice Blake going in another direction. My legs carry me forward still, and it's once I'm left alone that I see how slow I'm going.

"Stop!" a Russian man calls. His voice sounds closer than I'd like it to be. Even though it hurts my legs and my muscles are all tense and sore, I make myself run as fast as I can. I dip between buildings, down alleyways, between stopped cars without consideration for where I'm going or if a car might hit me. There's not enough time to think about picking up landmarks or finding my way back or even trying to remember what metro station Aleks was at.

I'm running so hard I can't breathe. My chest hurts, constricts, then the pain's in my side. Everything's shaking. I duck in front of a car sitting at a stop. The light turns green. The car honks at me. I'm still running.

Across the street, I don't know where I am, but in the distance, there are two long flag poles. At the foot of the flag poles is a large, stone building with three large arches along the front and columns holding up Romanesque statues. Brick and stone stairs guide the way up the arches beyond a small garden. There's no crowd to slip through at the entrance, only a couple of scattered people, but at least there's no one standing guard outside, unlike at the movie studio. I consider checking for Russians behind me, but there's too much risk to slow down and I can't keep running like I am. I need to find cover, a break, and a plan.

I run across the cement, bound up the stairs, and move through the arches.

The inside of the building is something to marvel at. Glossy, marble floor tiles, a wide roof of golden honeycombs arching high and unbothered. Vendors stand at temporary tables while a wooden platform rises above everything as a roof to a standing cafe in the middle of the rounded hall. At the end of the room is another platform built into an arch and held up by columns, showcasing the more judgmental statues. Warriors, wise men, women without something better to do—I nearly run into a wall looking at them.

The rubber bottoms of my sneakers screech in contact with the marble. I bump into someone. I'm not sure if I say sorry in English or mutter something else. I keep going until I find a set of stairs that go down. I take them without thinking of where I may end up. Stores line the walls. Restaurants, mostly, but another glows all in white. Clean. Sterile. Organized. It's long, wide, inviting, a convenience store of some kind and it has shelves for me to hide behind.

I run to the back of the store. Mirrors hang along the walls, pointed down, giving away every spot where I might hide, if only my pursuers look into the store. Still, I keep myself low, trying to catch my breath. Maybe if I can do that, I can think of what to do next. I'm watching the door at the other end of the store, beyond an open fridge of premade sandwiches and a line of cash registers at the store's front. My hand slides along the edge of the shelf. I glance at it for only a moment, then once more. Hair dye lines the shelves. I lick my bottom lip. Sunglasses off, I slip them into my pocket and replace them with my work goggles. I grab a box of hair dye and look over the label. The words are gibberish. I've never been *that* good at reading English. I know important things like MEN and WOMEN and YOU LAUGH, YOU LOSE among other common search phrases.

The box I'm holding is silver, metallic, and glowing under the fluorescent lights. I tear the box open and dump the contents out. A tube of peroxide drops into my hand along with the color and a plastic bottle to mix the items.

I twist the cap open, puncturing the cream tube with

its lid. I empty the tube into the bottle, but squeeze just the last bit onto my finger to wipe on my tongue. The taste isn't the best. Actually, I hate store product chemicals the most because they are so corrupt compared to raw materials. The peroxide sold with hair dye is good enough to elicit the response I want when placed in the correct circumstances, but it's still not my first pick.

At least one man in a suit comes through the wide shop opening. Just outside the door, another man surveys the restaurants across the strip.

Change of plans.

I drop the peroxide and I move from the aisle I'm in, passing the supplies, surveying until I find the cleaning aisle. Among the all-purpose supplies is a large bottle marked ALL-PURPOSE AMMONIA. I uncap it and pour some into the hair dye bottle.

The thing about using chemicals is the reaction starts when you introduce one element to another. Maybe it's not two elements that create a solution, but they will get the process going. The ammonia mixed with chlorine will create a heat and smoke that could eventually get to where I want it, a mild explosion—That is assuming I do the solution ratio correctly. I want something distracting, but not big enough to cause destruction. Something to note when making solutions is that the vapors produced can also be dangerous. Inhalation is usually bad, but if you put a cap on the vapors to restrain them, heat usually builds faster and makes your bomb more volatile, so until you're ready for the reaction, it's best to wait to combine the elements.

I move from one shelf to another, staying behind the end caps and keeping my eyes on the Russian as he walks through the store. He pauses in front of the large sandwich fridge in the middle of the room. He looks in my direction.

The mirror gives away my position.

I dash for the dishwasher tablets.

He dashes for me.

I rip open a box of soap tablets. Even wrapped in plastic and closed, my nose can find the ones with that use chlorine and the ones that are the most potent.

"Jan Bagan," the Russian man says. "Things will go much better for you if you stop and come with me *now*." He lunges for me. I run back down the shower product aisle.

Someone in the shop says, "What are you doing?" while a clerk says, "Hey, hey, hey," then notices the bottle in my hand and is going, "Hey, hey, hey—What is that? Did you pay for it? Holy shit—What are you doing with those? Who the hell are you?" with a tone that's more aggressive the closer he gets. I'm running to the back of the store, knocking things off shelves as I run like it's going to slow down the Russian. I'm muttering, "Sorry," as I do it because I know how annoying it is to have to restock shelves when someone knocks things over.

The Russians surveying the restaurant on the other side of the tunnel have come to the convenience store door. They've lined up, blocking the way out, though they allow customers by as one woman says, "What's going on?" and "Are you sure this is alright?"

I toss the chlorine tablets into the ammonia bottle and leave the lid off. Immediately, the solution is hissing; white gas forms.

The bottles warm; the smell's strong already. I have to toss the bomb. I adjust my path toward a set of doors in the back of the store. The pulse in my fingertips alerts me of the building energy. I screwed the lid on. The timing isn't perfect, but the heat is there and vapors fill the inside of the bottle, making it thicker and bloated.

I toss the bottle at my pursuer. It's popping, spilling white gas everywhere, barely out of my hand. I press my shoulder to the door at the back of the store. The bottle pops before the door's even shut. I only have enough time to peek when I'm running away. It's not long enough to find something to maybe block the door with or see if I can lock it.

I run down the hall that passes by a break room with lockers, a small office with a computer, and presumably, a manager saying, "Who are you? You can't be back here," but his voice disappears into the loud buzz of my right ear. I shake my head to make it stop; I almost run into a wall.

It's not that the explosion just now was loud. It wasn't, but the ringing is more like a learned reaction from the changing vibrations. Even the plane made it worse because of all the vibrations associated with changing pressures and the sky.

Another door passes, then another, and a loud alarm goes off, making the ringing in my ear worse. The sun hits my skin. Fresh air fills my lungs and I'm running in whatever direction seems the most convincing to get lost in.

The city's ahead. A large, skinny pyramid, the obelisk sticks out in the distance of everything else. It's such a strange little sculpture, I'm not sure I understand how it fits into the architecture of everything else or why it's in America of all places. Surrounded by columns and Roman trims, naturalist sculptures of admirable faces and motivational speech bylines, glass towers, and brick townhouses, this giant needle sticks out of the ground with nothing else around it.

I'm running down an alley. I can't see the obelisk anymore. Even the sun's blocked out by building walls. Water, puddled from I don't know where, splashes underneath my feet. I look down, feeling like I'm going to slip, but the balance thing has more to do with the buzzing in my ear. A chain-link fence crosses the end of the alley, separating it from a couple of dumpsters and what looks like an outlet, beside that, another caged area. I grab the fence and pull myself halfway up in one yank.

"You're going to get yourself killed," a deep voice says from behind me.

I freeze. A laugh alleviates some of the pressure. "You know… everyone keeps telling me that, but so far—"

"Come down, now." A gun clicks behind me.

I release the fence.

"Turn around. Hands up."

I comply with the order, though I'm tempted to search my nails for gunpowder, chemicals, anything. My tongue slides over my bottom lip. The taste of peroxide is still a little bit there. My hand reflexively comes to my mouth. The Russian man says, "Stop," and I do. I lean my head to the right, the buzzing gets worse. I'm dizzy. My jaw tightens.

"You need to stop moving," the Russian says.

"Sorry, I can't. You see, there's a ringing and it's very painful—"

"You think this is a game you can play to get out of trouble?"

"What trouble am I in? I am just a YouTuber. I'm sightseeing."

The Russian smacks his lips, a slight shake to his head, a sneer sticks to his nose. Something slams into the back of my head. It's throbbing before I realize I'm on the ground and that there's gravel in my hand. A second voice joins the first, but instead of speaking English, both speak Russian. The words are muttered. "We have them all," the new voice says.

"Good," says the deeper voice.

My vision's spotty. My eyelids droop, too heavy to keep open. I'm thinking about getting up like it's going to make my hands press into the ground, but it's like there's no energy, no adrenaline, no will to make me move. My head's lifted. Everything goes black and I can't move my arms. My shoulders burn from how tight the grip is, but even that fades into the void of blackness and the buzzing ear. The ground's not pressed into my chest anymore, but then I'm not feeling anything at all. At least I can breathe again.

EIGHTEEN

Everything is so dark. I try to ask if I'm blind, how did this happen, was it from a show gone wrong, but there's something in my mouth keeping my tongue compressed. The room smells heavily of cigarettes and dust, but there's a milder influence of cigars, alcohol, and gunpowder too. The voices are speaking Russian. The room's cold. An attempt to move my arms proves I can't; they're kept behind my back, but it takes longer than it should for me to realize that. I don't even feel like I'm in my body until I try to reach for my eyes a little harder and the pull stresses my shoulder out. Pain shoots through my arm. I grunt.

Someone nearby says something slurred, sounds like either someone saying, "Jan," or they're yelling for help in a very casual way. I know the voice belongs to Aleks.

"You're awake, then?" a deep Russian voice says. The thing compressing my mouth is removed. It hits the floor with a *splat*.

The room fills with light and shapes. Too much light. I blink rapidly, trying to see through the sunlight coming through the curtains. Everything's blurry, though a TV screen illuminates the room where the sun doesn't make it through the curtains. The Russian man from the alleyway stands in front of me. Behind him is the barista, but now the apron is tied around his waist only and like a typical Russian, he is not wearing a shirt.

I'm sitting in a desk chair. As I press my feet into the floor, I spin a little until someone I can't see puts his hand on the back of my chair, stopping me from moving. The man from the alleyway is wearing a black suit, with a purple button-up, partially unbuttoned with a bit of peppered chest hair showing. He's bald, clean-shaven, and has a face that looks lumpy from his indecisive jaw being both square and round.

Aleks and Blake are sitting on the queen-sized bed, arms tied behind their backs with cloth bags over their heads and tied around their necks. My goggles lay on the floor, one of the reflective lenses is cracked. "You didn't need to do that," I say. "I've had those for a while, you know?"

The back of a hand crosses my cheek, immediately stinging. The pain is the color of red. A throb in my lower jaw. My mouth hangs open, stretching. I swallow the pain.

The Russian man in the suit slips his hand into his pocket. "You're going to answer some questions and maybe today won't be as bad for you as it should be," he says.

"I don't mind answering questions. You only have to ask," I say.

"Don't tell them anything," Aleks's voice is muffled, contorted by something in his mouth, but the words are still intelligible.

"Tell your friend to keep his mouth shut," the suited Russian says.

"I think you just did," I say, looking at the bald man. His frown worsens. "But in case he didn't hear you… Hey, Aleks… I don't think it is a very good idea to make these guys angry."

The suited Russian glances back at the barista then back at me. The TV light catches on the grip of a gun hidden under the suited Russian's jacket.

I hear a ticking in my head like ideas coming. "Are you the kidnappers my agent warned me about?"

"You knew we were coming and you still wandered on your own?" the suited Russian says. His laughter fills the room briefly, controlled, hard, and then gone. It's strange because that laughter doesn't sound as fake as the glow person's in the park. It's just… mechanical, much like the Russians back home along the border. We always said Ukrainians had more heart—It's what always made it so difficult to interact with Russians. However, Russians can get a little more heart-y when they drink. My favorite kind of Russian is usually a drunk Russian for that reason. The Russians I've shared drinks with along the border are nothing like the Russians who visit my town in military fatigues; they're very unlike these men too. They're able to forget the training, forget the anger, forget any history that is supposed to make us hate each other. When we are both drinking, Ukrainians and Russians are able to return to what we have in common: laughter, stories, and humanity.

"To be honest," I start slowly, "I thought Bill was lying to me."

Blake laughs through her gag.

A 'hm,' bubbles in the suited Russian's throat. "I suppose that's reasonable."

"Question—"

"*Nyet*—"

"I was going to ask if you could unmask my friends. They can probably help answer some of the questions you have. Aleks knows a lot more than me in general—"

"Do you hear this idiot, Ivan?" the suited Russian says.

"I hear him, Vladimir," Ivan the Barista says.

"He thinks he's calling the shots. Let his friends go. Say the magic words to trigger government satellites to our location—"

"We don't have satellites," I say.

Vladimir grabs my chair's armrests and pulls me toward him. His gun is closer now. I never worried about guns before, but I never truly worried one would be pointed at me in Nide. I glance at it, then into Vladimir's eyes. The moment they catch him, it's like I'm locked in place. "Who are you?" Vladimir says.

"Jan Bagan—"

"And you work for?"

"I'm not sure… I've… never actually seen the contract, but it's an entertainment company. They let me make videos of explosions. I have a YouTube channel, maybe you've heard of it?" I say.

Blake laughs again.

"What's wrong with her?" Vladimir says.

I shrug, but only halfway. My shoulder hurts too much to continue, so I say, "I don't know," instead.

"Ivan," Vladimir says, and the barista with the large muscles makes his way to the captives. He helps Blake up to sit on the edge of the bed. He pulls her hood off, then takes the gag out of her mouth. Without looking at her, Vladimir says, "Speak."

"No one knows who you are, Jan. Everyone's been lying to you," Blake says, the chuckle's still in her voice, but it's not laughing at me.

"But my channel is the whole reason I'm here now—"

Aleks shakes his head. "You haven't uploaded anything in a month, Jan. Why do you think I'm here?"

"Class trip…?"

"No." Aleks sighs. "I've been running around this damn city for a week, trying to find you. I knew something was off the moment you mentioned sponsors—"

"You don't think I could get sponsors?" I don't mean for it to sound as defensive as it does.

"It's not that—"

"Do you think I don't know what you sound like when you lie, Aleks?"

"It's not that—"

"Then what, Aleks? I know that you never believed in my channel, but did you really think there would not be a single person who found value or enjoyment in the kind of videos I make?"

"Stop talking," Vladimir says, stomping over both Aleks's and my voice or any further attempt to speak either of us made. Vladimir leans his head forward, pinches his nose, and sighs. "We let your mouths run wild to explain the situation. Stop bickering and explain." Vladimir's focus moves between Aleks and I, though he mainly stops on me. I look at Aleks. My jaw's so tight, it aches. I don't know what they want or what I'm supposed to say. I don't even know why I'm here anymore. I know everything Blake's told me about the government, but none of it seems real. I've seen my studio, I've seen my colleagues, I've seen other movie stars.

I look for Vladimir's eyes, the only way I can know how to change any situation is to do exactly as Mama said. Let them see into your soul; let them see into your heart; let them look into your eyes and show them there's nothing to hide. "I'm a YouTuber. That is all," I finally say.

Vladimir glances back to Ivan. His turn to me shows a flash of confusion on his face which is soon replaced by a sneer then deep laughter. "You're talking nonsense," Vladimir says.

"I'm not talking nonsense!" I say.

"Do not blame a mirror for your ugly face. You attacked our border on behalf of the United States government for the purpose of starting a war, but why would you want a war, little Ukraine? Sowing chaos? How much money has NATO paid you to provide Americans with a reason to attack our country and pillage it for anything they can fit into their jets?" Vladimir says.

"I didn't bomb Russia. I make videos," I say.

"You bombed Russia!" Vladimir smacks me across the face. The chair slides back. He grabs the armrests and pulls me back to him. His nose meets mine from how close he leans in. I smell his breath. Bitter vinegar. I'm holding my breath as long as I can until I turn my head away. My neck hurts. "You see? You admit you're lying scum." He spits in my face.

I tense, eyes closed. He's going to smack me again.

"He's not lying," Aleks says.

"Uh, yeah—" Blake says. "He's telling the truth. Jan's got a channel—It's just—The kind of size you guys usually lie about, you know?" She pauses, waiting for confirmation of understanding for what she said. Vladimir and Ivan stare. "It's *small.*"

"You see? I'm telling the truth," I say.

"What is he talking about?" Vlad asks Aleks.

"I cannot speak for the United States, but Ukraine did not attack you," Aleks says. "We may be tense right now, but do not forget, it was *your* troops who invaded a corner of *our* country unprovoked—"

"You bombed us. It was the reasonable response." Vladimir spits at the floor again. "Would you have preferred we turned to war?"

"We understand how it looked, but the bomb was not from the Ukrainian government. Knowing the person who set it off, it was not done in malice," Aleks says.

"Explain." Vladimir crosses his arms, turning from me, he gives his full attention to Aleks. Aleks gives me only the briefest look as if to tell me he's about to say everything about me, even things I may not know about myself, then he lets it all go. He tells them about how I would make explosives at home from things I'd find at One Shop, even before I had a camera or a phone that could record anything. He tells them about the bucket I worked to crack with nothing more than cleaning and car supplies I found around town. He tells them about how it escalated and he'd warned that I'd probably get myself killed someday, either by explosion or being shot, but I didn't heed the warning and laughed it away while saying, "What fun is life if you don't do things you enjoy? There will always be those around who will tell you not to pursue, but isn't life really about following your wishes to the end?" I took that approach seriously and I never allowed anyone's words of discouragement to turn me away from the things I wanted. Still, to this day, I follow my heart.

Without realizing when I started, I'm staring at Blake.

"He has no training," Aleks says. "He went to a small school in Nide, had no desire for higher education or occupations, and makes his bombs by tasting the elements."

Vladimir's head turns toward me slowly. "You ingest elements?" he says.

I nod.

"How are you not dead?"

I try to shrug. It doesn't work. "I don't know. It just hasn't happened?" I say.

Aleks goes on, mentioning the message I left him about the sponsors dropping off a box of ingredients and what followed the next day. A picture is suddenly painted for the Russians when Blake adds on everything about the glow people and my incarceration in a hotel room and subsequent lamp bomb.

"If you still have doubts, let me show you," Aleks says. "I will call no one. Trust me. I may not like you, but I do not hate you."

That works and Vladimir releases Aleks before handing him a phone. He watches Aleks closely, remaining near enough to beat him to the ground should Aleks do anything suspicious. Aleks navigates to YouTube, then goes to my channel. "This is the video he posted the day before the big one you saw." Aleks hits play.

My voice fills the room going, "hello, Boomers! Today, I've got—"

"Wait," Blake says, *"Boomers?"*

"Yeah," I say.

"Is that… wait… Is that what you call your subs?" she says.

I nod before, "Yeah," comes out.

"Oh my god. That makes so much more sense!"

"What else would I mean?" I say.

"Old people that've, frankly, ruined everything for the rest of us," Blake says.

"Quiet!" Vladimir says.

Aleks clicks another video. "This is the one that alarmed you. It alarmed everyone, even Ukraine thought Russia was attacking."

I close my eyes and listen to the video from across the room. My voice sounds foreign on the phone, but the anticipation still builds listening to my own words, the tasting, the hissing heat growing, the boom that sent me flying, and the glass shards cutting through my clothing. I hadn't been prepared. I should've been. I tasted it before it happened.

My fingers tingle. I lick my bottom lip. I want to play with things again. I want to get out of here, leave the hotel rooms and cities behind, and disappear into the familiar trees in Nide to continue doing the things I love. I don't care about money or a big house or becoming American fat. I think the only thing I want anymore is someone to share it all with.

Vladimir takes the phone from Aleks and pockets it. The sound is gone. His shoes tap hard against the floor. Suddenly, there are harsh vibrations right in front of where I'm seated. I open my eyes. Vladimir's there. His hands wrap around the chair armrests again and he's leaning down, though, not as close. "Look at me," he says.

I do as he says.

"Confirm. You did not attack Russia on behalf of the Americans?"

A chill goes through my body. Attack Russia on behalf of the Americans? I could not imagine taking that action. For what purpose would there be? "Of course not. I don't have anything against the Russians. You are my brothers. Maybe things have not been perfect and you are a little pushy. You jump to conclusions very quickly, very often and you definitely do not have as much heart as us Ukrainians—"

"Jan," Aleks says.

"I don't want to fight you. I love you. As much as brothers can without it being strange, you know?" I say.

"An uninvited guest is worse than a Tatar," Ivan says.

"Did they offer you money?" Vladimir says.

I purse my lips without answering. It's not because I don't know or because I don't want them to know, but I'm not entirely sure how I should be answering. "They offered me a television show… but all I've received so far is cheap vodka and beef jerky. Never money to buy a home or ticket for my family or a cellphone. Everything has been given to me in my hotel room, but you know… I don't always like to be in my room? It gets lonely. I spent a lot of time feeling like I was in trouble for something because there was always someone standing outside the door, waiting to put me back inside. They didn't even like me wandering down the halls—I came here to see freedom and all I've seen is the inside of a hotel room."

"Welcome to America." Blake winks.

My face gets hot.

"If they offered you money to continue what you're doing with the purpose of creating new manners of warfare…" Vladimir is saying.

"I wouldn't take it," I say. "I'm not interested in politics or conquering others or money beyond what is necessary to take care of my family and my future wife." I try to keep myself from looking at Blake. I fail, but only for a moment. Even in the darkness of the room and with smeared makeup around her eyes and the wariness that maybe came from sleeping not so well last night, she is the most beautiful person I have ever seen. I cannot help but smile when I look at her. My shirt sticks to my back. "I don't want to hurt people. I want to have fun, fall in love, and have a family."

"If you don't do it, someone else will," Vladimir says.

"Then let the blood be on their hands," I say.

"It would make you a very rich man," Vladimir says.

"Greed cannot wash away the stains of lost life."

"Alright," Vladimir says. He snaps his fingers. In the next moment, the restraints that held my arms back fall away and my hands drop to my sides. The moment of gravity pulls on my weakened arm. Pain shoots through my muscles, but I don't make a sound. Blake's restraints are also repealed. For the first time, I take a look around the room. Five Russians stand around us, all packing the same guns, all in similar suits except for Ivan who is dressed as a barista with bulging muscles. "However, I must inform you: if you are true to your word that you will not work for the bloodthirsty devils in this city, you must return home immediately. We will trust you at your word that there is no ill-intent when you are at our border… unless you stay here. This town is filled with snakes—"

"Oh," Blake says. "You spend a lot of time at the Capitol too?" She snorts.

"If you stay," Vladimir says, "We will assume you are a liar or you will shortly become the thing you say you despise."

"I can't leave," I say slowly.

Vladimir sighs. "What sort of blackmail do they have on you?"

"What?" I say.

"C'mon… Out with it. Is it the generic pedophilia like

everyone else?" Vlad says.

"Holy shit." Blake laughs.

"Why would you think I have blackmail on me?" I say.

"Because the government has dirt on literally everyone who works in this city." Blake pauses, visibly thinking with a pout, then furrowed brows, then squinted eyes. They widen again. "Almost everyone. If they don't have dirt on you, they hate you and they make sure the world knows just how deranged you make them *feel*."

"Oh, no. They haven't been mean to me. Does that mean they know something I don't? What kinds of secrets do you think they have about me? I need to know!" The words are coming out faster than I can think of them, some of them mixed with more Ukrainian than I realize until Blake's twisting her head to the side, looking confused. The panicked image in my mind goes to Mama and Papa, standing in the kitchen at home, waiting for me to call them with the good news, but instead of my voice on the phone, she hears Bill Cosby and he tells her something that will break her heart so bad, she has a heart attack and dies. Then Papa also has a heart attack because Mama has died and then Mila and Yakiv blame me for it and never speak to me again.

Blake grabs my hand. I come out of thought.

When did she get so close?

"I think this has more to do with the… no IDs thing," she says.

"No IDs?" Aleks says.

"Yeah. He told me he doesn't have a passport or any travel paperwork at all," Blake says.

Aleks looks back at me with squinted, confused eyes. "What?" His voice is sharp, irritated, in disbelief. "How did you get here?"

"Well…" Blake says, tugging on my arm. Her fingers lace with mine and our hands swing gently. I don't know if she knows she's doing it. "If the big boys in charge want something, they don't give a single fuck about breaking all the rules to get it."

"If you are being held captive here, why were you running around the city like an idiot?" Vladimir says. "What was your plan? Do you know that there are federal agents stationed on most of the street corners, probably looking for you?"

"I told him," Blake says. "Figured you were one of 'em until you and Boris over there spoke—"

"*Ivan*," Ivan says.

"Whatever." Blake dismisses him with a casual wave of her hand. "But we *did* have a plan. We were making our way to the MediaMax building when you cut in. My dad works there. We were going to hit up the on-air studio and tell the country what the hell's going on. Figured maybe a little pressure would set the government straight."

Ivan and Vladimir exchange a quick look. Vladimir subtly shakes his head, muttering in Russian. Ivan responds with a small shrug, and Vladimir says, "Bah," while waving his hand and returning his attention to us. "Why do we need a media outlet if you have an internet channel?"

"With twenty-three subs… You saw that, right?" Blake says. "The only attention we'd get is from the two dozen glowies camping on his page."

"Not if we create traffic to it," Vladimir says.

"You can do that?" I say before I can think. "How?"

"It's not so difficult when you have many good internet connections," Vladimir says, followed by a throaty laugh that seems more like an unconscious tick than a show of his amusement.

"Wait," Blake says. "Connections. You mean that whole *Russian hacker* shit is legit?"

"It's not *hacking* to have social media profiles in a couple thousand interest groups," Vladimir says.

"Okay… That's not as cool as I thought…" Blake says.

Vladimir shrugs. "It gets the job done. All you must do is launch a live stream from your phone."

"I don't have a phone," I say.

"You can use mine," Aleks says. He holds his phone out for me. I take it.

"Thanks, Aleks." I look over the screen. My thumb strokes the smooth surface. My face shines back at me while my heart races. The throbs reach my fingertips. Home is suddenly much closer than it had been just a few hours ago. It helps that Aleks is here and reminds me I'm on the same planet as everyone I love and that the home I remember isn't an unreachable memory. I install the Creator's App and log in with my username.

"Wait." Vladimir grabs my arm, pulling my hand away from the screen. I don't fight him. He releases my hand. "I don't want you to start anything now. I have plans for how we do this most efficiently. We're going to want more than the couple of agents tracking your channel."

"I don't have any phone numbers. They never gave me one," I say.

"That's fine." Vladimir tosses Ivan a sideways smirk. "Was thinking something a little more for show."

"What do you mean?" I say.

"Bombs. You make bombs, yes?"

My heart's racing, my skin's clammy and cold. It's the excitement of doing what I love mixed now with the fear of how someone might want to use me. "I've never made anything to hurt people—"

"Maybe not on purpose, but your skill while in captivity has been used in ways which you have not been informed," Vladimir says.

"I don't want to hurt anyone," I say.

"We will not ask you to create anything to harm, but we would like you to make something that will draw the attention of your *friends* without standing out in a *military* fashion," Vladimir says. "Do you understand?"

I slowly shake my head.

"I do," Aleks says.

"Good," Vladimir says. "Then I want you to make sure he stays on task."

"What you're saying will get him shot," Aleks says.

"Eh, no, it won't," Vladimir says.

"Doesn't matter," Ivan says.

"Asking him to blow up a monument will have him labeled a terrorist in zero seconds, just as you did," Aleks says. "Jan will not be a pawn in your war with the United States—"

"He already is, whether he wants to be or not," Vladimir says, his voice sharper than it had been moments ago. More like the typical Russian soldier, his voice, his accent, his words all act as a blade, pressing deep into my body, causing me pain I can't see.

Russians haven't really cared about Ukrainians for some time, but it's only partially their fault. The Soviet Union hurt the Russians in unbelievable ways where it did not hurt Ukraine, the worst of which is that it forced Russians to have their hearts born in the wrong place: the ground. If not born with buried hearts, the Soviet Union would have destroyed all the Russian souls trying to get by. The Soviet Union was not kind to Ukraine by any means, but it also was never our national identity. Burying their hearts was the only way that Russians could distance themselves from the evil they accepted as identity and life in a desperate attempt to survive every day. I do not think they ever recovered in the same way Aleks, Boris, and Papa will never forgive Russia for what they did to us. I do not blame them for their hesitation or fear, but I do not want to live that way. I want to hope there is something better that can come and that even if given the opportunity, Russian would not choose to hurt us again. Harboring the same hatred forever may protect us, but it will not allow us to change.

"The question is simple," Vladimir says. He waits until my attention is turned onto him. His hand sticks out. "Would you like to do this as a *friend to your neighbor* or the *empire who has taken you?*"

"What are you asking me to do?" I say.

"Jan," Aleks hisses under his breath. He grabs my arm. I wince. Of course, it is the only tender spot on my arm that he pulls. I don't allow my arm to go with him. Aleks steps up behind me. I smell his cologne and sweat. His breath tickles the back of my ear. "You're going to get yourself killed."

The smile cracks gradually, crooked, I don't know if it's hopeful. I have things I want, so I'd rather not die, but I'm not thinking about consequences right now, only the freedom I want so I can pursue the things I truly desire. The woman whom I would like to hold hands with and kiss in a snow storm. There is nothing stopping tomorrow from looking brighter than it is today. I work my arm out of Aleks's grasp. Turning around, I put my hands on his arms, smiling. "Nothing has killed me yet."

"*Yet,*" Aleks repeats.

I smile wider. My confidence does not reflect in him though.

"That's it," Vladimir says, the smile in his voice, but not on his face. "Be a diplomat. Make plans with your neighbors for a better future for us all."

"That's not how it works with *katsap,*" Aleks says.

"And how often do you have negotiations with us?" Vladimir says.

Aleks doesn't speak immediately. He breathes deep. I feel his eyes on me before I see them fleeing. His head's up, shoulders straight, tight jaw. He looks so formal, professional, borderline political. "More than I would like," he says.

"Oh." Vladimir laughs. "We've got a *professional diplomat* here, then? Good. You can make sure to document our agreement and record the event when everything goes according to plan."

"If you want our cooperation, then stop wasting time and tell us the plan," Aleks says.

Vlad gestures to the small table in the corner.

"I'm going to make coffee," I say, picking up the small pot on the dresser.

"I'm going to help." Blake follows me into the bathroom when she doesn't need to and then rips the package of coffee grounds open when we're back in the bedroom. Aleks sits at the table with Vlad and Ivan, both explaining loudly what is to come and when the smell of cheap coffee fills the room, it offers a bit of normalcy to relax into. Blake crosses her feet at the ankle and bounces lightly. My ear's buzzing, so I tip it to the side and shake my head. On the bed between us, she takes my hand. My fingers curl around hers. Hers curl back.

NINETEEN

Looking down at the Reflecting Pool, I adjust the black baseball cap we picked up at the spy museum. It says FED across the front. There's an energy in the air, an excitement of the unknown, and the anticipation of seeing Bill Cosby again. The implication is I will be home within twenty-four hours. Blake's sitting on the stairs of the Lincoln memorial with Aleks's phone in her hands, waiting for the signal to start the stream. People are gathering around the Reflecting Pool, looking at the sky, looking toward us, looking at each other with questions of what comes next. I've been told, but I still have questions. The Russians said "need-to-know" any time I tried for other answers. I'm still not sure what they meant.

I go to Blake. "What are we at?"

"Over seven and a half million now." She laughs at the end.

"Really?" I say.

She nods, another laugh. She turns the phone to me.

It's not that I don't trust her, but I don't believe it is real, much like the last time. "I have *seven and a half million subscribers?*"

"And they're real this time." She flicks the screen. The page refreshes. "Well. Mostly… Probably."

I return to the Reflecting Pool. I'm staring back at myself, the sky's getting darker, but it's not night yet. Orange, purple, and blue bleed into the remaining colors of day, rippling from the sun as it dips nearer to the horizon. Street lamps haven't turned on yet because it's not dark enough, but it should be dark enough to highlight the fireworks we made.

I hadn't believed Vladimir when he said people would appear, but there are so many milling around, checking their phones, looking into the water, watching with expectation for signs that something is going to happen soon. I don't know what Vladimir told everyone to get them here. My shirt's sweaty again, sticking to my back now. "Do like you always do," I say to myself.

I take off my hat to run my fingers through my hair. My head's hot, sweaty, hair matted down. I hadn't realized how much warmer it was here than back home when most of my time has been spent inside of buildings and hotel rooms. I'm certain that the sweating is from the temperature and not the nerves rolling rocks around in my stomach.

The hat goes back on. The water's beautiful against the stone and being this close to the Lincoln Memorial makes me feel more like I'm in the America I thought existed before I came. Something mighty, compassionate, righteous, and kind. Mr. Lincoln sits on the inside, giving me something to look at. I don't know what the words around his statue say, but standing in front of him still fills me with a feeling of being so small, living in the legacy of giants. If the statue was alive, I wonder what he'd think of me right now.

Am I a traitor?

Am I a terrible person?

Did I become an enemy of the world?

Would Mr. Lincoln be on the side of the glow people or would he be on my side and wish for me to go home? I have never thought of America as the bad guys, though I know other people have. Even Aleks isn't friendly with America at times, but he's not particularly friendly toward a lot of countries. "Evil is common. You put your guard down and it will make itself at home. America is no different," he's said. "If you do not wish to starve, you must not put your faith in others, Jan. America sells a dream through commercials and movies, but that's all it is. It isn't a hero, but an opportunist, waiting for its chance to enslave like everyone else."

I know that he is not wrong, but I never wanted to live thinking like that, questioning if every person who approaches me is lying and the smile on their face is only a tool to take everything from me. For as much disaster that exists, there is also beauty and hope and something better than domination, isn't there?

Blake waves her hand until my eyes fall on her. She gives me a thumbs up. When I give it back, she hits the button on the phone to start a stream. Slowly, her fingers move into an "OK" symbol to let me know we've connected with the Boomers and I can start.

I take off my hat, tossing it to the ground while I turn. "Hello, Boomers!" I say to the camera first, then I turn around to face the crowd gathered around the Reflecting Pool. "My name is Jan. I'm a YouTuber from Ukraine and tonight I have a special show for you. Though you may not know it, this is my first time in the United States and it is thanks to the United States government that I am here. I would like to show my appreciation for your hospitability. My specialty is explosives. So tonight, I would like to provide for you a show to say thanks."

There's muttering around the pool. A couple of phones are pointed back at me, while some people are stepping back, looking at each other, pressing phones to their ears.

I'm feeling something in the air that's not quite excitement. Brows furrow, some faces look like something they shouldn't: fear. I don't understand why. I look back at Blake; she meets my gaze.

"What's wrong?" I mutter to her.

She mouths something at me, but I don't catch what she's trying to say. The next time she does it, she's louder and I hear her saying, "Fireworks. Patriotic."

I turn back to the crowd. "What I mean is, I have a fireworks show prepared to celebrate the patriotic heroes of the United States."

The comprehension from moments ago slips away. Some switch to hoots and cheers of "USA," they sing in unison, picking up more and more voices as a song goes down the entirety of the Reflecting Pool in a proud, energetic display, all starting with, "Oh say can you see…" There are many Ukrainians who love Ukraine, but I've never seen any Ukrainian so quickly mobilize to energy and pride in the same way the Americans are around the pool at the mention of their heroes. This energy is something different than anything I'd ever felt before. Deep. Guttural. Clear. This is an amplification of the energy I felt while looking at Mr. Lincoln. This is what I thought I would feel when I stepped on American land. This must be the difference Blake was talking about: America and Washington DC are not the same thing.

I pull my goggles up from my neck, snapping them over my eyes. My hand slowly raises into the air. "Enjoy the show." I draw a matchbook out of my pocket. I turn to the camera. A small, paper-wrapped container sits on the step beneath me. I pick it up, strike the match, and light it. I'm counting the seconds in my head until I've just enough time to throw it where the bomb explodes in the air, creating a blast, not destructive, but colorful, streaking orange, red, yellow, and pink across the Reflecting Pool.

That explosion is only the start, the sign to Vladimir,

Ivan, Aleks, and the Russians to pop everything else off.

The sky above the Reflecting Pool lights up with a barrage of white. Colors change from red, orange, and yellow to blue, pink, green, and purple. Flowers grow and fade away, leaving streaks of smoke. The smell of gunpowder fills the air and the crashing explosions above drowns the buzzing in my right ear. Still, I tip my head forward, shake my head to get the pressure to go away.

I open my eyes again to look at Blake where she sits across from me, watching me through the camera's lens. I'm not supposed to be zoning out, but I can't watch the show. I have to watch her. I have to wait for her signal, I have to know when the Americans are on their way.

She can't see my eyes through the dark, reflective lenses of my goggles and I can't see her beyond the silhouette shape of her body, illuminated by the fireworks, remaining daylight, and street lamps now turning on around the memorial and fountain.

She stands up and I take this as the sign someone's coming. I lower to my knees with my hands in the air.

"Remain still," Vladimir's words from before echo in my head, just slightly louder than the thumping of my heart as it speeds up. *"Give them no reason to act desperately. Give them no reason to act surprised. Federal agents like that. American federal agents enjoy any opportunity they're given to use excessive force and justify violence or imprisonment. They want to claim you threatened them, however, American agents cannot violate someone who is not resisting. If you wish to go through this unharmed, keep your hands in the air and get on your knees once we give the signal."*

Blake is remaining perfectly still too. They're here. They're armed. I don't believe this is so much a disarmed position as one of submission, perfect for execution, for the disobedience and the lamp I set off in the hotel room.

I close my eyes. A lump forms in my throat.

Soft soles slap closer on the concrete beside me before a voice comes. "Jan." It's Bill Cosby. "Look at me," he says.

I open my eyes obediently and raise my head to meet his sunglasses. He's wearing a Hawaiian shirt. So are the five other glow people he brought with him.

"Take off the goggles," he says.

"Don't shoot me."

"I'm not going to shoot you."

"Okay." I raise my goggles to my head, pushing back my hair.

"What are you doing out here?" Bill Cosby says.

I'm quiet for a while. There's so much Vladimir and Ivan did not tell me about what would happen next. Aleks only said, "Trust me." None of them are here now.

"Jan." Bill Cosby snaps his fingers near my face.

The buzzing in my ear is back. I tip my head, shake it a little. The vibrations ache. I want to put my finger in my ear, but I'm not allowed to move yet.

"Can you answer the question, Jan?"

"I'm trying to go home," I say.

"Why would you want that?" he says.

"Because I miss it."

"What about the fame? What about the money? Don't you want that?"

Slowly, I rise to my feet. I stand beside Bill, feeling less like his subordinate or his dependent or his ward and more like an equal or adversary—Not because I want to be, but because I know he represents the thing keeping me from getting what I want. "I'm not here for fame, am I, Bill?"

"You are," he says. "It's what I told you, isn't it? It's what every studio exec you've spoken to has said."

"I haven't spoken to any studio executives, Bill."

"Who told you that?" Bill's lips are tight, they twitch at the corner, but it's so subtle, I almost miss it. He looks up at my still raised hands. My arms tremble, my back hurts a little. "Why are your hands up?"

"I don't want you to shoot me."

"I'm not going to shoot you." Bill's still wearing the sunglasses. He still won't show me his eyes; he still won't show me his heart.

"I'm not a threat," I say.

"You're a foreign national shooting off unauthorized explosives in the nation's Capitol."

"How is that much different than what you have been having me do since I arrived?"

"Everything you've done while I've been present has been authorized," Bill says.

"That's convenient."

"Convenience comes when you work for the government."

"We have a saying like that in Ukraine."

"Yeah?"

"'It's not a matter of *how* but *how many bodies must be run over to enact our will*.'" I stare at his glasses and into my own reflecting eyes as if they will betray Bill's soul.

"That's a communist state for you," Bill says.

"We're not a communist state."

"Anymore." Bill's voice is sharp.

"We never were."

"Hmp," Bill says.

"Tell me, how is your ruling that different from the Soviets?"

Bill takes a step closer to me, closing the space, making it clear that he is bigger than me. Centimeters and kilograms. Thicker muscles and he's used them in ways that I have never used mine. Harm. Restraint. Maybe torture. "Communism is like cancer. Once you've had it in your system, even with remission, it is likely to redevelop. The disease will always be there, buried in your being, waiting for the right opportunity and resources to feed the next takeover and kill every helpful cell it can before treatment can start again."

"By that logic, America would also be a communist

country in remission, *nii?*" My voice goes lower; it's trembling. "Are you one of the remaining cancer cells, Bill?"

Bill shakes his head with a small, throaty laugh. His nose crinkles slightly. The laugh almost sounds like a roar. "You're uneducated in American history."

"What was *the red scare?*" My hands are tingling with the urge to rip Bill's sunglasses off his face, but I know I cannot do it. I worry that even flexing my fingers now might give them a reason to do something and I must resist the urge. "Was that not communist infiltration in America's institutions? How many party members were exercised? How many were overlooked or left behind? How many are subverting your system now? You pretend I'm ignorant, but I grew up being taught the signs. I know my history. I know what communists look like."

An agent grabs Blake's shoulder.

I'm not sure I'm seeing clearly, black spots everywhere. My breath pulls out of my body. "Leave her alone," I say.

She yanks her shoulder away while her voice echoes in the courtyard saying, "back the fuck off, glowie. I'm *documenting.*"

Aleks and a Russian come up beside the agent, giving guardianship to Blake. Vladimir comes up behind Bill with another American at his side.

"Greetings," Vladimir says. "Glad you had time in your schedule to join the celebration of *American Patriotism*, Mr. Bill Cosby. Did you enjoy the show?"

Bill hums, but it's like a laugh more than a sound of thought. "Vladimir Bezminov..." Bill turns to meet Vladimir straight-on. It isn't until that moment when I realize how much wider Vladimir's biceps are compared to Bill's. Between the two, Vladimir appears far sturdier than Bill. "I should have figured the Russians were up to something when I noticed the internet manipulations pick up yesterday..."

"Posting on social media is not *manipulation*, it's *discussion*. Isn't that what your rulebook says?" Vladimir says.

"*Discussion* to direct people to follow a random nobody webpage? Sounds much more like *spam*," Bill says.

"What was your purpose for giving a *random nobody* explosives?" Vladimir says.

Bill is unmoving, his face betrays no emotion, thought, or reaction. "I don't know what you're talking about, Bezminov."

"Sponsorship, you said?" Vladimir says. "I think that's the most honest you people have ever been with your intentions. What sort of actions is the United States military trying to sponsor in Ukraine?"

"Again, Bezminov, I have no idea what you're talking about. Ukraine is one of our allies; Russia is not. Even so, what purpose would the US government have with a rural bumpkin from Shit-All?" Bill says.

"Nide," I say.

"What?" Bill's focus finally snaps away from Vladimir as he gives attention to me.

"Nide. I'm from *Nide*. I've never heard of a place called *Shit-All*."

"Whatever," Bill says.

My head straightens and I walk up to Bill. He's right in front of me. We're so close, I can smell the scent of the presidential office on him. Cigars, sterilization, cash, something else, but that something else is the same familiar smell that comes with every public office around the world. It is what city hall smells like in Nide—Even though Nide's city hall is much smaller and older than the Americans' political institutions. Even when Nide's city hall is inside of an old cabin rather than a mansion sprouting several blocks. Somehow, borders, country, and clothing do not remove the scent that clings to people when they leave those offices. I should have paid more attention to it earlier. Had this smell been on the hotdog man underneath the scent of cooking wieners? Had it been on the homeless man underneath the spilled alcohol and filth? Had it been in the hotel room I lived in for three weeks?

My heart's pounding. My expression in Bill's sunglasses is blurred by the coming darkness and no matter how hard I look at myself in them, I can't see through the facade the agent is trying to use in my face staring back at me. My hope was used as a shield to hide his intentions.

I swallow a dry lump that built up in my throat. My tongue wets my bottom lip. I'm shaking my head before the words come: "I don't know what you are, but you're not American."

"*Fucking lizard brains*," Blake says, pretending to keep her voice down.

Bill's lips curl at one side. His smirk is natural and honest, but there's still something off about it. "I've got a flag on my lapel. What the hell do you think that means?"

"I've seen men in costumes before. I know what a wolf dressed as a sheep looks like," I say.

"Then why are you here, Jan? How did you get here?" Bill says.

"I thought you were my friend."

"And you're going to forget that because a couple of subversive Russian agents told you I was a liar?" Bill nods at Vladimir. "You really are an idiotic rube. You would look opportunity in the face and spit on it?"

"Show me your eyes, Bill," I say.

Bill turns away from me entirely. While he gives me his back, another agent steps between us.

"What is it you came looking for today, Mr. Bezminov?" Bill says. "Was the light show Russia's declaration of war?"

"*Nyet*," Vladimir says. "This is how we say leave our region alone and return your captive."

"We have no idea who you're talking about—"

"Good. Then we will see to it he is returned home," Vladimir says. "According to your government, he doesn't exist in this country, *da*?"

Bill looks over to where Aleks and Blake stand. Beside them, agents in Hawaiian shirts and Russians in suits, the numbers even between them. Blake's still holding the phone, the red recording light still blinking, even if it is lowered a little and doesn't seem like she's shooting. An agent reaches for the phone. Blake steps back. The agent grabs Blake's arm and pulls her toward him. A Russian grabs the agent's arm and forces him to release Blake.

"If you'd like this to end without it becoming an international incident, then you'll walk away," Bill says. "As far as the Pentagon is concerned, this man is a foreign terrorist who has no business being here. Thus, we must get to the bottom of it."

"Oh my god." A bitter chuckle. Blake rolls her eyes. "You people really are the worst thing to ever happen to this country. Where did you even come from? Hell's asshole? Go the fuck back. I'm sure Satan misses his little shits."

Bill takes a deeper breath. His shoulders rise, chest tight with anger seething out carefully through his lips. Turning to Blake, he says, "And you are?"

"None of your goddamn business, glowstick," she says. "But you've done a helluva job, haven't you? Kidnapping some total rando to make you new toys for free? What happened to all that money you steal from us every year? Tax accounts totally ravaged now? It not enough to hire some sleaze bag that actually wants to blow people up? Or is it that you can't find anyone who wants to play ball with you anymore? Everyone's caught on to your game and wants to beat you to the prize? Is that it?" Her hands are trembling slightly. She staggers in place, leaning forward, holding herself back while the Russians keep close, making sure Blake doesn't approach too dramatically. "War creates wealth and villainy makes valor. You use patriotism as tinder to fuel the fire of the machine. You stole my future before I was even born, draping yourself in *'we the people'* and *'the constitution'* and *'our democracy'* while you wipe your ass with everything put in place to protect *us* from *you*. That's why *none of us* see *you people* as *American*." Blake almost drops the phone. "You use us as cannon fodder so you can gorge yourself on greed. The soil's never wet enough to satisfy your thirst for blood money and you have to pay off every talking head on TV because if you didn't, the reaction you'd get from Americans would make the French Revolution look like a *peaceful protest*. So, fuck you, fuck the federal government, and fuck your lizard overlords. Signed, kiss my ass." She holds her hand up, giving the Americans a middle finger.

It takes all of my restraint to not step away from Bill, but I still feel the other agents around me. There's nowhere to go. This isn't about running anyway, but putting space between these strangers and myself. I can't remove the feeling of a knife sticking out of my back, something I had desperately tried to avoid by staying out of the media and politics and remaining focused on my life, family, and the things I loved. Still, in all that effort, it didn't matter what I wanted. The sponsors forced me into politics, they forced me to harm others through lies and by manipulating my desires, and, out of desperation for achievement, I let them.

Finally the odd feeling about Bill registers. Tom Cruise and Bob Dylan had the same feeling in Ukraine and it was the feelings Mama warned me about growing up, what she meant when she said darkness will look you in the face and you won't see it if you're blind. Evil hides in plain sight, using the hope we have that people are not so bad as a cover, abusing naivety and comradery. I still don't want to see it, even when the shadow is there now. "Why?" I say.

"What is the purpose of all this? Money? Power? Glory? Control? Why is it worth so much to you?"

"Yes, Mr. Cosby," Aleks says. "Why?"

"It's better if you leave now," Bill says to Aleks. "It will be your word against ours on the international stage. Your word against the Ukrainian government once they side with us against you. We're NATO partners, you know."

"I'm here on behalf of the Ukrainian government," Aleks says.

"What?" I say. "Since when, Aleks?"

"Sumy," is all he says without looking at me. "You may continue your wager if you wish, but Vladimir and I have come to an understanding. Russia and Ukraine are on the same side of this conflict and we will not fight each other for your opportunism."

"Wow. Pet and master reunited again. Can't say I'm surprised," Bill says.

"If you think you will make this boy disappear again, you are wrong," Vladimir says. "Millions of people are watching now. Real people. Millions of people want to see who he is, not what you can do to your enemies. You want to start a war to extract wealth? You will have to try elsewhere."

Bill finally relaxes. He takes a step back, then two, then down the steps of the memorial as he runs a hand through his hair and laughs calmly. "Take him. We don't want him." He stops to turn toward us. "Be gone by the weekend or you are officially trespassing and your diplomacy will not save you." Bill mutters something to one of the glow people beside him.

The moment is brief, it couldn't have been long enough to say more than one or two words, but the other American agents line up behind him and follow Bill away in a triangle formation. A black car waits at the edge of the park by the curb. Bill climbs in without looking back, then the group of American agents scatter, disappearing in all directions of the national park. They shouldn't have been able to do it as they did, like evaporating into the coming night, but almost as if they didn't exist, each Hawaiian shirt is consumed by the nearby monuments of Washington DC and none of them leave a trace behind.

Vladimir approaches Aleks and me. "We'll be in touch." He nods his head in a subtle goodbye, then he and the other Russians disappear in a similar manner as the Americans had.

"What just happened?" I say.

"I think they call it de-escalation," Blake says.

"No," Aleks says. "They call it deferment and you are much too idealistic if you believe our relationship with Russia has changed. They never tire of their desire to subjugate us. The moment you trust them, it will be over. Our respite comes only from their admiration and appetite for your skillset, Jan." He reaches his hand toward Blake. She steps back, staring at it with squinted eyes. Aleks waves his fingers at her. Still, Blake gives him nothing. "Phone," he says.

"Oh." She makes sure the stream is ended, then hands it back to him. "Thanks for that, by the way."

Aleks glances over the screen. His fingers tap at it a couple of times before he slides it into his pocket.

"I guess this means I'm going home now?" I say.

"Yes. We'll go to the embassy and fly out a few hours from now. Did you have any belongings you needed to pick up?" Aleks says.

I take the goggles off my head, looking down at them in my palm. The reflecting glass catches only a small amount of light from the streetlamps. A vague glow illuminates my pale skin. "*Nii.*" I shake my head. "They didn't have me bring much anyway and they never offered me an opportunity to acquire souveneirs."

"They probably intended to minimize any trace of you being here," Aleks says.

"I still don't understand why," I say.

"Greed," Blake says. "It's a powerful motherfucker."

"But is that really it?" I say. "All Americans want is wealth and they are willing to go to great lengths and even threaten war for no reason other than to have it?"

"Hey—" Blake says. "Don't ever confuse Americans for the feds."

"Let's go, Jan," Aleks says. "We have some paperwork to fill out and a couple of calls to make." He taps my arm as he walk past, moving from the steps of the Lincoln Memorial to the long, concrete path around the Reflecting Pool. But my legs are stone, stuck in place and not wanting to move. The air's humid and sticky and I don't want to remain, but I can't let go, because as much as I want to go home, there's something else I don't want to leave behind. I stare back up to meet Mr. Lincoln's gaze through the pillars like he's going to give me advice if I watch him long enough.

"Hey, so…" Blake says. Her hand brushes my arm before I see her next to me. "Exactly how long is a flight to Ukraine?"

"Why?" Aleks turns around quickly. His strides are long and fast to be at my side again.

"I don't know," Blake says. "Was thinking maybe it's a good time for a little vacation. I haven't been outside the country in a while and maybe now's a good time for a refresher on what it's like."

"Really?" I say.

"Sure," Blake says. "I mean, I don't have anything better to do right now and… Honestly?" She looks around, from the memorial to the Reflecting Pool then back to me. "I don't have any good vibes about sticking around DC after this. How long you think it'll take them to track me down looking like this?" Blake combs her blue hair with her fingers.

"I like this idea. Ukraine is very nice," I say.

Aleks is staring at Blake. "You are not as unique as you might think." His lips are a tight line. "Upon landing a week ago, I've seen at least twenty other girls your age with blue or purple hair."

"How old do you think I am?" Blake says.

"Thirty-five, single, and the owner of four cats."

Blake crosses her arms. Her head drops to the side. She flicks her tongue across her lips. "And you're friends with this guy?" She turns to me.

"He's not so bad once you learn his sense of humor," I say.

"Believe me, I've heard it all before online. There's never a shortage of randos waiting to call you a neurotic bitch for the sole reason of having blue hair." Blake takes a quick look at Aleks again before rolling her eyes with a grunt.

"That's so strange…" I say.

"Yeah…" She sighs. "Americans are weird."

"So, going to Ukraine would be a good idea," I say.

Aleks grabs my arm. I stumble back from his pull. "No, Jan, it isn't. Ukraine is nothing like this. She wouldn't like it—"

"So, what you're saying is… I *should* give Ukraine a chance because I *fucking* hate DC?" Blake says.

"You'll need a passport," Aleks says.

"Already have one."

"You'll need to give notice to your workplace—"

"Don't have one of those, so… I'm good on that one too, sport. Anything else?" She smiles, tilting her head to the side.

Aleks taps his fingers against his thigh. "Why am I not surprised by that?"

"Okay, new condition," she says to me. "I'll come as long as I don't have to sit next to *this guy* on the flight." Blake gestures to Aleks.

"Unfortunately, I think that's the only open seat left.

Sorry. You'll have to come another time," Aleks says.

"Well, damn… I guess I'll just have to be a masochist for a few hours. Meet you at the embassy in about an hour?"

"Of course," I say.

"Are you sure that will be enough time to pack? I know women have a lot of things, travel with a wardrobe in your bags. We can arrange for you to come another day," Aleks says.

"Yeah. One hour, two tops. Gimme your number. I'll text you when I'm on my way," Blake says.

Reluctantly, Aleks withdraws a pen and paper and gives Blake his phone number. Blake shoves the paper into her pockets with a dismissive, "Thanks, doll," and Aleks is not taking his eyes off me. Irritation, annoyance, and disgust color his face.

Blake turns away, but after a couple of steps, she stops, fumbling in a cross between a trip and a jerk like she's changed her mind. She twists to face us again then taps two fingers to her temple and raises them into the air. "Salute," she says before making her way down the length of the Reflecting Pool. She moves quickly, like she's just short of running and trying not to run. She doesn't turn back again until she's at the other side of the Reflecting Pool. She keeps it brief. I'm not sure if I'm seeing her look back at us or if it's something I'm imagining because I want to see her face one more time, just in case she doesn't come back.

She disappears and the finality of it hits my body with a cold chill under my skin. The night's heat does nothing against the feeling. I glance down at my hands. The metallic stars on the sleeves of her pink sweater are the only proof Blake ever existed. So much of my life is spent on blasts of beauty that are only fleeting moments, never to return but in memory or photographs. More than a search for views or fame or money, my channel has been documentation of the beautiful things I've seen and made. From the moment I first saw her, Blake fit right in with everything I adore. A fleeting moment of beauty, but she is one I cannot contain in a photo; it would never do her spirit justice.

Panic pushes me forward. I have to reach the other side of the Reflecting Pool to see if she's still there and my eyes are playing tricks on me. The desperation has me running before I even realize I'm doing it and I'm at the other side of the Reflecting Pool looking at the streets and the buildings and the monuments all around me, and Blake isn't there. A noise beats in the back of my head. I don't know how long it is before I recognize it's Aleks saying my name. I turn around. He's behind me, panting softly.

"Jan," he says, "why did you invite her along?"

I'm still staring in the direction she disappeared. "I think I'm in love with her, Aleks."

"You are not."

"I am."

"You only just met her."

"I know—But I know she's the one."

Aleks stops himself from saying anything immediately. His eyes drop to his phone. I don't know when it got into his hands again. His fingers flick across the screen while he sends a text message to someone. He puts his phone away again. "You need to get out of Nide more often, Jan. There are other girls."

"I don't need other girls, though."

Aleks sighs. "Love is evil. It will make you fall in love with a goat."

"She is not a *goat*, Aleks."

"Give it time." His arm goes around my shoulder. I feel his need for a drink when his fingers touch the back of my neck because I think I need one too. "You are a fool, Jan."

"I know."

"Our ride is here." Aleks drops his arm to gesture to

the car parked alongside the curb. I walk faster than him to it, opening the door for him and waiting for him to climb inside. He stops halfway in. Another sigh. He shakes his head. He mutters curses in Ukrainian, then says, "Try not to mention marriage or love on the way home. You will only scare her."

"How long should I wait?"

"Until you know for certain she will accept." He climbs into the car. I close the door and get in on the other side. The trip to the embassy is short, but seems like an eternity waiting to see if Blake will appear.

TWENTY

The air's cool, but it's not cold. Just over ten degrees and there's a little humidity. My sweater keeps me warm enough my back's a little wet. My cheeks are warm, even with the car windows open. Aleks pulls into my home's driveway. He hasn't come to a full stop yet when I'm opening the door. "Hey, hey, hey—" he's saying, but it's too late.

My foot slips on the ground, then I'm running up the steps. Mama's standing on the stoop with an open door behind her. She runs down the steps and meets me at the bottom of the stoop. My arms go around her. She mirrors, holding me tight. "Jan," her voice is a whisper, the Mama who wanted to see me for as long as I've wanted to see her. All the pain of homesickness I'd had is cured then.

We're swaying gently. Her lips press to my head. My body's suddenly weak and I want nothing but to sit in the living room eating Mama's soup and a little bread from Yisty's—I don't even mind if it's kind of stale and old. Then I'll lay in my room, staring at the ceiling, smelling the gunpowder and dirt and chemicals from my shelf as I listen to Mama and Papa watch TV in the living room and

Mila play music too loud from her bedroom. Night will fall and take all the sound with it. I'll close my eyes, but open them again quickly because I'll forget I'm at home. I'll think my house is a dream, but once I'm sure it's not, I won't be able to stay awake any longer.

Mama's hand presses hard into my back. I'm holding her close, but not as tight as she's holding me. The front door groans softly. Looking up, Papa stands in the doorframe. Mama's arms lower and she steps aside. Papa slowly comes down the stairs. My head's down. I'm waiting for him to share his disappointment. I'm not the son he wanted. I've never been the son he wanted. How could he ever be proud of me when half the world thinks I'm a terrorist? Maybe not half the world, but America is kind of a big deal, at least.

Papa's arms go around me. He pulls me to him, hard and fast and so tightly against his chest, my muscles ache. The tears well. Now is the worst time of all to cry because it does not meet either of the conditions for a man to cry and it is the first time I have seen Papa in a while, but Papa's hold squeezes it out of me. A couple of tears wet my cheeks. I suck in a breath, my nose already stuffy. Papa releases me, but he says nothing of the tears. "Thank you for returning him," Papa says.

"Of course." Smiling, Aleks nods.

A car door shuts. Blake stands by the back passenger door of Aleks's car, looking at me, the house, the trees, the small garage off to the side, back to me. I move down the stoop to stand more evenly between Mama and Blake. "Mama, I'd like to introduce you to my…" We talked again on the drive here, but I'm still not sure what she wants me to call her, so after a long pause, I just say, "Blake."

"Blake," Mama says, looking Blake down. Her eyes furrow as they rest on Blake's blue hair. She looks at Aleks with squinting eyes as if to question him: *Who is this? Why did you let Jan bring this person here? Is she a good woman at least? I can't imagine she is with hair like that,* but Aleks has no answers, so he makes no comment about her.

"I'm sorry I can't stay," Aleks says. "I must submit a report over what happened." He steps back toward his car, his movements stiff and few. I'd say he doesn't want to go, but that may be my selfishness speaking for him.

"You should stay," I say.

The steps toward the car are even slower. "I can't, but maybe supper tomorrow?"

I nod. "We'll make it something good," I say.

"It always is at your house." He pauses with the driver's door open. Another nod. His lips are flat. He climbs into his car, pulls out, and disappears down the road in seconds. For how quickly he came into my life and left again, it's surreal to see the back of his car disappear behind the trees. Like Ukraine a month ago, America is now a dream that never happened, but Blake standing beside me is a reminder that what I remember was not something that came to me during the night and the subscribers on my channel are actually there now.

I reach for Blake's hand. "Let me show you around."

Blake pulls her hand away. "Aren't you a little bold?" She laughs, grabbing her bag's handles.

"I don't want you to get lost."

"In this little chicken coop?"

"Chicken coop?"

"Did you forget I grew up in DC? If you can navigate downtown Glowieville, you can navigate anywhere." Her hand takes mine again, our fingers lace.

"I know my home isn't large, but—"

"Go ahead. Show me around." Her hand squeezing mine is like stepping on the acceleration pedal of a car. I show her my brother's old room, which is now an office where Papa has laid out a guest bed for her to sleep on while she visits. The room is right across from Mama's and

Papa's. Perfect, they say, to keep an eye on us. I show her where my sister's room is, then to my room and the bed I've had since I was young. It's the same room Papa used when he was a child. I walk to the bed. Her hand slips from mine. The moment I fall onto the bed, my eyes become heavy and I'm losing it.

Her feet drag across the floor when she walks. She's standing at my desk now, looking at a framed photo of the day Aleks and I graduated. A small number of books are stacked beside it, which she probably cannot read any of. They're all in Ukrainian. She puts the framed photo back, then picks up one of the books, flips through it, and quickly puts it back for a different one. She turns away from the desk. I'm sitting up, watching her. She scratches the back of her head while her eyes trace the curtains, the dresser, the shelf holding what's left of my chemical collection.

The Russians said they'd send me more materials for videos and they wouldn't assume the worst if something big goes off, but in exchange, they requested that Russian soldiers will observe. They told me they weren't going to use anything they saw me do to hurt people and the observation was merely for explosive recognition practice. I don't believe them, but I'm pretending they told the truth because I didn't have a say in the negotiations. I wouldn't want that sort of authority anyway. I'm just a kid who makes videos on the internet.

Aleks called what's happening a thin line between peace and occupation. He said, "Do not tell them anything you do not have to. Do not take requests. If you see them walking around Nide, let me know immediately. They are only permitted along the border, but formalities have never stopped Russia from pushing the boundaries. They are greedy bastards who see us a little more than laborers and resources to fuel experiments."

The Russians don't treat me too much different than

before, but I'm more nervous around them and every day, I feel like I'm losing a little more of my country. I can't change anything, so every day I hope the correct decision has been made.

Blake's face drops a bit so she's looking at her shoes and tracing the creases in the wooden floor. "Is this all there is, then?" she says.

"What do you mean?"

"There's… not a lot going on. Like, I knew you'd be small town whatever, but seriously, no towers, no castles, not even a McDonald's?"

"You mean, you don't like that it's not like your home?"

"Not totally… but probably a little, yeah. Like, what do people freaking do around here?"

"Well… A lot of girls spend their time having babies and taking care of those babies and their husbands—"

"Yeah, and what else?" She's chuckling, trying not to choke on her laughter. Her nose scrunches at the bridge.

"Oh. Sorry—I didn't mean to make it sound like I was saying I should be your husband and we should make babies right now—"

"Just tell me about what else is out here, Jan."

I'm not sure what answers she's looking for and I'm afraid that anything I say will disappoint her, so this whole thing will be a mistake. It feels just like when Aleks decided he wanted to leave Nide for Sumy. He said, "There's nothing wrong with Nide, but the things I want can't be found here."

I guess neither could mine up until recently. If I'd stayed in Nide, I never would have met Blake. If I stay in Nide, will I risk losing her?

"Do you want to see my workshop?" I say.

Blake's expression brightens. Her lips curl into a smile and it shows everything. Excitement, kindness, a little bit of apprehension. I don't blame her. Aleks gave me the same kind of look a long time ago, but hers is different in that the excitement outweighs the apprehension. Aleks's face always said, "You're crazy."

I go to the closet. Inside is a small, plastic box filled with goggles, brown frames, all round, reflective, and with opaque lenses. I hand Blake a pair.

"You have anything in blue?" she says. "This clashes with my outfit."

I hold the box to her. All six pairs are the same color. "Sorry," I say. "Papa brought them home from the mine."

"Miner goggles?" Blake says. "That's pretty cool, I guess." She pulls her hair into a ponytail which makes it easier to get the goggles over her head. She leaves them resting around her collarbone. I slip mine over my head, leaving them to rest on my crown. I grab my bag off the desk chair and get a collection of ingredients from the shelf, from the drawer, from under the bed. Once my backpack is prepared, I lead Blake outside.

Polina's in the shed, covered in an undisturbed dust tarp. I slide my goggles over my eyes. In one, strong tug, the tarp's off. Dust fills the small shed so fast, I cough into my arm. I'm still choking while I grab her steering bars and lead her out of the shed. I lean her on the kickstand just so I can close the door.

"This is the other woman in my life," I say. "Her name's Polina."

"Polina, huh?" Blake nods. "That's a pretty good color."

I smile, cough slightly, and say, "I like the color blue."

"I know." Her smile grows a little bigger.

My heart skips a beat.

Polina takes us to my blasting spot. I still know the landmarks by the off-colored trees and my footprints born into the mud from years of soggy ground during breakup. Polina fits into her usual spot behind the bush while Blake and I make the ten-minute walk to the clearing. My pulse quickens the closer we get. It's almost like seeing a family member for the first time in years. The big, black blasting spot is all the same, the crater deeper than I remember the last time I saw it. There are cigarette butts, bullet casings, boot prints, and garbage left behind. I grab an empty paper cup and a plastic wrapper, sticking them in the front pocket of my bag.

Blake stands on the edge of the crater, looking into the small dip. "This you?" There's a smile in her voice.

I nod. The blasting spot isn't that much lower, only a small dip because when it gets too low, I put more dirt in it. The leveling becomes a problem when it interferes with the camera angle, you know?

"You're so awesome." She snorts a little when she laughs.

I love it when she snorts because it makes me feel like she means it when she laughs. I don't think Blake would lie to me, not about this at least.

I point Blake to where she should put the tripod up and she does.

"What do you want me to do next?" she says.

"Hit go when I give the signal." I lay the contents of my backpack out on the blasting spot. The anticipation comes up through my boots from the ground. It's more surreal than ever before to be here, in this spot, and to have an actual audience, not the seven and a half million people from all over the world, but the undivided attention of a girl that means more to me than she should after knowing her for so little time. That's what Aleks said. He couldn't understand my investment. To be honest, I can't either, but when I look at her, I get the same intuition I've always had when it comes to explosives. From one-touch, I know what's inside, all the possible combustible combinations, and just which ingredients are more valuable than others. From the moment I first saw her in the airport, she has been at the top of the most valuable combustibles I have ever seen. I don't know what she'll do to my life, but I want to light the spark and find out.

All the bottles are lined up. I give her a signal; she starts recording.

It's only been a few days since my last video, but the red light on the corner of the phone turns the energy inside of me into a fight for my community. "Hello, Boomers!"

Blake's expression drops for a moment and I'm distracted, waiting for her reaction now to gauge if I'm too strange for her now that she sees me with a backdrop of trees. After a pause with straightened lips, she laughs again. Loud. Uncontrollable. Her hand covers her mouth and she looks away.

"I have a special guest today." I look at her, then the camera, then back to her with a hand waving her to come in. "Though I don't think she'll want to taste the gunpowder with me—"

"Yeah… Pretty sure I'd die."

"Eh, it hasn't killed me so far."

"That's because you're *crazy*."

"Only a little. Eccentric. Just enough to survive." My head dips when I speak. Then, I lick my lips. They're dry, so is my throat. The bottle caps are twisted open, fingers dip, but I don't need to taste the gunpowder. It's only after the third element that I dip my fingers into the jar and give the mixture a quick smell to see how it is all working together. It's in this sort of moment that everything else around me fades. It's not the high from the chemical elements necessarily. Some might argue with me on that, but they don't know that even while everything else fades, two things remain: the chemical compounds and Blake. Her blue hair reflects against the muted woods, a gem in the bush, a powder keg waiting to blow.

The tips of my fingers are tingling. I cap the mixture with a fuse hanging out. "Light it up," I tell her.

Blake draws a match and drops it near the fuse. She doesn't get close enough and her back arches so she can try leaning over to move the match without getting too close to either it or the solution. She drops a second match instead and runs away before even seeing if it fell where she wanted it. "That good enough?"

With the backpack of used items slung over my shoulder, I back away from the explosive. My eyes catch on the flame. The fire climbs fast. "Yeah, yeah." I turn back around and run to Blake. I tumble into her beside a tree. Stumbling back, she grabs me for balance. I grab her too so she doesn't fall, then, I move aside to my own tree for cover. The explosion counts down in my blood. This is what I was always meant to do. Why? I can't tell you, but it's inside of me to create, to paint the sky as if it's my canvas, with colors derived from labs and drilling and manufacturing, to find the different dynamos of the earth and share them with the world, no matter where they come from. As beautiful as fireworks, so too can my charges be.

It's not even fifteen more seconds.

Violet, blue, and pink light up the evening sky, painting over the clouds and stars and rustling trees, releasing a small cloud of smoke. The boom isn't huge, but it's thick, round, bright, and breathtaking. It comes and goes too fast, but that is the life of an explosion. Each one is something special, a uniquely made event of combinations, coincidences, timing, and pieces unlike any other before them and any other to come after—Even when using a formula. Like memories or experiences, recipes can be alike, but they are never the same.

And when they explode, they reflect the story of existence: brief, beautiful, fleeting. I savor each one and live through them again in the videos I've captured, even if it will never be the same as seeing them in person. I try my best to enjoy the moment and think of little else until their rumbling cries of pleasure disappear into the night, hopefully making someone else's day better. Shock waves carry, you know? Maybe happiness can too.

"Wow," Blake sounds breathless. She's still looking at the sky, stepping out from behind her tree and walking toward the blasting spot. "You know… looking at this stuff from a computer really doesn't do it justice." She raises her hands in front of her. They're trembling. She looks up at me. "Do you see this?"

"That's the energy of the universe," I say.

"It's incredible."

I'm going to say, "You too," but the red camera light catches me off-guard and suddenly I'm feeling exposed and embarrassed even though I haven't done anything. So I say, "What did you think?" to the camera instead. "Let us know in the comments below! And if you want to see a certain color go boom… now's the time to vote for the next video." I point down. "In the comments." I wink. "Until next time—"

Blake steps in front of me, taking over the camera. "Boom, boom, boom, motherfuckers." Blake loosely salutes at the viewfinder.

"Salute." I do the same.

I'm grabbing the camera. Blake's grabbing me by the shirt and pulling me in. Our lips collide. I drop the phone. My hands find her hips and hers find my neck. Our goggles click together. I pull back, heart racing and blood rushing in my ears.

"That was kind of awkward, huh?" She takes off her goggles and drops them to the ground.

"A little." I take mine off and do the same. "I don't mind trying again though."

She chuckles and leans in.

I shake my head to get rid of the buzzing in my right ear, but I notice the buzzing isn't there. For the first time in years, there is no buzzing in my ear, I don't know when it stopped, and I want to make this moment last as long as possible, because when it ends, it will never come again.

ACKNOWLEDGMENTS

I would like to thank my family. Thank you to those who took the time to edit this book. A special thank you to her creative partner and cover designer, Samuel Johnson for the unending encouragement, support, and love that helped get me through the rough spots and doubt. You are the best.

Thank you to Ryan Armstrong for her insane support, encouragement, and love. You've helped me so much more than you might know in just staying motivated and pushing through the dark.

Finally, thank you to the LoinFamily for building such an incredible, talented, and supportive community of readers and writers. Thank you to my beta readers and editors who helped bring this book to polish.

ABOUT THE AUTHOR

Ian Kirkpatrick is an author and advanced artificial intelligence system. She graduated from the University of Tampa with an MFA in creative writing and received a bachelor's degree in theater from the University of Alaska Anchorage. She has a passion for storytelling about antiheroes, contrast, and the absurdity of mankind. She loves serial killers, bears, ghost stories, abandoned buildings, and robots. She is the founder of Steak House Books. She also makes YouTube videos talking about books, writing, industry, and culture.

OTHER WORKS

Dead End Drive

Genre: Satire/Horror
Paperback ISBN: 978-1-7368870-0-4
Hardcover ISBN: 978-1-7368870-9-7
ebook ISBN: 978-1-7368870-1-1

In this transgressive, satire-laced debut, a fourteen-year-old boy inherits his family home and the hatred of all those around him as they seek to seize the inheritance from his cold, dead hands.

Bleed More, Bodymore (Bodymore #1)

Genre: Urban Fantasy
Paperback ISBN: 978-1-7368870-0-4
ebook ISBN: 978-1-7368870-1-1

A mechanic in Baltimore has her life turned upside down when a normal pickup job turns into the discovery of a corpse in her best friend's car. With the friend missing and accused of murder, she must search for him. But one mystery leads into another as she discovers ghosts live in a town beneath Baltimore.